The Streaker

The Tale of a Modern-Day Cynic

Jackson Forelle, Esquire

Published by Tidemarsh University Press Tidemarsh University Press
A Division of Tidemarsh University
Docemus quia sub lege tenemur
www.TidemarshUniversity.com

First Edition
Published April 2025, Tidemarsh University Press
ISBN: 979-8-9985785-0-2
Multiple illustrations by Ms. Sax's third-grade class at Seaford Elementary School
Printed in the United States of America

For the Fam—those still paddling out, those in the flow carving it up, and those who've already caught their last wave to the shore

Book Disclaimer:

~~Although I am an attorney, nothing in this book should be considered as having created an attorney-client relationship between myself and any reader, and nothing herein shall be considered legal advice.~~

~~There are inherent risks in undertaking any extreme sport, such as kiteboarding, surfing, and martial arts, including the risks of severe injuries, death . . . .~~

~~You should consult with a doctor before undertaking any new exercise program and . . . .~~

~~The information in this book is not intended as, and shall not be understood or construed as, financial advice and is not a substitute for financial advice from a professional who is aware of your individual circumstances. There are inherent risks in quitting your job. . .~~

Dogs and philosophers do the greatest good and get the fewest rewards.
— Diogenes of Sinope

Well, what the heck! I went and did my best.
And by God, I really tasted something swell!
And for a moment, why
I even touched the sky.
And at least I left some stories they can tell.
I did!

— Jack Skellington, *The Nightmare Before Christmas*

Foreword

By Judson A. Breckendorf III, Ph.D., Chair of the Endowed Henry Bernard Professorship and Department Head of the School of Philosophy at Tidemarsh University

It seems that I have been caught up in some unholy deal with the devil that those at the helm of this fine institution have made with one Jackson Forelle, Esq. Apparently, as part of this grand bargain, without having obtained my advanced approval, my skilled services have been bartered off like a loaf of bread or a truckle of cheese, as a result of which I have been commanded to write a foreword for Mr. Forelle's book, *The Streaker*. I have to say that I was a bit surprised, considering our past dealings, that Mr. Forelle would even want me to undertake this task. Nevertheless, as I have no choice, I will now meet this commitment as best I can, in good conscience.

So, as I sit here drinking my second glass of a surprisingly gifted Meritage, I set to work to write an honest assessment of this novel. In doing so, I suspect that these pages will never see the light of day, which is, frankly, fine by me. After all, I would prefer not to be associated with this particular book. Perhaps the best way of preventing such a connection—while still maintaining my obligation to write this foreword—is by delivering a frank and candid assessment. However, before I memorialize my thoughts on this piece of work, I believe it is proper for me to address a few other preliminary points of order.

Upon first glancing at the title of Mr. Forelle's book, I assumed he had written about something of which I knew little. I assumed that *The Streaker* chronicled the antics of overweight, beer-guzzling sports fans who enjoyed shedding their clothing and bounding around sports arenas, jiggling to the horror of the crowds. Upon further inspection, I noticed the tagline and concluded that the title of the book constituted a symbolic reference to the ancient Greek Cynic philosophers.

For those who spend their lives outside the academic circles of philosophy, you should know that, besides having written and published several prominent books concerning the great debates of modern and ancient philosophy, I am also the primary draftsman of one particularly well-regarded textbook titled *The Anatomy of Philosophy* that is heavily used in introductory philosophy courses at several prestigious universities across the country. Note that this should not be confused with the book *The Philosophy of Anatomy*, which is full of many sorts of quackery. If you were to ask the vast majority of my colleagues, I am confident that they would confirm my particular expertise in the realm of ancient Greek philosophy. I make mention of these facts, with all due modesty, to explain why I would normally be the perfect choice to write a foreword for a book that is ostensibly intended to delve into considerations of the Cynic philosophers of old Greece. To put a finer point on it, it is not the purported subject matter of the novel *The Streaker* to which I object as much as the author of the book.

For the life of me, I still do not know why Dr. Smyth chose Counselor Forelle to write a book describing the esteemed professor's island-hopping exploits through the Caribbean last summer. I have always had nothing but respect for Dr. Smyth, and he is well-regarded as both a scholar and an educator in philosophy. Also, I understand he has been generous to our university as of late. Of course, the book reveals that Mr. Forelle represented Dr. Smyth in the course of Dr. Smyth's adventure. As a result, I can't help but wonder if there was some coercion involved in Dr. Smyth's selection of Mr. Forelle. Perhaps Mr. Forelle knows more than he discloses in this tale? Also, the fact that Dr. Smyth did not himself write this foreword begs the question of whether the book was even condoned or authorized by Dr. Smyth. I am unable to confirm either way as to this speculation due to Dr. Smyth's current unavailability.

With that, let me briefly discuss a key historical figure that is relevant to the book. Specifically, I would like to talk about the old Cynic philosopher Diogenes. Although the teachings of Diogenes clearly provided motivation for Dr. Smyth's travels, for some inexplicable reason, Mr. Forelle has chosen not to mention him by name until deep into the novel. I will now take a moment to remedy this error.

I have written about Diogenes on multiple occasions. There is a well-known story about the man and his brief interaction with Alexander the Great that does an effective job of illustrating some basics of Cynic philosophy. The story takes place not long after Alexander's ascension to the Macedonian throne in 336 BCE when he had occasion to travel to Corinth in south-central Greece. The new king was only around twenty at the time and had not yet set out on his campaigns to conquer much of the known world. Because of this, he was not yet known as "the Great," so I will just refer to him henceforth, for the sake of simplicity, as Alexander in lieu of a more cumbersome title such as "Alexander, Still Looking to Make a Name for Himself" or "Alexander, Later to be Proclaimed as Great."

With this in mind, I will continue the tale. While in Corinth, Alexander took time out of his busy schedule to seek out Diogenes, who already possessed some level of notoriety as a famous philosopher in the school of Cynicism. By the way, the word "cynic" is derived from the ancient Greek word *kynikos,* meaning "dog-like," as the Cynics believed that emulating and living the simple life of a dog was a noble pursuit. You see, Cynics rejected social norms and structures and the accumulation of wealth, which they saw as a distraction from obtaining the mental clarity of living "in accordance with nature." It is believed that Diogenes was around seventy when he encountered Alexander and was living in a barrel with no material possessions.

Young Alexander and his entourage found Diogenes sprawled out in the grass, dozing in the sun. As Alexander walked up and stood over the lying man, a small crowd quickly gathered. The locals were obviously curious to watch the exchange between the two famous figures.

"I am Alexander, the king," Alexander said.

Diogenes replied, "I am Diogenes, the dog."

"Why do they call you this?" Alexander asked, already knowing Diogenes's reputation as a Cynic.

"Because I fawn on those who give me anything, I yelp at those who refuse, and I set my teeth in rascals."

Deciding he wanted to put Diogenes's ascetic beliefs to the test, Alexander offered to give him anything he wished within his powers. All Diogenes had to do was ask.

Diogenes, who was still lying down and looking up at the ruler of all Macedonia, conceded that yes, there was one thing that Alexander could do.

"Then speak it," Alexander commanded.

To the surprise and amazement of the men and women who had been watching the exchange, Diogenes replied, "You can stand aside and stop blocking my sun."

The story concludes that as Alexander walked away and left Diogenes to his convalescence, he smiled and told the men who were accompanying him, "If I were not Alexander, I would want to be Diogenes."

Although several scholars, including myself, question the accuracy of a few minor aspects of this reported event, it is an enjoyable little tribute to Diogenes and to Dr. Smyth's aspirations.

With that, I believe it is next customary in a foreword to provide some insights into the author and his credibility. The first descriptor that comes to mind when I think of Mr. Forelle is unadulterated bravado. Why else would he consider himself fit to climb the existential terrain touched upon in the novel without having the appropriate qualifications to do so?

I easily learned a great deal about Mr. Forelle on the website of his law firm, Forelle & Reichle, P.C. I affectionately refer to the group as "the comfortable fish firm," as I learned from a colleague of mine in the foreign language department that both named partners have family names of Germanic origin. "Forelle" means "trout" in English.

I consider this fitting as it places Mr. Forelle in the same broad aquatic characterization of a shark, only less threatening and impressive. Reichle is likely a derivation of Reichel, which can be interpreted to mean "a little bit rich." I have no idea as to whether Mr. Reichle is rich or impoverished but must presume that he has made some profit from the extorted settlements reached by his partner against Tidemarsh University. Regardless. I have noticed that people who have accumulated some level of wealth don't like to call themselves "rich" nowadays but instead say they are "comfortable." I was thus able to derive my pet name for the firm, "the comfortable fish firm."

In reviewing the law firm's website, I learned that Mr. Forelle obtained an undergraduate degree in engineering right here from

Tidemarsh University and he obtained his law degree from here as well. It is a bit disturbing that a double alumnus from our fine school would take such obvious pleasures in repeatedly suing it. Maybe he just has a grudge from one too many parking tickets issued by campus security.

I went back and reviewed our curriculum for the engineering program at Tidemarsh, and I confirmed that not a single philosophy course is required to graduate. Likewise, Tidemarsh School of Law does not even offer a philosophy class for their aspiring Sophists. Apparently, the school of jurisprudence has chosen to skip the teachings of Socrates in favor of skills development—like issuing endless vexing subpoenas or cunningly contorting facts in marathon depositions.

As a result, based upon the education he received here in the engineering discipline, I suspect Mr. Forelle could likely design with basic competence a shed or other rudimentary structure that would not collapse in a minor windstorm. However, it is also likely he received absolutely no formal training in classical philosophy. I certainly don't ever recall seeing him in one of my classes.

To be fair, perhaps a detailed understanding of philosophy is not necessary to write the book at issue as Dr. Smyth is qualified to write on the subject and, after all, Mr. Forelle only chronicles Dr. Smyth's adventures. I am sure many writers delve into subjects in which they are not experts. Still, Mr. Forelle also has no credentials as a writer or journalist. After an exhaustive search, I have concluded that Mr. Forelle has thus far failed to defraud a single agent into representing him or con a single publisher into placing any of his work into the public domain. I was not even able to find a magazine article written by him.

So, you are likely asking yourself why I am writing this foreword, as it is now abundantly clear that I am not a great fan of Mr. Forelle's work. Unfortunately, I am limited in what I can say pursuant to the nondisclosure and non-disparagement agreement I recently signed. However, I can give a bit of background as to how I came to know Mr. Forelle. Apparently, based on his less-than-lucrative writing career, he has not quit his day job. Mr. Forelle and the comfortable fish firm have represented several members of the fairer sex in matters involving alleged unfair treatment here at the university. In fact, one such client was a recent graduate student of mine. As a side note, I still fail to understand exactly what is wrong about complimenting one's appearance, or their footwear, for that matter.

As I alluded to at the start of this writing, the administration of our university settled the matter with my former graduate student, also known as She Who Is Not to be Complimented. As part of that settlement agreement, the attorney for the university requested Mr. Forelle sign what is referred to within the legal community as a "put down your pen" provision, meaning the university would settle on his client's requested terms if Mr. Forelle committed to never suing the institution again. I have been told that, at first, Mr. Forelle balked at the idea, but for some inexplicable reason, he abruptly changed his mind on the condition that Tidemarsh University Press publish his book and, to add insult to injury, that I write this foreword. Having now undertaken that task in such a manner as to not tarnish my integrity, I will also put down *my pen* and send this document to Mr. Forelle, feeling confident that it will quickly be deposited into "the round file."

If, in the extremely unlikely circumstances he includes this foreword at the beginning of his novel and you have now purchased his book, I highly recommend that you promptly return it to the store and demand a full refund and instead purchase *The Anatomy of Philosophy* by Judson A. Breckendorf III, Ph.D. It can generally be found in the academic section of the bookstore.

Preface

by Jackson Forelle

I had heard many things about the Smyth family, both while I was growing up and throughout my career in Yorktown. It's not a big place, and as a local lawyer, I'm privy to much of the scuttlebutt that goes around town. The Smyths were one of those prominent families in the area. Everyone in town knew Max was a successful businessman and also knew he only had one son, who wasn't interested in taking over the family business. Instead, his son had pursued some type of academic career. By all accounts, Max was a self-made man and came from a construction background. I think he was a brick mason when he was young and then started building homes. That's how he got the money to buy his first scallop boat, and things just grew from there. Within five more years, he owned a half-dozen of the vessels.

I don't know what happened that caused things to start going downhill, but it was the talk of the town for some time. People love to see someone they know succeed almost as much as they enjoy watching that success evaporate. I asked his son, Rye, about this a few times, and it was clear he really didn't want to talk about it.

My involvement in this story is perhaps not that significant. Still, because I felt Rye's quest was so interesting and because I played at least a minor role in the adventure, I felt compelled to write about it. When I approached Rye with the idea, he was happy to oblige. Frankly, I think he had bigger fish to fry and was only mildly intrigued by the idea of me memorializing his journey. He told me he had tried to write about it himself but had given up, and so if I wanted to give it a shot, I was free to do so. Despite his indifference to my plan to write this book, he was kind enough to give me all the

14

notes he had taken on his trip, which were extensive and detailed. Rye explained that he no longer needed them and that I was free to use them as I pleased. Although some of the information I obtained from these notes, as well as my interviews with Samuel, Kaia, and Nori, was secondhand, I believe the book is generally an accurate depiction of events.

Also, I would like to thank Judd at Slack Tide U—which is what me and my friends called Tidemarsh University when we attended there—for his thoughtful foreword for this book. I would like to give him particular credit for the new moniker for our law firm, "the Comfortable Fish Firm." You see, since our representation of Rye, we have developed quite the reputation within the commercial fishing industry, and our admiralty practice has flourished. Sometimes, you just need to "lean into" things. As a result, we have added Judd's suggested tagline to our letterhead, along with a suitably haughty-looking shark standing upright with the assistance of a walking stick and sporting a monocle to boot. I was able to find a copy of my first sketch of our new trademark. Keep in mind that I drew it on a bar napkin while drunk. I can assure you the final design was much more refined and impressive.

We've enjoyed working for several of these small seagoing businesses operating in the region. Many of them have a number of minor matters that require regular legal attention. These companies are too small to need "in-house" counsel and have instead chosen to hire outside counsel on an ad hoc basis. You could say that we have effectively become their "out house" counsel. The characterization is particularly well suited when you consider the fact that we handle all kinds of shit for them.

Also, to be clear, I, of course, gave Rye the opportunity to write the foreword to this book. He indicated that he was flattered, but he was just too busy to dedicate sufficient time to do justice to the project. Certainly, given his current undertakings, this is more than understandable. Despite his busy schedule, he still took time to meet me for drinks the other night. I took the opportunity to share Judd's draft foreword with Rye. Upon reviewing it, Rye told me that Judson Breckendorf was an obnoxious blowhard and that the man had written an equally scathing review of one of Rye's academic papers. In fact, Rye was so upset that, his other obligations be damned, he offered to take the time to write a foreword befitting this book.

I gave Rye a little background about how the foreword came into being. I explained to him how, during the mediation, Tidemarsh wanted me to agree to never file suit against them again. I decided that if I was going to agree to that, I may as well get something out of the deal. I wanted Tidemarsh to publish my book because they'd worked with some well-received authors over the years, including a couple of laureates. More importantly, they recently published a book by a local author on backyard chicken keeping that really took off.

I threw in the bit about Judd writing the foreword as an afterthought in my settlement offer. I meant it more as a joke than anything else and really didn't think the university would go for it as part of the settlement. I was surprised when they came back and agreed without even discussing it with Judd. I think the administration was a little pissed off that the school had to write a big check due to Judd's unwanted advances toward my client. Maybe they decided a little salt in the wound might deter future bad conduct.

When Judd was compelled to draft the foreword, I figured, at best, he would write a couple of caustic paragraphs about how the book was worthless and call it a day, in which case I'd have a good laugh and toss it. But when I read what Judd sent me, I knew that I had struck gold. I guess he just couldn't pass up the opportunity to bloviate about himself. As a result, I was happy to include his unedited foreword as part of this book.

As to his comments regarding the merits of this novel, I will leave it to you, gentle readers, to decide if I have something worthwhile to say and whether I conveyed this information in, at least, a mildly entertaining fashion. Just please remember that I am, after all, a lawyer and not a writer nor a philosopher.

Part I

Chapter One

Most people don't realize it, but pretty much anyone can get buried at sea. I'm not talking about scattering ashes, either. What I'm referring to is disposing of a complete body. I was skeptical about this at first and thought the final interment in the deep blue was reserved for those in the Navy and such. I had to look it up myself to satisfy my curiosity. You can't legally chuck your dead cat or dog overboard, but you can toss a dead person into the drink.

You don't even need to get a permit. All you're required to do is notify the EPA within thirty days after the burial. Not surprisingly, there are a few other regulatory requirements. You need to be at least three miles offshore, and the water must be at least six hundred feet deep at the dumping location. Maybe the term "dumping" is a little harsh, but after talking to Rye, that's the best word I can think of to describe the funeral service for his father, Max.

By the way, federal regulations prohibit a burial at sea by means of an open-air pyre, which, if you ask me, is unfortunate. I think a lot of guys have had at least a fleeting interest, at some point, in "going out" engulfed in a glorious ball of fire. Despite my own curiosity, I'm not certain I can put my finger on the allure of earthly departure by nautical barbeque. Maybe we're holding out hope of waking up in an oversized beer hall, surrounded by scads of attractive and salaciously dressed—or perhaps less than dressed—people of the preferred gender. Still, all things considered, I understand why the feds don't allow it. I mean, what happens if the fire fizzles and fails to complete the job? I suspect having a "Pittsburgh rare" body washing up on the beach could really ruin the old family picnic and result in at least a solid decade of counseling for the kiddos.

But the idea of just dropping me in the open water after I die, as-is and unheated, freaks me out a little. Maybe it shouldn't. I understand that there are monks in Tibet who will occasionally chop people up upon their demise and feed them to the eagles and other large carrion birds that live in the high mountains. It's called a sky burial, and it represents generosity to other living beings. Maybe it's not that different from being eaten by a bunch of fish.

Rye told me that only a handful of people had been invited to take part in his father's burial. Max's sister was there even though the two hadn't really gotten along for the last several years. I think their relationship had devolved into a state of mutual tolerance, at best. A few men that Max had worked with over the years were also on the boat. They weren't the bankers and businesspeople, either. A couple of the guys had worked on the water for a living. One was a former scallop boat captain who had worked for Rye's dad at some point. Another man was a house framer and had remained friends with his father ever since they had worked construction together in their early twenties. They were all pretty old but nice and told Rye the types of things they were supposed to, like how they liked his father and were going to miss him.

The steel scallop boat that was transporting them was close to a hundred feet long, and it took them several hours to get offshore at cruising speed. This was mainly because the boat was kept in Yorktown, and they had to motor twenty miles down the bay and past the Chesapeake Bay Bridge-Tunnel before heading out into the Atlantic. It wasn't a windy day, but there was a low-pressure system several hundred miles offshore, and this was causing a steady swell.

The ceremony itself was damn strange. I guess all funerals are strange, but this one stands out more to me. There was some minister there from a church Rye's father apparently belonged to. This was a surprise to Rye. As far as he knew, his dad hadn't been to a church in years.

There were three readings. The first reading by the minister was from Psalms. "Those who go down to the sea in ships and ply their trade in great waters, these have seen the works of the Lord and his wonders in the deep." The minister's second reading was from the Book of Matthew. It was the verse about Jonah being in the belly of a great fish for three days and three nights. I guess this is where Max figured he was heading. The minister then handed Rye the final reading pursuant to his dad's written instructions in his will. It was a quote from *The Fountainhead* by Ayn Rand that said, "The only thing that matters, my goal, my reward, my beginning, my end is the work itself. My work done my way." My first thought when Rye told me this was that maybe his father was trying to make a postmortem connection with Rye. Maybe it was the closest thing to philosophy that Max understood and believed in. Then again, maybe Max just wanted Rye to deliver his final middle-finger salute to everyone that had pissed him off over the years.

After the readings, two of the men Rye had met on the ride out lifted Max out of a casket-shaped fiberglass container. They had Max packed on ice like a fish. He was also wrapped up in some kind of white shroud, so you couldn't see any of him. The two guys were big dudes, and it was a good thing because Max wasn't a small guy, either. Max was also wrapped up in some stainless steel chains so he'd sink faster. I guess the chains also make sure you don't float back up later. They're insurance that you go down and stay down.

One of the two burly men grabbed Max's feet, and the second lifted him by his head. They shuffled to the back of the boat carrying him and then paused at the back rail, which was well over waist-high. The men realized they had to really get under Max to lift him up high enough to clear the rail—maybe by using a "clean and jerk" method you might see someone do in a weight room—or they could stand back farther and get a windup to toss him over. The man holding Max's head made the call when he said, "On three."

Everybody was holding their breath, worried that Max wouldn't clear the rail. The two guys carrying him must have had the same thought because they threw him extra hard, and he sailed back and hit the water a good ten feet behind the boat. Rye was so stressed watching the whole maneuver that he didn't think to look down into the water right away, and his father was already out of sight by the time he walked to the rail to look for him.

As soon as the boat arrived back at the docks, Rye had to rush to make it to the memorial service on time. He'd forgotten to pick up his suit the day before, so he swung by the Kentucky Fried Cleaners on the way to the funeral home. Having grown up in the area, I still remember waiting with eager anticipation as a child, having heard a would-be franchisee was bringing the Colonel's secret recipe for fried chicken to Yorktown.

For those of you who are too young to know this, Colonel Sanders was a real person. He was really a colonel as well, although not a military one. In Kentucky, the governor has the authority to issue "letters patent" and thereby bestow honorary titles on citizens in the state. The highest title given in the state is a Kentucky Colonel, which Colonel Sanders was. I guess the governor was damn impressed with that chicken. There's a long history of letters patent that flows from English law. A slightly less prestigious example of a

21

letters patent—at least in the eyes of a chicken-lovin' Kentuckian—is the Prince of Wales, which is traditionally given to the male heir apparent to the English throne.

For some reason, I don't think the Virginia governor has the power to issue letters patent. The closest thing he has to bestow a special status on another is the authority to give out license plates with low-digit numbers. If you see a Virginia license plate around with a number between one and one hundred, that's somebody who's got some connections in the governor's office. Somebody who has a plate with numbers between a hundred and a thousand is special, too, but just not as special as someone with the lower digits.

I've never actually asked a police officer whether there's an unwritten policy to cut these folks a break if they're speeding, but I expect there may be. Someone told me that at one time, the police couldn't even run these plates to find out who the vehicles were registered to, but the state legislature—most of whom had the coveted plates—changed the law because they were afraid of a public backlash if it came to light. As a mere mortal without any significant political connection, I just have a good old regular license plate with a combination of six letters and numbers. That's okay with me, though. There are also benefits to anonymity.

The aspiring Yorktown KFC franchisee also didn't have a title or a magic license plate that could make a summons disappear. He hoped he could one day wield that type of power and intended to start down this path as a Chicken Lieutenant in Yorktown. Unfortunately, it never happened. The rumor at the time was that an existing KFC franchisee in a neighboring community—he was probably a Chicken Major or at least a Chicken Captain, as I heard he was operating in several locations—objected to the proposed restaurant in Yorktown.

Apparently, the Yorktown location was too close to one of the existing restaurants under the all-powerful franchise agreement. By the time this came to light, the Yorktown building was nearly done, complete with its signature red-striped, pointy mansard roof. Knowing he was outranked, the man who had hoped to diversify Yorktown's chicken offerings gave up and sold the building to someone who wished to open a dry-cleaning business in the community. Not wanting to waste money and tear down a perfectly functional, albeit slightly funky, roof, the new owner just painted the roof's red stripes black and opened up. This spawned the first—and likely only—Kentucky Fried Cleaners.

Rye picked up his suit and proceeded to the funeral home to change. Because I didn't personally know Max and had not yet met Rye when Max passed away, I didn't go to the memorial service that evening. I remember there were a lot of people who went to it. The funeral home is located just down Route 17 from my law practice. In reviewing Rye's notes, it became clear to me that he was really struggling with the loss of his father. The death apparently sprouted a thought the night his dad died. At first, it was just a passing thought.

It was a question he had asked himself before, typically at times when his life was in transition, like when he was trying to figure out if he really wanted to get his Ph.D. The question he posed to himself was, "What should I do with the time I have left?"

He figured the thought would pass. But in the following days leading up to the funeral, the question didn't subside. Instead, it increased in frequency and volume, making it hard to shut out. The question also morphed into the truncated version of "with time left." Academia loves acronyms nearly as much as the military, and it's likely Rye's many years spent at universities that caused his subconscious to further abbreviate the invasive thought to WTL, pronounced as *Whittle*. This was the cadence Rye could not escape at the memorial service. At the time, Rye couldn't help but recognize the appropriateness of the acronym because he felt like the obsessive thought was whittling away at his sanity.

Rye walked outside even before the memorial service had wrapped up. He'd been feeling a little dizzy ever since he got off the boat. That wasn't surprising. Because he'd spent nearly the entire day in those rolling swells of the bay and ocean, I'm guessing he was a little landsick. I've experienced this many times after spending a full day on the water. It's like the Earth isn't steadily rotating on its axis anymore but instead has become off-kilter and has picked up a bit of a shimmy. Kind of like a spinning top before it collapses. I thought it was just me who got this, but then I read about it in a Jack London story and realized it wasn't uncommon. It usually goes away in a few hours, but it can last longer. I expect that, between being off-balance and the emotional trauma of the day, Rye was having a rough time.

As he stood on the porch of the funeral home, Rye spotted the guys in the parking lot who had tossed his father into the sea earlier in the day. They were shaking hands with a couple of other old dudes. They looked like they were saying their goodbyes. Rye suddenly had a desire to leave as well, but he knew it would be rude to go before all the guests departed. Rye was still enviously watching the men in the parking lot when he felt a tap on his shoulder and turned to see Ernest Harker standing behind him.

I have known Mr. Harker for a few decades and have gone up against him in court multiple times. Most people call him Ernie. Practicing law in a relatively small community has some advantages. There are only so many of us around, and it's not unusual for the few lawyers in the area to have several cases against each other in a year's time. Because of this, most lawyers aren't inclined to pull a fast one on a colleague. That's one reason I'm more careful in my occasional dealings with lawyers from Washington, D C, New York, or other big cities. Those folks can sometimes go their entire careers without ever crossing swords a second time with the same attorney, and in that type of environment, lawyers are less worried about making enemies.

Ernie Harker was an excommunicated Washington, DC, attorney who apparently decided he had had enough of the grind up there and wanted to make a go of it here in the area. Unfortunately, even though he had only practiced up in our nation's capital for a few years, he just couldn't shake what he'd learned during that time.

Don't get me wrong. Ernie could be friendly when he wanted to be, but it often meant he wanted something in return. I told somebody once that dealing with him was like trying to grab a snake out of a burlap sack. Not only is it always slippery, but it's also hard to tell if you got the head or the tail.

"Oh, hello, Ernest. I thought you had left already," Rye said.

Ernie had introduced himself to Rye a little earlier in the funeral home and told Rye he was the longtime attorney for his father. He attempted to talk to Rye about some "important business matter," even though several other people were waiting to talk to Rye in the receiving line.

"I hung around in my car for a bit. I thought I might catch you when you were leaving," Ernie said as he swished around a small disposable plastic cup that was empty except for a few residual ice cubes.

Rye picked up on the smell of alcohol on Ernie's breath. "I hope I didn't keep you waiting too long. How about I call you tomorrow, and we can talk then?"

"It's no problem. I never pass up the opportunity to attend a funeral or a memorial service. I usually pick up a good amount of work from them. Everyone thinks about their estate plans when someone dies. Nice job on the respite food, by the way. The scallops wrapped in bacon were a nice touch. Usually, when I go to these things, there's just crappy finger food, but I really filled up here. Nicely stocked full bar, too," Ernie said as he swished his cup again and then jiggled the last few pieces of ice into his mouth.

Rye, who had not eaten all day, responded, "My father told me several times when I was young to never let someone leave your home without offering them food and a drink. I thought he would want the same thing for his service. I just hired a caterer to handle it all."

"*My* father always said that the best-tasting food and drink is the food and drink that's bought by someone else. I'm not sure where he got that from. I should look it up," Ernie said with a shrug. "Anyways, I needed to talk to you about your father's business dealings. I'm still trying to make him some money, and there's a bit of urgency here."

"Ernest, I don't expect my father has any urgency to make money at the moment," Rye said.

"Yes, yes . . . of course," Ernie stammered. "I mean, I am trying to make *his estate* some money."

Rye said nothing.

"Your dad was a great man," Ernie continued. "At one point, he was one of the wealthiest men around here. I think he owned a dozen scallop boats at the height of things. Eight here in Yorktown and another four that he docked down in Hampton."

"Yes, that sounds right," Rye responded flatly, not recalling exactly how many boats his father had owned.

"Of course, he lost nearly everyting. I hate to say this, Rye, but he made some terrible decisions over the last few years. I tried to keep him on track, but he just wouldn't listen. You know . . . the whole horse and water thing. And your dad could be more like a mule than a horse when he set his mind to something."

Ernie's phone rang before Rye could respond, which Ernie answered, holding up his index finger to signal he would just be a moment.

"I'll call you back in a few minutes," Ernie said into the receiver.

After a pause, he hurriedly added, I'm at the service now. Bye."

"Sorry about that," Ernie said. "As I was saying, your father made a damn big mess of things. I did his estate plan, and everything goes to you. Unfortunately, I don't think he had much left. He still owned his home, but it's heavily mortgaged. There may be a bit of equity there, but not much, and the cost of a real estate agent will eat that up. The personal belongings in the home all go to you, though. I saw he also had a small life insurance policy for his burial expenses, but looking at the spread you put on, I'm sure that's gone now."

Feeling exhaustion settling in, Rye said, "Ernest, if it's about the house and his personal effects, can we talk about it later? The service just ended, and I'm quite tired now."

"Actually, it's about the *Miss Elizabeth*."

"Who?"

"The *Miss Elizabeth*. It's the boat you were on earlier today for the burial."

"Huh, I never caught the boat's name," Rye muttered.

"Well, your father still owned her, free and clear. She's run-down and a little beat up, but I think she's still basically seaworthy, or at least she's not in immediate threat of sinking. The boat has been mostly laid up at the docks of the scallop company. As far as I know, your trip earlier today was the first out in quite a long time. I understand the dredges and rigging are shot, so she can't work right now. It will cost six figures to get her in working order again, and your dad didn't have the money to do it."

"I understand," Rye said, thinking that he didn't have that kind of money lying around, either.

"I've been talking with another client of mine for the last few months who's also in the scallop business. He had made an offer to your dad to buy the boat. I think your dad had basically agreed to sell it, but he hadn't signed the final paperwork yet. The offer is still open. I can get you a hundred thousand to sell it as it sits. I actually have the paperwork in the car if you'd like to sign the agreement now."

"Thanks, but I need to think about it," Rye said with a sigh.

"Sure, but don't take too long. I think it's a good deal, and that kind of money could make a real difference for someone like you. I know academia doesn't pay that much. Not that it's not a worthy pursuit," Ernie quickly added. "What is it you teach? Psychology, right?"

"Philosophy."

"Of course. I knew it was something like that. Get back to me as soon as you can. Call me at my office," Ernie said as he headed to his car while calling someone on his cell phone.

Chapter Two

The following day, things hadn't improved for Rye. He sat in his windowless office at the university with his head buried in his arms on a desk covered in a mix of academic papers and textbooks. He'd been there for over an hour trying to rally himself. With great effort, he lifted his head and studied the watch on his wrist that his father had given him some years ago. Rye saw that it was nearly time for his 10:00 a.m. section of Philosophy 210—*An Introduction to Ancient Greek Philosophy.*

He mustered enough strength to stand up and walk down the dimly lit hallway to the classroom. He hadn't slept for days, and his mind was more disheveled than his office. The decision regarding the scallop boat had added a new variable to an equation that was already unsolvable in his compromised state. Rye questioned whether he should have even come in to teach. There were only a few classes left in the semester, and certainly, the administration would have understood him taking some time off.

Rye rounded a corner and entered a narrow indoor corridor that connected the philosophy building, where his office was located, to the chemistry building, where his Philosophy 201 class was waiting to be taught. Rye's other classes for the semester were located even farther away, and Rye wondered who he'd pissed off to get such crappy classroom locations. One of the neon tubes in an overhead light was flickering, and Rye's left eye twitched in unison with the strobe effect on the surrounding hallway walls.

Rye slipped into the classroom and walked past a diminutive man with a white beard and round glasses who was exiting. He recognized the man as a well-regarded chemistry professor. Rye had never actually spoken with the colleague, but there was a rumor that the chemist had made a fortune inventing an everlasting urinal cake after being inspired by a psilocybin-induced lucid dream where Willy Wonka was a plumber instead of a candymaker. The little man smiled broadly and offered a hello to Rye as he passed. Rye half-heartedly attempted to smile back as he shuffled absently to the large wooden desk at the front of the lecture hall. He didn't look up but instead pulled out a rickety wooden chair behind the desk and plopped down in it.

The classroom was one of the smaller auditorium-style rooms with the seating area sloping up toward the back. It was designed to hold around a hundred students, even though only about half that number were taking Rye's class. The last students trickled in, but Rye just sat motionless and studied at the wood grain veneer that traversed the desk. Some students continued to talk with one another while others were engrossed in their phones or computers, but after more time passed, an uneasiness settled in and the classroom began to focus more on the stock-still professor sitting at the front of the room.

Rye had been planning to continue his discussion about Socrates, but now, at the last minute, he decided to jump ahead to what had traditionally been the lecture he saved for the last class of the semester.

"What are your most important considerations going to be when you graduate with your degree and start looking for a job?" he asked as he raised his gaze to the quiet room.

One of the male students sitting in the middle of the classroom immediately answered with enthusiasm and said, "Money!"

Rye stood and walked to the whiteboard at the front of the room and erased the hieroglyphic chemical equations from the previous class. He wrote "MONEY" in large letters on the right side of the board and circled it.

"What else?" Rye asked.

"Work-life balance," another student volunteered. "I don't want to work myself to death."

Rye went to the left side of the whiteboard and wrote "WORK-LIFE BALANCE."

"Anything else?" he asked.

A young woman in the front row then said, "I want a job I enjoy, and I want it to be fulfilling."

Rye added "ENJOYMENT" and "FULFILLMENT" to the left side of the board under WORK-LIFE BALANCE and then wrote in larger capital letters underneath the word "HAPPINESS" and circled it. He then went back over and sat in the chair behind the front desk again.

"Now, let's do a little thought experiment. I'm going to give you all two choices—an existential fork in the road," Rye explained. "If you take the road to your right, upon your graduation from this institution, you'll take a job that is very lucrative. Let's say you're going to be employed as the head of sales for an international urinal cake company."

Several students laughed, recognizing the innuendo about the chemistry professor who had just left the room.

"You'll make a great deal of money. In fact, you'll have more money than you can easily spend. You will be able to buy just about any house you wish and any car you want. You can even get one of those vanity license plates. Perhaps something like 'LUVWEE' or 'PISSCAKES.'"

More students laughed.

"You'll be able to buy all the other niceties our modern-day society can provide you," Rye continued. "However, there is a catch. You will *hate* this job. The job will not be mentally stimulating but mundane. You will wake up every morning despising the idea of going to work, and you'll need to drag yourself out of bed. The short walk out your front door and down your driveway to your very expensive and bedazzled car will feel like a trudge across a ten-mile soggy bog while wearing the latest in high-tech swimming flippers. You'll grow to detest the trademark best-selling scents of Bubblegum Brook and Cotton Candy Cataract. Oh, and there's also a second requirement in our thought experiment that's tied to taking the path to the right. You'll need to commit to taking this job for twenty years. At that point, you can quit, and you will have enough money to do whatever you want for the rest of your life.

"Okay, now let's talk about the path to the left," Rye continued. "Somebody give me an example of a job that you think might fit these criteria."

The student who had said she wanted a job that she liked said, "How about a kindergarten teacher?"

"Maybe for you. That sounds like the worst job imaginable for me," the girl sitting next to her objected. "A bunch of little kids running around and screaming with runny noses and snot bubbles."

"I want to blow stuff up," a student near the back of the room interjected.

"Fine," Rye said. "So, let's agree that the perfect job is subjective. For the sake of argument, let's just say that the job everyone would love is a kind of kindergarten mad scientist. This person goes around with a rolling cart to the different classes and blows things up and conducts other interesting experiments. Can we all get onboard with that?"

Several of the students nodded in agreement.

"So, if you take this road, you will pursue a career upon your graduation that is not lucrative, but is a career that you will love," Rye said. "The job will be mentally stimulating and fulfilling. You'll get to come up with all kinds of interesting experiments. From erupting volcanos to exploding bottles filled with Coke and Mentos, the kids are going to love them all! Just to be clear, you'll be able to make a decent living doing this. You'll buy an inexpensive car, like a used Toyota or something, and you can still get a vanity plate. After all, it costs like ten bucks at the Virginia DMV to get custom plates. Maybe it says 'C4 4 KIDS.' After several years of work, you'll also be able to purchase a modest but nice home. You'll need to live on a budget and save for things like vacations or other large purchases. If you take this road, you'll work until you can no longer do so, whether that results from physical or mental decline. There will be no 'golden years' of retirement for you. However, that will be fine because you don't want to quit your job. You'll get up every morning and can't wait to get to work. You'll be so happy that people might start to avoid you because you're just too damn upbeat. So, these are the two choices you have. Everyone who would take the path to the right and take the money, please raise your hand."

Rye scanned the room and saw all but a few students had raised their hands. He pointed to one of the young men in the middle of the class who had his hand up in the air and asked, "Why?"

"Because I want to have nice things," the student explained. "I want a nice house and a kick-ass car. I don't have a problem with urinal cakes if they make me rich. Hell, I'll put a big sign out in gold letters at the security gate of my mansion that says 'Wizz Manor.'"

More laughs erupted from the class.

"I understand," replied Rye. "But you would have a place to live and basic transportation if you took the other path. Is this worth twenty years of your life? Think about it. That's likely a quarter of your life—and that's if you're lucky! Are you really willing to give that up for nicer stuff?"

"Let's face it, Professor, stuff is important."

"Why?" asked Rye. "I mean, my car isn't expensive, but it gets me to where I want to go. I don't live in a mansion, but I don't believe I would be any happier if I did."

The student thought for a moment and responded, "It's more than the stuff, I guess. I want to be successful. The person who sells the piss cakes might get laughed at, but he's successful."

"Why does that person sound successful?" asked Rye.

"Because he has money. He has the expensive house and expensive car. That's what success is."

"Says who?"

"Everybody! Just look around!"

"And this is important to you?" asked Rye.

"Well, sure. Everybody wants to be successful."

"So, to ask this question again in a slightly different manner, you're willing to spend twenty years of your life in misery so other people will see you as a success? Does that really make good sense?"

"I think so," said the student in a wavering tone.

After a brief pause, a young woman who had been sitting quietly in the classroom raised her hand.

"Yes?" Rye asked, pointing to her.

"Professor, what if we want the best of both? What if we want to make a lot of money and have a job we love?"

"That's an excellent question," responded Rye excitedly as he jumped to his feet. "The problem with that scenario is . . . ." Rye swayed back and forth for a moment, trying to steady himself, but then promptly collapsed, striking the side of his head on the floor as he landed.

Chapter Three

When Rye awoke, he was disoriented and thought he was in his bedroom back at home and that he needed to get moving. He felt like he was late for something, but he didn't know what. Then he heard the voices of several of his students who were standing around him and calling his name. He panicked for a moment. Tenure or not, he might have a problem explaining to the dean why he had multiple students in his bedroom. In his state of semi-consciousness, he tried to recall if orgies were strictly forbidden in the faculty handbook. As he sat up with a jolt, he looked around and realized he was still in his classroom. Rye took a deep sigh of relief.

"Are you okay, Professor?" one student asked.

"I'm fine, I'm fine," Rye stuttered, trying to get himself oriented.

"Professor, we called 911. They're on the way," the student explained.

Rye tried to stand up, but he was clearly still dizzy.

"Professor, just stay put. I think you hit your head."

"Perhaps you're right," Rye said, rubbing the left side of his head and feeling a large bump. "What happened?"

"You just fell over. You've been out for five minutes."

"I see," Rye said. "And where am I now?"

By the time the paramedics arrived, most of the students had left, but a few lingered to make sure their teacher was okay. The male and female paramedics were wearing matching khaki pants and navy blue short-sleeved polo shirts with some type of smartly embroidered logos on their left pockets. The man was also wearing a matching navy visor. Both of them looked very young to Rye, and he thought they looked like they belonged more in a golf tournament than in an ambulance.

"What'd you shoot on the back nine?" Rye asked the young man.

The paramedics just looked at each other, and the woman asked a student what had happened. She then leaned over to examine Rye's head and found the large knot on it. As she straightened back up, she noticed Rye staring at her chest. Rye's eyes caught hers looking down self-consciously at her neckline to make sure her shirt wasn't too far unbuttoned.

"Don't be alarmed, young lady. I wasn't looking at your breasts. I was trying to count the snakes," Rye noted with a hint of embarrassment.

The woman looked confused. "You see snakes?" she asked as her eyes shot around the room. "Ed, we may have a problem. Either our patient is delusional or there are snakes around here, and you know how I am about snakes," she said to her fellow paramedic.

"Your insignia," Rye further explained.

The woman looked down at her shirt again, this time to inspect the logo of the local EMT group, and noticed that there was a staff in the center of the insignia with a snake wrapped around it. "Oh. It's just one snake, I think," the woman said with a chuckle.

"That's good. It happens to be the Rod of Asclepius. Asclepius was the Roman god of medicine and healing. I met him at one of the dean's cocktail parties a few years ago. Nice enough guy, but like a lot of Italians, he didn't have a good sense of the personal space we Americans are comfortable with. He was also kind of handsy. You know what I mean? One of those guys who's touchy-feely. I don't think it was really sexual, but it still made me a bit uncomfortable. Hell, maybe he was coming on to me. I've never been very good at reading those kinds of signals. Regardless, he's known to have some extraordinary healing powers and was damn good at prophecies as well. Some people get the Rod of Asclepius confused with the Staff of Caduceus, which has two snakes and sometimes wings at the top of it. That staff belongs to Hermes, and he really could be a bit of an asshole. He drinks too much and makes inappropriate jokes," Rye explained. "All in all, I think the Rod of Asclepius is a better pick than the Staff of Caduceus for your logo."

The female EMT looked at Rye quizzically. "Maybe we should take you in and have you checked out. Are you feeling dizzy?"

"Yes, but I've been feeling dizzy for two days now," Rye said, referring to his land sickness.

"Okay. Let's have the doctors look at that for you," the woman suggested.

"Only if you think it's necessary," Rye replied.

When Rye arrived at the emergency department of the hospital, a nurse quickly took him back to a room, put him in a paper gown, and took his vital signs. She then quickly disappeared and told him to wait for a doctor. The hospital was busy, and it took a youthful but tired-looking resident some time to make it to Rye's room. As the doctor walked in, he discovered a thin, middle-aged man pacing the room, sinewy arms and legs jutting awkwardly from an ill-fitting paper gown. The man muttered to himself as he moved, his wiry frame in constant motion.

"Excuse me, Mr. Smyth?" the doctor interrupted.

Upon hearing this, Rye spun around quickly, looked the doctor squarely in the eye, and rushed to him with his hand extended to shake and said, "Ah, you are the medical doctor, correct?"

The doctor was clearly taken aback by Rye's wide eyes and overenthusiastic mannerisms.

"Yes . . . yes sir, that's correct," the doctor sputtered.

"Humm, you appear a little on the young side and entirely too healthy," Rye said, eyeing the doctor suspiciously.

"I'm sorry. I don't understand. Would you prefer a sick doctor?" the resident asked.

"By the dog, that is exactly what I want! It is only a doctor who has been very sick himself who will have the best understanding of how to treat an affliction. The sicklier the doctor, the better, in my opinion!"

Amused by this response, the young doctor said, "I don't think there are any particularly old and sick doctors available now. How about you let me take a look at you?"

"Are you sure?" asked Rye. "I would think that a fine facility like this would have multiple feeble practitioners of the medical arts around who have managed to narrowly escape the jaws of death on some previous occasions."

"Well, I had my appendix removed a few years ago, if that's any consolation," the young doctor managed.

"Hum, not very harrowing by today's standards. After all, it's not even a vital organ, is it now? I believe it is a holdover from our earlier ancestors to aid digestion back when they ate grass and tree bark and such. Nothing more significant? I'd feel better if it was a gallbladder. At least it still does something. A kidney would be even better. Oh, a heart! Yes, a heart! Now, if you had your heart removed, you'd have my full and undivided attention!"

"I have good news for you. You see, my heart was ripped out in third grade by a girl named Vicky Davis when she pushed me out of the sandbox and told me that we couldn't play together any longer," the doctor explained.

"Ahh, excellent. Then let us proceed," Rye replied as he sat down on the examination table. "You know, I am a doctor myself."

"Really? What kind?"

"The kind that considers the entire patient—his health, his mind and his soul."

"Functional medicine?" the doctor asked.

"Of course not. You really must think more broadly," Rye explained.

"Theology?"

"Heaven forbid, no! I am a Doctor of Philosophy, and by that, I mean that I hold an actual Ph.D.—one grounded in the field of philosophy. If you had occasion to see it, the piece of paper on my office wall would demonstrate that I obtained the degree from the same illustrious institution where I now impart knowledge. Did you know that 'philosophy' means 'love of wisdom,' and that, based on its Greek derivative, 'doctor' means 'teacher' or 'instructor,' such that a Ph.D. basically means someone with a love of wisdom who is qualified to teach it?"

"No," the doctor replied, appearing anxious to get the conversation back on track.

"Well, it does. The problem is that they now give Ph.D.s to people graduating from all types of fields, including degrees that are more vocational in nature. What I mean to say is that they even give them in fields that are better suited to a journeyman—such as someone seeking a career in mathematics and physics. So, I ask you, just how is one supposed to differentiate oneself when one's Ph.D. is actually rooted in philosophy?"

"I . . . I don't know," the doctor stammered as he walked over and inspected Rye's head. "So, tell me what happened."

"I don't fully know. I remember walking to my classroom, and now I'm here. I believe someone told me I fell."

"I see a good bump on your head here. Is this where you hit the ground?"

"Young man, do you not recall me just telling you I don't know what happened?" Rye said. "I am wondering who it is that is injured here. Perhaps I didn't give you enough credit for your prior surgery. Were there any complications or long-term effects?"

"Okay, just relax. Do you have a headache?"

"Perhaps a bit."

"Any other symptoms?"

"Relief."

"Relief from what?"

"I believe that knock on my noggin has dislodged those pesky creatures that have been driving me to near insanity. If I had realized that it would only take a good thumping to do so, I may have committed this act of self-care days ago!"

"I'm not sure I understand," said the doctor as he checked Rye's reflexes.

"My head is finally clear! I feel the veil has been lifted because of this minor incident, and an opportunity has now presented itself for me to undertake something of great importance."

"What's that?" the doctor asked, intrigued.

"Oh, it would take far too long to explain to you, and I fear your beliefs may be too ingrained into the system to listen."

"I see," the doctor responded, deciding it would be best to drop this line of questioning.

"Can you tell me what the date is?" he asked.

"It's a Friday."

"Can you give me the actual date?"

"I rarely try to keep track of extraneous information that can be looked up easily. Superfluous data crowds the mind unnecessarily with triviality and detracts from analysis that is more important."

"I see," said the doctor. "I'm just trying to determine if you may have some kind of head injury," the doctor said as he removed a small flashlight from his pocket and shined into each of Rye's eyes. "Can you tell me who the president is?" he asked.

"The president of what?" Rye inquired. "I can tell you that the president of the International Society of Philosophical Analysis is currently a learned gentleman named Lucius something, if I recall correctly. He has written extensively on cross-cultural moral patterns with an emphasis on interpersonal features."

"I was actually referring to the United States."

"Oh, I don't think it's a good idea to discuss politics with your doctor."

"You're making this quite difficult," the doctor said with a sigh.

"I assure you that is not my intent."

"Your reflexes appear to be fine, but I think you likely have a bit of a concussion. Perhaps we should run a few tests, but I'll talk to the attending physician."

"I don't see any need for any tests," said Rye. "I have been a relatively healthy person and, as such, have generally discounted my need for physicians. If you're healthy, you don't need one, and if you are very ill, you will probably die, and what's the point of needlessly extending that process? Especially because such an extension may not be an enjoyable process."

"Still, I think we should just make sure you haven't suffered a more serious injury."

"I appreciate your input, but I would like to leave now. I have decided I have a great deal of planning to do."

The attending doctor flipped back through Rye's admission notes and must have noticed that Rye had been brought from the university, supporting Rye's story. I say this because the doctor reluctantly agreed to release Rye and told him to come back in if he started feeling worse.

Upon leaving the hospital, Rye immediately drove to the university. He headed to the dean's office, where he put in for leave for his last few classes and indicated that he would not be giving a final exam but would assign a paper instead. Rye then went down to his office and sent out an email to all his students confirming that there would be no final exams but instead directed all of them to write a paper analyzing the merits of living *in accordance with nature* as advocated by the ancient Greek school of Cynic philosophers. He then logged into the university grading system and gave every student in his classes an "A" for their final grade, knowing that the grades would not be posted until after the semester had ended.

Chapter Four

Rye decided it was time for him to inspect his newly inherited vessel, so he hopped back into his car and drove to the waterfront. It was a little after 3 p.m. when Rye drove through the rusted open gates of Yorktown Scallop Company. This was where Rye's father had always docked his boats. There was nothing fancy about the place then, and it hadn't improved with time. There was a wooden bulkhead that ran along the waterline and two massive piers that jutted out into the tea-colored brackish creek. The piers were bleached gray by the sun, with dark, tar-colored pilings that extended above the decking to a height of nearly ten feet.

There were also several truck tires wrapped around each piling to create a makeshift fendering system so that boats wouldn't get damaged when seas got rough or if a captain came in too hot. Many of the tires had frayed over the years of baking in the scorching summer sun, resulting in some of them sprouting random tufts of white rubber hair. Rye remembered seeing the tires on the pilings for the first time as a child when his father brought him here. At the time, the tires reminded him of the old carnival game where you could win a prize if you threw a small plastic ring around the neck of a Coca-Cola bottle. Rye had pictured large men throwing the tires up in the air and around the pilings in the same way.

Yorktown Scallop company also had a small brick office, a tool shed, above-ground fuel tanks, and a large industrial metal building for processing and freezing the scallops. There were nearly a dozen scallop boats docked at the pier and along the wharf, each between eighty and 100 feet and weighing close to 150 metric tons. The boat hulls were painted various shades of blue and black, but their sterns were all oxidized red from the overflow of saltwater that drained off the decks when scallops were hoisted by the dredge. The large steel riggings of the boats were painted white and pointed skyward from the boat decks.

As Rye rolled to a stop and stepped out of his vehicle, he could see a good deal of commotion going on with several men up on one of the boat decks and more below on the pier. The deck crane was lowering a pallet stacked with large white bags, which Rye knew were filled with scallops from a trip. Rye scanned the boats, but he wasn't sure which one was the *Miss Elizabeth*, even though he had recently been on her for his father's burial. They all looked pretty much the same, and the way the boats were docked, you couldn't see their sterns where the names were written. Rye climbed out of his car to ask someone which boat was his, but everyone was too busy to take notice of him.

The young man operating the forklift appeared to be struggling to get it aligned with the base of the pallet that had been lowered onto the dock. There was a weathered and shirtless old man with a long beard trying to give the operator instructions from up on the boat deck while also laughing at the younger man's lackluster operation of the forklift. "Back her up farther and try and get it lined up better and try not to back into the water!" the old man yelled down.

"No shit," the young man yelled in response, obviously frustrated, as he took another shot at getting the piece of equipment aligned with the pallet on the narrow pier.

"Get a move on, boy! You're holding us up!" said another man who was operating the deck crane on the boat.

A large man came out of the processing building and walked quickly past Rye in the parking lot and toward the docks. He was wearing jeans, a gray T-shirt, and white rubber work boots. The man was obviously annoyed and was muttering to himself.

"Excuse me, sir," Rye interjected as the man walked by.

The man did not look at Rye but focused his gaze on the activity ahead on the dock and simply replied, "Give me a minute."

As the man in the gray T-shirt approached the forklift, Rye heard him yell, "What the hell you doing down there? You said you knew how to drive a forklift!"

"I do!" the kid on the forklift shouted back. "This damn thing is messed up. I think it's the transmission or something. It's all jerky when I stop, and besides, there ain't enough room to get lined up right without ending up in the water."

"Show me," said the man in the gray T-shirt as he leaned back and rubbed his chin.

The forklift driver pulled up to the pallet again on the dock and tried to line up the forks with the openings of the pallet to pick it up, but he failed once again.

"I'm telling you something ain't right on this thing," the young man said again.

"Bullshit," said the man in the gray shirt. "Get the hell off there and I'll show you how to do it," he added as he walked over and climbed on the machine as the young man stepped off.

One of the men up on the boat yelled down, "You sure you want to do that, Port? You still remember how to run one of them things?"

Several of the men standing around laughed.

"Quit screwing around! We got to get this goddamn boat unloaded!" the man in the gray shirt yelled back as he quickly backed up the forklift within a few inches of the edge of the pier and realigned it. He then came forward and immediately picked up the pallet. He looked over at the young man, who was watching him sheepishly.

"Nothing wrong with this goddamn machine. You're new. I don't mind that you don't yet know how to operate a forklift, but don't tell me you can if you can't. We can teach you, but be upfront with me! Lead, follow, or get the hell out of the way! You head into the icehouse and help unload the bags."

"Yes, sir," the young man said, deflated, as he turned and walked away.

"Lower the next pallet!" the man on the forklift yelled back up to the boat.

Rye continued to watch the men work for another twenty minutes before someone else took over operating the forklift, and the man in the gray shirt walked back up to Rye. As he approached, he said, "What can I do for you? You looking to buy some scallops? We don't usually sell retail, but I reckon we can sell you a bag."

"No, that is not my intent, sir. What is your name?"

"Port," the man said flatly.

"Port? Like the wine?" Rye asked.

"Like the port side of the boat. I'm left-handed," the large man explained.

"I see. Well, Mr. Port, I am here to inspect my boat."

"It's just Port, and what you mean, your boat?"

"The *Miss Elizabeth*, if I am not mistaken."

"Oh damn, you're Max's kid. You're a teacher or something, right?"

"Yes, you are correct."

"She's the one at the end of the wharf over there," Port explained as he pointed to the last boat down at the end of the property. "She's a goddamn mess."

"I would like to make an impromptu inspection of the vessel if that is agreeable."

"Come on, I'll show you," Port said with a shrug as he started walking down the pier.

Rye and Port walked down to the end of the pier, where Rye's recently inherited scallop boat sat. As he walked across a wooden plank that ran from the dock to the stern of the vessel, he glanced down and observed the boat's names set out in flowing script lettering, "*Miss Elizabeth*, aka *Fat Lily*."

"Why on earth did someone choose that rather unflattering nickname for my vessel?" Rye asked.

"Because she's fat. She has a wide beam. She don't run too fast either but lumbers along pretty well through a good sea," Port explained as they made their way aboard.

Rye hadn't paid much attention to the vessel when he was out on it the day before. He was just too distracted at the time to care about what boat he was on. But as soon as he boarded it, his nose registered the familiarity of the boat's smell. It wasn't overwhelming, but it was unmistakably present. It reminded Rye of seaweed that had been sitting in the sun too long, tossed with a hint of ammonia.

"What exactly is that aroma?" Rye asked.

"Money," Port responded. "That's the smell of scallops, or their remnants, anyway. Them little bits left on the deck can get rank over time. Damn near impossible to get them up completely, even with a good scrubbing."

Rye walked around the black metal deck that looked solid despite some peeling paint and patches of rust. He noticed several hatches, a deck crane, the dredges, and a few worktables that he assumed were used to process the scallops. He also eyed the back rail, over which his father had tossed over and into the sea.

"What's below the deck?" Rye asked.

"You got the crew quarters, a small galley, and a head."

"A head of what?"

"A head—you know . . . a place to take a crap and shower and whatnot."

"What a strange name. I would have thought that a tail would have been a better choice for a name than a head. Are the quarters spartan?"

"Spartan? What the hell does that mean?"

"Are they basic and without frill?" Rye explained, a bit annoyed.

"Yep, they're basic. Nothing frilly about this boat."

"Sounds perfect. Can we look?"

"Why not? Follow me," Port said as he led Rye below.

Rye followed Port to a steel door leading down into the interior of the boat. The men descended a narrow set of metal stairs and into an equally narrow hallway. Rye followed Port down the corridor toward the bow of the boat. The hallway was lit with dim red lights mounted on the walls and encased in small metal cages. Port showed Rye a bunk room located on the port side of the bow. There were three sets of metal bunk beds in the room that were bolted to the exterior wall of the boat. The room was narrow, with little floor space beyond the bunks. On the starboard side of the boat, there was a similar-sized room that had only one bed. Port explained that this was the captain's quarters. Port then showed Rye the galley and engine room.

"From where does one control this vessel?"

"Come on," Port said as he took Rye back up a separate set of stairs that emerged next to the wheelhouse. Rye stepped inside and observed a strange confluence of old and new. There was a chair in the center of the room for the captain that was mounted on a swiveling steel post that reminded him of something in a barber shop. There were multiple windows across the front and sides of the wheelhouse that gave a good view of the outside environment despite their obvious thickness. Like the rest of the boat, the room was constructed of steel, but it was trimmed out with a dark wood interior and there was a nautical ship's wheel mounted on the center console, just in front of the captain's chair. The wheel had been made from some type of dark wood and had several layers of varnish that had likely been added over the years, which added a yellow tinge. Rye estimated that it was around two feet in diameter.

In contrast to these classic features, the front console area of the boat held multiple modern pieces of electronic equipment with a plethora of knobs, buttons, blinking lights, and brightly colored screens.

"What is all of this?" Rye asked, looking around at all the electronics.

"That there is your propulsion controls to set your speed and such, along with your navigation, radar, GPS, communications, plus a few other things."

"This appears to me a bit more complicated than I expected and entirely unnecessary, if you ask me," Rye said, eyeing all the controls and equipment suspiciously. "Still, the world has changed, I suppose. It turns out that I may need some slight instructions."

"Instructions for what?" Port asked, looking confused.

"Operating this craft, obviously," Rye responded.

"You ever run a boat like this before?"

"Not precisely like this, but in my youth, I spent several months voyaging on a beautiful Polynesian double-hulled vessel traversing from Hawaii to Tahiti. She was quite a spectacular craft at a little over sixty feet. She was constructed of wood and had two masts, and you steered her by means of a paddle of sorts."

"That right?" Port asked, not sure what to make of this description.

"Absolutely. We completed the voyage using only traditional navigation techniques, mind you. We used the sun by day and certain stars you could see shortly after sunset to maintain our course. Did you know you can also follow the course of certain migratory birds to navigate the open ocean?"

"Can't say I did," Port responded, scratching his head.

"Well, you can. It can be quite useful. We actually took a few pigs and chickens on the journey as well. We were attempting to simulate the travel methodology of the ancient Polynesians. Overall, the trip was an amazing success. Unfortunately, however, we failed to encounter any significant storms."

"Unfortunately?" Port asked.

"That's correct. We hit a few squalls along the journey, but nothing that was overly threatening. That was quite a disappointment."

"You ain't making a lick of sense, man."

Rye ignored the comment. "Anyway, back to the task at hand. I'm afraid I'm a bit rusty on my celestial navigation, and seeing you have all this equipment already in place, I may as well make use of it."

"Why you want to learn how to run this boat anyhow? I don't see you as wanting to run scallop trips. Besides, I heard you're selling the boat."

"You have heard incorrectly," Rye responded. "I have use of this stout craft. I would like to embark on a journey in search of enlightenment. I seek to live in accordance with nature!"

"What the hell are you talking about?"

"I believe I spoke plain English," Rye responded, looking puzzled.

Chapter Five

It was just past 5 p.m. when Rye pulled into the parking lot of Bar 17. The bar was located right off George Washington Memorial Highway, commonly referred to by the locals as Route 17. This place had been through several renditions over the years, including a country and western theme in the late '70s, complete with a mechanical bull. Rye had never been to the bar before but knew its reputation for having a rough crowd, including a number of bikers who frequented it.

Rye was looking for someone and was confident he would find him here. Specifically, he was looking for Samuel Keene. In fact, Samuel is the common connection between Rye and myself, and it is this connection that led to my involvement in this story. Rye and Samuel had grown up in the same local Seaford neighborhood—one of the smaller enclaves that make up the Yorktown community. Seaford was founded in the early 1600s, and it was originally called Crab Neck. As a child, I found the original name of the area more than a bit confusing. As far as I knew, crabs didn't have necks. The original name of the adjoining community, Dandy, caused additional consternation in my youth. That small community had originally been christened as Fish Neck. I could at least picture what a fish neck might look like in theory.

It was only later in my life that I realized the names were derived from the multitude of crabs and fish originally harvested from the narrow "necks" of land where the communities were located. The area continued to be populated in the later twentieth century by watermen who made a living setting crab pots and collecting oysters using hand tongs. Present-day Yorktown was more of a suburb to the adjoining Newport News, where the shipyard still dominated the employment scene. That's not to say that Yorktown didn't still have some folks who worked the water for a living. I have dealt with many of them over the years and have observed a few common traits, including a certain pride in making your own way, a general distrust of the government, and a strong aversion to taxes.

They had been friends when they were little and went to the same elementary school. After school, they spent many afternoons trudging through the marshes in search of adventures, catching crabs, and avoiding snakes. Rye had moved away in the fifth grade when his parents divorced, and he left with his mother, who had taken a job out of the state. His father stayed in Yorktown, as he was already working in the scallop business. Rye had been mostly absent from Yorktown and Seaford since he left, but he visited his father occasionally. He spent most of his professional career teaching at universities in different areas of the country until around two years ago, when he took his current position at a nearby college.

Shortly before returning to the area, while catching up on the phone, Rye's father mentioned that the dock manager had hired Samuel Keene as a mate for one of the boats owned by Rye's dad.

"That's the kid you were friends with, right?" Rye's father asked.

"Yes, that's him. How is Samuel doing?"

"We'll see. He just started."

"I really should reach out to him. Please pass along that I hope life is treating him well."

Once Rye relocated to the area, he asked his father again about Samuel so that he could contact him but was disappointed to discover that his father had fired him due to failing a drug test. At that point, Rye felt it would be too awkward to contact his old friend.

Even though Samuel had not seen Rye for nearly forty years, Samuel made it to the memorial for Rye's father. When Samuel introduced himself to Rye at the service, Rye didn't recognize him at first. It was clear that Samuel had burned the candle at both ends and looked considerably older than Rye. It was during this conversation that Samuel told Rye he was at Club 17 pretty much every day, from 5 p.m. to close.

As Rye walked into the bar, he scanned the barstools. Because of the early hour, there were only a few people in the dimly lit room, and Rye was relieved there were no bikers in sight. Rye quickly spotted Samuel sitting at the far end of the bar, talking to the young female bartender.

Rye walked over. When Samuel spotted him, he quickly spun around on his barstool with a big smile and said, "Damn, Doc! I don't see you in forever, and now, two days in a row! What are the odds of that?"

"Hello, Samuel. This is not just a random encounter with an old friend. I have come here looking for you," Rye explained as he sat down next to Samuel.

"How'd you know I'd be here?" Samuel asked as he finished off his beer. "Oh, never mind, I told you, didn't I?" Even though the bar had just opened, Rye discerned a slight slur in Samuel's speech.

"You want another one?" the bartender asked Samuel.

"Damn right, and one for my friend, too."

"None for me, actually," Rye said to the bartender.

The bartender handed Stems another beer, and Stems neatly lined up his empty bottle with a few others that were sitting on the bar.

"Why do you leave them sitting up there that way?" Rye asked his friend.

"You see, I have had a couple of issues, you might say . . . like disagreements with the folks working behind the bar here. As to my tab and exactly how many beers I've drunk by the end of the night, me and Anna here came to an agreement that we'd just line up the bottles. Keeps arguments from happenin'," Stems explained.

"Yeah, unless you carry the bottles into the bathroom," the bartended chimed in.

"Look here, you don't expect me to take a piss without a beer, do you?" Samuel inquired.

"Fine by me, as long as the bottles don't end up in the trash in there."

"Never happens," Samuel said, grinning. "Anna, this man here is a big-time professor, and we were good friends back when we were about yea high," he explained, holding his hand about waist-high.

"Stems, you know about every damn soul livin' in this town," the bartender commented.

"Did she call you Stems?" asked Rye.

"Oh, that. That's what most everybody calls me now. I reckon a few still call me Sam or Sammy, but you're probably about the only one that still calls me Samuel, except my mom, maybe."

"How is your mother?"

"She's doing great. Still livin' in the same house down in Seaford and doing her own thing. I bought me a double-wide a couple of years ago and put it back on the big field behind her house. Ain't got to pay no rent that way, you see."

"I am glad to hear she is well. So, how did you derive the peculiar moniker 'Stems'?"

"The what?"

"Why do they call you Stems?"

"Oh, it's a bad joke. People used to say that I was always smokin' crappy weed. You know, that it was full of stems and stuff. I guess it just stuck somehow. Mind you, I only smoke good shit now. I reckon people oughta be calling me 'Bud.' You sure you don't want a drink?"

"Thank you, but no. I don't drink often. For some unexplained reason, I am impervious to the effects of alcohol."

"Say what?" asked Stems.

"It has no effect upon me."

"Damn, that sucks. Talk about bad luck. Why bother to even drink, then?"

"I generally agree, although I find sharing an occasional drink can set others at ease."

"I don't know. Maybe you should see a doctor or something. Just don't sound right."

"It is of no importance," said Rye. "I've come to you as I am looking for assistance."

"So, what do you need from me, Doc?"

"I am in need of your navigation skills."

"You came all the way down here 'cause you need directions or something?"

"It's a bit more than that. I inherited the *Miss Elizabeth* from my father, and I would like to take her on an excursion."

"That sure as hell sounds . . . interesting. Where you want to go?"

"I'm not sure yet, but somewhere where I can seek to live in accordance with nature."

"Sorry, Doc, but I don't really know what that means."

"You are not the first one to respond in this manner. Do you know a man named Port down at the scallop company?"

"Oh yeah, ol' Port. He runs the place down there. He's a bit of a hard-ass. You know, he's the main reason I got fired. He never cut me a break but just kept running to your dad about every little thing."

"I told this gentleman of my intent, and he just laughed."

"Not surprised. Tell me more about what you looking to do?" Stems asked, taking another drink from his new beer.

"I want to live as nature intended us to live. I want to follow the lead of the ancient Cynic philosophers and live a dog-like existence. We've moved too far away from our natural state. Instead of being outside and enjoying the simple pleasures of life, we spend our days living in large modern boxes with controlled lighting and climate. Most people spend endless hours in the evenings in these boxes looking at pictures on screens, and then in the mornings, they scurry off to work and go into different large boxes, where they spend many more hours looking at pictures on other screens. All these boxes just wall us off from all the beautiful gifts nature has to offer us."

"You got a strange way of looking at things sometimes, Doc. Seems like you got something against boxes. I find the things pretty damn useful, personally. If you got a lot of shit to carry, they can be pretty handy. If you're loadin' up at the liquor store, a nice sturdy box works a lot better than some damn plastic bags. Hell, no question my trailer ain't nothin' but a big box, but it keeps me warm and dry. Guess you could say that I'm a fan of the box."

"Perhaps, but I think you may be missing the point," Rye said, rubbing the back of his neck.

"No, I think I get it. You're thinkin' out of the box!" Stems said with a laugh. "You're saying you want to spend some time outdoors."

"Samuel, that is just part of it. Yes, immersing myself in nature will allow me to investigate a more fulfilling lifestyle free from many of the trappings of modern society. But I have a much bigger agenda that I have yet to disclose," Rye said.

"I'm all ears, Doc."

"I want to write a book about these experiences. A great and important book. A book that is certain to shed light on these invisible trappings. A book that, without doubt, will change the world!"

"Doc, if you want to write a book, can't you do that right here? I'm not sure, but I think a lot of them good writers spend a lot of time in bars," Stems commented as he looked around the establishment. "Hell, I bet I can get you exclusive use of one of the booths here. You know, I got me a bit of pull around here."

"I appreciate the offer, Samuel, but to write a book of this significance and magnitude, I have decided I need to travel and find others who have chosen this path. By the dog, Hemmingway traveled to Madrid during the Spanish Civil War to gain firsthand insights for one of his greatest books, and he was merely writing about some skirmish. What I am planning to write is far too important an idea to rely upon purely theoretical discourse. This is surely the pathway to success! I need to live these experiences myself and interview others about their experiences. If we travel to the right place, we are certain to find boundless examples of those who have escaped the invisible prison and are thriving in the simple bounty of nature."

"And you figure *Fat Lily* is the best way to travel?"

"What's wrong with that? It sounds as if she is a capable craft."

"Last I seen her, she was capable enough. I'd need to check her out. I heard from one of the captains down there that she ain't been out scalloping in a while. Sitting too long ain't none too good for boats. All kinds of bad stuff can happen when engines ain't being run."

"Stems, I can tell you she was running fine the other day. You know, we used her to bury my father at sea."

"No shit?" Stems said loudly. "Damn, I figured you just cremated him or put him in the ground, like most other folks. Good for Max. I wouldn't mind going that way," he mused. "Still, even if the boat's running okay, she's a far stretch from some yacht or pleasure craft."

"All the better," replied Rye. "A yacht may be the ultimate culmination of buying for status. It becomes less about its function and more about how impressive it is to others. The *Miss Elizabeth* sounds perfectly functional. Besides, yachts are designed to have all the decadent comforts of a modern home. I want a very basic abode."

"She's pretty basic, Doc. No question," Stems said.

"Excellent, Samuel! Just think of it. Enjoyment of the natural world and the forsaking of all the societal constraints that prevent us from living freely and speaking honestly! It will be a magnificent field study!"

"So, where you want to do this field trip?"

"A field study," Rye corrected. "A place where I can observe others who have seen fit to reject the oppressions of modernity. Based upon some of my anthropological studies in my early career, I believe we should head south, likely to the Caribbean."

"The Caribbean is a big place. Maybe you should look to narrow that down a bit."

"Perhaps. Do you have any suggested guidance on this subject?"

"Humm, a buddy of mine spent a couple months down in the Exumas, if I remember right. He said it was a pretty big group of live-aboard ex-pats down there. I bet they got some of them old hippie types that got sick of the grind up here in the States. Sounds like maybe that's the type of folks you're looking to talk to. I think it's a bigger scene in the winter, but I expect there'd still be some there this time of year."

"That sounds acceptable. I want to get started immediately. If something were to happen to me before I can complete my writings, it could be a calamity for all humanity. I feel like Michelangelo rushing to finish the Sistine Chapel before his death!"

Stems said nothing but took another drink.

"So, Samuel, are you agreeable to taking this trip with me?"

"How long do you want to go for?"

"An undetermined length of time. My summer is free, and then I can decide in a few months whether I wish to return at all."

"Well, I've just been cutting grass for some folks for a livin' lately. You know, I make a lot less than I did on the boats. If we do this thing, you reckon you can give me a good reference and get me back in the good graces down at the docks?"

"Stems, I would do everything within my powers to repair the relationship."

"You know, I've run them boats a bunch of times, but never really been the official captain of one. Captain Stems! I like the sound of that! Sounds a little like a pot-smokin' superhero!"

"Yes, or perhaps the host of a children's educational television program that promotes science, technology, engineering, and mathematics," Rye said with a chuckle.

"What?"

"You know . . . STEM education."

"Huh."

"Err . . umm . . . actually . . . perhaps the superhero with the cannabis is better."

"Damn right! So you're sayin' I'd be runnin' the show, right?"

"You would certainly be in control of the helm of the *Miss Elizabeth*."

"If I take off, I guess some of my clients would have to find someone else to cut their grass for the summer. But worse comes to worst, I expect I could pick them back up when we get back. Would it cost me anything?"

"I'll cover all the expenses."

"Food, drinks, and everything?"

Absolutely. So, are you game for the trip of your life?"

"What the hell, Doc. Nothing ventured and all that."

"That's the spirit!" Rye said with a broad grin. "You know, speaking of ventures, there's one other thing about traveling by boat that appeals to me," he added, as his smile faded, and his expression turned thoughtful.

"What's that?"

"I am looking to experience the sublime."

"Oh, those guys rock! It's hard to beat the old Sublime, but I'm not a huge fan of the new stuff."

"There's a new type of sublime?" Rye asked, confused.

"The band, right?"

"I'm not talking about music," Rye explained, a little flustered. "I'm looking to experience the pure power of nature firsthand. You know how the ocean can go from calm to dangerous in an instant? I can imagine the fierce wind and perilous swells!" Rye said excitedly. "I'm not sure a person can fully understand what it means to live according to nature without seeing firsthand its full fury!"

"I've experienced that once already. Believe me, you're not missing nothing there. Once, we were 150 miles offshore on a scalloping trip and had to call in an SOS. We were taking on a good amount of water in one hell of a storm. We somehow limped in, but just barely. The Coast Guard was doing flyovers. I'd be happy to never experience that again."

"You are a lucky man. It sounds . . . spiritual," Rye said.

"Doc, if we are gonna do this, I need to make the call when we sail. I'm good with a few months in the tropics on a boat, but I ain't interested in doing any crossings in bad weather and putting my ass in a sling. Sorry, but that's a deal-breaker."

Rye paused for a moment but then ultimately nodded his head in agreement, although he was clearly disappointed.

"When do you want to leave?" Stems asked.

"As soon as possible. Full speed ahead and balls out! That's what I say!" Rye said, regaining his enthusiasm.

"Oh, that's a bad idea, Doc. I've done that before, and you want to keep them guys protected. They ain't really designed to be swingin' free like that."

"What are you talking about, Samuel?"

"Balls-out. It's a bad idea."

"It's an engineering term."

"A what?"

"It's referring to the metal balls that were historically used as centrifugal governors in steam engines," Rye explained.

"Not where I'm from."

"Oh, forget it," Rye said. "I would like to go as soon as possible."

"We got to get provisions for the trip."

"I really would prefer not to take anything besides the necessary fuel for our destination."

"How you suppose we're gonna eat? More importantly, how you suppose we're gonna drink?"

"For food, I thought we could catch our meals. I recall my father has an impressive array of fishing equipment at his home that is now mine."

"Man, we need to get some food for this trip. You should see how we stock the boats for a scalloping trip. We don't skimp there."

Rye sat contemplatively for a few moments. "If it is absolutely necessary, I can go to the store and obtain provisions. I will purchase a reasonable quantity of the food and water."

"That's a start, but I'm gonna need more to drink than water."

"You know, my father also had a serious wine collection, which is mine now, I suppose. I think he also kept an assortment of beer. I see no reason you cannot go by there and retrieve these items if you wish."

"Where's the house?"

"It's in Earl Cobbler Estates at 521 Goldlung Lane."

"I tell you what. You go to the grocery store tomorrow and load up on food, and I'll go by and get the fishing gear and a few other *necessities* for the trip, including the beer and wine. You say everything there is yours?"

"Yes."

"I may as well grab a few things to make the boat a bit more comfortable."

"It is important for me to minimize my possessions on this excursion," Rye explained, sounding leery. "That's one of the main points of taking the boat."

"Yeah, yeah, I got it. But that's you, not me."

"Fine," Rye relented. "But don't be excessive."

"Sure thing, Doc. You got a key?"

"My father always kept one under a planter by the back door. But you likely will not be able to gain entry to the neighborhood. They are strict with the security at the twenty-four-hour gated access. Most of the individuals that reside there believe that the ultimate proof of ownership of certain possessions stems from one's ability to exclude others from the use of those possessions."

"I ain't worried about that. You just leave that to me," Stems explained. "Tell you what. Let's plan to leave first thing day after tomorrow. That'll give me time to get the stuff and go by and check out the boat and make sure she is ready to go. I may have to put some fuel in her. How you want me to pay for that?"

"How much will it be?"

"I'm thinking we need 500 gallons to get down around the Bahamas and back. Say maybe three grand. You have a credit card I can use to fill her up at the marina?"

"Why do we need enough fuel to get back?"

"I was just thinking maybe we'd be coming back at some point. Not always that easy to find a place to buy fuel when you get out in the sticks. Tell you what, let me check the fuel levels tomorrow, and we can go from there."

"That's agreeable. Thank you, Samuel."

"Let's meet at 8 a.m. at the docks the day after tomorrow," Stems said, smiling as he ordered another beer.

Chapter Six

There was a reason Stems had agreed, at the drop of a hat, to take off on an extended excursion with his old friend. Stems was in the grass business—but he made most of his money growing it, not cutting it. He had planted a good portion of the back field where his trailer was located with a hybrid strain of marijuana he had painstakingly developed over the last few years. The blend was able to simultaneously lift you up and calm you down—like jumping on a trampoline while sitting in a beanbag chair.

Stems had figured out that cutting lawns gave him the perfect cover to sell his product to a more affluent clientele without raising suspicion. That's why he was confident he could pick his business back up when he returned. Nobody in the area had weed that rivaled his.

Stems woke up early the next morning as he knew he had a lot to do. This was something to which he had not been accustomed at the time. He quickly dressed, smoked a joint, and then went outside and emptied the large, enclosed utility trailer that he used for his landscaping business. After unloading the lawn mowers, weed eaters, and other equipment he used to cut grass, he then hooked up the trailer to his pickup truck and headed to Earl Cobbler Estates.

Thirty minutes later, he arrived at the guard shack at the entrance to the subdivision. I've represented several residents who have lived here over the years. There are some fine folks there, but others tend to be a bit uppity. The design and development of Earl Cobbler Estates decades earlier was personally overseen by one of the heirs to the controlling interest in a prominent Virginia tobacco company. The neighborhood and its meandering golf course were constructed along the banks of a mosquito-infested bog, which was marketed as a "pristine nature reserve." The development was also conveniently located a short distance from one of the company's large cigarette manufacturing plants.

At the time, the heir envisioned he would ultimately move to the area and believed that, without a top-notch, exclusive housing development, he would have difficulty luring his well-heeled compatriots to the area. After some initial fits and starts, the neighborhood was built and managed to attract a group of new residents. These folks consisted primarily of some of the more affluent locals as well as individuals and families that had relocated from the northeast.

Although most of these people were financially "well-off" by traditional standards, their bank accounts didn't quite hit the mark for the heir of the cigarette fortune. In fact, most of the new residents actually had jobs and worked for a living. Sure, someone with the heir's level of wealth might, on occasion, *need* a doctor or a lawyer, but that didn't mean he wanted to hang out with them! Even more troubling to the heir, almost all of his friends quickly lost interest in Williamsburg, Virginia, when they discovered that there were only a handful of limited bars in the town. Ultimately, the heir decided that moving to the area was a lost cause and stayed in New York. After all, he could use his private jet to come down and check on the factory when necessary.

Stems rolled to a stop at the closed entrance gate and security building of the subdivision, and a burly man with a shaggy red beard stepped out to meet him. The man was wearing a khaki-colored uniform and a matching baseball cap.

"What's up, Stems? You're a couple of days early this week, ain't ya?" the guard asked with a smile.

"Yeah, man, I'm heading out a town for a bit so thought I'd get Mrs. Oswald's yard done before I go."

"She's such a nice old lady," the guard commented. "She'll stop sometimes on the way in or way out and talk to me for like five or ten minutes. Some of the other residents will get annoyed waiting for her to move. She's always super happy."

"Oh, yeah, she's great."

"She's not like most of the other people that live here—the ones that look permanently pissed off whether they're coming or going. I try to smile and wave, and they just scowl back at me. I don't even know how they get their faces all twisted up like they do."

"Lots of practice," Stems commented.

"Man, if I write one of them a ticket for speeding in the subdivision, you should see how pissed off they get!"

"There's somethin' I've been meaning to ask you. How is it you guys can write tickets in the first place? I thought you had to be a cop to do that."

"You do, but the local sheriff deputized all of us security guards for when we're in the neighborhood. So, we're pretty much as good as cops here on the property."

"No shit?"

"Yep, we can do it legally, but pull over one of the curmudgeons around here and write them a ticket, and they'll waste no time telling me their homeowners' dues pay my salary."

"Maybe they got a point there."

"Maybe, but if they didn't want us enforcing the law in here, what's the point of having us around in the first place?"

"The people that live here just want you to enforce the law against *everyone else*. People like me, I reckon," Stems commented.

"Got that right. Hey, if you're gonna be out of town for a while, can you hook me up?"

"Sure, what do you want?"

"That depends. How long you gone?"

"Not sure. Maybe a few months."

"Damn. How about a half-zip, then?"

"Hold on. Let me see," Stems said as he rummaged through his center console. "Here's two quarters," he said as he pulled out two tightly rolled Ziploc bags packed with weed that he had recently harvested and handed them to the guard. "That's $200 total."

"Guess I'll be looking to pick up a little overtime," the guard said as he discretely removed the money from his wallet and handed it to Stems. "Later, Stems," the guard added as he raised the gate.

Chapter Seven

Stems backed his trailer into Rye's father's driveway, walked around to the back, and found the key stashed underneath a potted plant right where Rye said it would be. He entered through one of the back French doors to the large living room of the home and let out a long, slow whistle.

"Jackpot," he said aloud.

In short order, Stems located the wine cellar in the basement. Rye's father had the custom-built room constructed shortly after he moved into the exclusive subdivision. The man didn't even like wine that much. Still, he had the limestone that lined the walls of the cavernous room brought in from a quarry in central Virginia at great expense. The wine racks that extended the entire length of the two side walls to the room cost even more and were reclaimed and transported to the United States from a dilapidated chateau in central France. There was also a large and impressive three-inch-thick slab of dark wood with a twisted and gnarled live edge that sat upon four wine barrels in the center of the room. The imposing centerpiece was used as a table for wine tastings. Along the back wall of the room sat two mammoth, industrial-looking stainless-steel refrigerators. Many of the wines stored in the racks were collectibles, and Rye's father used the room in the past as a display to impress bankers and business executives. He never drank the exceptional wines but memorized what was most important about them to recite as necessary. The room was now dusty and felt like a tomb to Stems.

Stems admitted to me that he knew absolutely nothing about wine but felt it was obviously a waste for all those bottles to be sitting and collecting dust. He was of the belief that alcohol was drunk, not gazed upon. As a result, he felt that these neglected wines were essential provisions for the upcoming trip. Stems started randomly pulling out the bottles from the rack, but most of the labels were in French and there was little he could discern about them. He decided it would be best to take as many as possible, as he figured that, based upon their aged appearance, most were likely to turn bad soon. He began placing several upright on the polished marble floor as he thought about the best way to get them loaded as efficiently as possible.

Stems ran upstairs from the cellar and grabbed a stack of beach towels from a linen closet and then returned to the cellar. He spread out two of the towels on the floor and carefully laid out a half-dozen bottles on their sides in each. Stems pulled the ends of the towels together to create two makeshift slings and then carefully lifted the towels—one in each hand. He awkwardly held the towels out from the sides of his body with his dominant right arm higher than his left, resulting in him looking a bit like an off-kilter human Roberval scale.

Stems made it up the steps and to his truck. He placed the bottles in the truck's bench seat, having decided that this was safer than transporting the wine in the trailer. By his third trip, Stems was making good progress, but he was already getting winded and his shoulders were aching.

Looking to further expedite the process, Stems pulled a comforter off a downstairs bedroom in the house and dragged it into the cellar. He spread the comforter on the floor and put another twenty bottles on their sides in the middle of it and then pulled the four corners together. Stems hoisted the sack of wine up over one shoulder. The bottles clanged together as he walked up the stairs, but he managed to get them to his truck. He slid the bottles, comforter and all, into the floorboard of his vehicle in front of the passenger's seat. He successfully emptied the wine from the cellar when he repeated this maneuver with a second comforter he found in the downstairs bedroom closet. When he returned to the cellar, he next checked the large refrigerators and was excited to find four cases of German beer in each, which he quickly transported and stacked in his trailer.

Stems next reconnoitered the rest of the large residence. He went into the attached three-car garage and quickly located the fishing gear Rye had described. It was all neatly stacked against one of the exterior walls. There were multiple Penn and Shimano rods and reels of various sizes, including smaller rods with spinning reels and large offshore rods and reels designed for ocean fishing. Rye's father had been a consummate fisherman for years and regularly went sports fishing in the outer banks of North Carolina. Although the equipment had not been used for some time, Stem's inspection revealed that it was all in excellent condition and had been well cared-for. It took several trips for Stems to get all the fishing equipment into his trailer.

Stems next spotted a ping-pong table that was folded and stood against the back of the garage. He remembered someone telling him about some billionaire putting a $300,000 self-leveling pool table on their yacht. This gave him the idea that perhaps a ping-pong table would be appropriate for their scaled-down excursion. After all, Rye wanted to keep things minimal, and a ping-pong table seemed to fit that bill. Closer inspection of the table revealed it was on wheels, so Stems easily rolled the table out through one of the overhead doors and into the back of his trailer. He also located several paddles and ping-pong balls in one of the garage cabinets and loaded those as well. Stems then went back inside the house dragging a few cardboard boxes he had found in the garage and proceeded to the kitchen where he loaded up many of the pots and pans along with much of the dishes and silverware, having decided that the galley of *Fat Lily* could use some sprucing up.

After Stems loaded the kitchen items, he walked back into the house and surveyed the living room furniture, which included a large brown leather couch and matching recliner and a massive flat-screen TV on the wall. Stems paused for a moment, trying to heed his friend's advice, but his willpower collapsed when he pictured himself lounging on the back deck of *Fat Lily* watching television. With great effort, he dragged the heavy recliner outside and into his trailer. In his attempt to duplicate this feat with the couch, he broke off one of its legs that got caught on the front door threshold. Still, he loaded it anyway, followed by the television. Feeling accomplished but running out of steam, Stems retreated farther into the trailer to locate and open one of the still-cold imported beers. He then plopped down on the recliner in the trailer to try it out, bouncing up and down on its seat cushion to verify that it would work for its intended purpose.

After finishing his beer, Stems went back inside to peruse the home for any other items that might have been *necessary* for the trip. He ultimately worked his way upstairs to the main bedroom walk-in closet, where he found a large open gun safe. It contained a few expensive-looking double-barreled shotguns with intricate engravings on their wooden stocks. There were also several boxes of shotgun shells in the cabinet, along with two boxes of skeet and a skeet thrower sitting farther back in the closet. Stems had only shot skeet a few times in his life, and that was over the water off the back pier at one of his buddy's homes in Seaford. Still, Stems thought that skeet shooting was another activity pursued by cultured men of leisure, so he loaded all these items into his trailer as well. Declaring his trip a success, Stems locked up the home and left for the docks with his spoils in tow.

Chapter Eight

Stems drove into the parking lot of Yorktown Scallop Company and pulled up as close as he could to the pier where *Fat Lily* was docked. He scanned the facility and only saw a couple of men milling around at the far end of the parking lot near the icehouse with shovels in hand. Stems didn't recognize the men and was relieved to not see anyone from his checkered past at the facility. He boarded the vessel, proceeded to the bridge, and started the large diesel engines that powered the boat. The engines fired immediately and idled nicely with a steady hum without putting out any smoke. From this, he could tell the boat had been run recently. He was also happy to see that the boat was full of fuel.

When Stems climbed off *Fat Lily*, he noticed that the two men he had seen when he arrived meandered over to the docks and were eyeing him suspiciously.

"Howdy," Stems said as he approached the two men.

The larger of the two men, who was six feet tall with long, dark hair in a ponytail and a short beard, answered.

"Hey buddy, what's up?"

The guy was stocky but had a bit of a belly, partially hidden by an oversized, faded black Tidemarsh University T-shirt with the school's mascot Ophil the swamp opossum looking a bit rabid.

"Port around?" Stems asked.

"Naw, man. He's off doing some shit somewhere else. Something you need?" the other man, who was thin and clean-shave, but had tattoos covering both arms asked.

"I'm the new captain of *Fat Lily*. Call me Stems," he offered in response.

"Hey man, I'm Paco, and this here is Brody," the thinner man said, nodding at his friend.

"The boat's running good," Stems commented. "Somebody been keeping her up?"

"Yep, boss man been starting her every week. Heard the owner was thinking about selling her."

"I don't know nothin' about that," Stems replied. "I could use some help loading some things on the boat. You guys up for giving me a hand?"

"You know that ain't really our jobs," Paco explained. "The crew usually handles that."

"Yeah, I know. I'm the only crew on this trip, and I was hoping you'd help a guy out."

"Maybe," Paco said with a grin, looking over at Brody. "Boss man ain't gonna be back today, but it'll cost you."

"I got a fine case of imported beer with me that's got your name on it if you'll help me unload that trailer."

"What da you think?" Brody asked Paco. "We could take some beer up and work at the hunt club this weekend. Probably a good weekend to put up the new deer stands. I got me a good spot picked out. It'll be just like going to the meat market."

"I don't know why you even want to bother with it this year. You didn't shoot shit last year except a chipmunk," Paco said, grinning.

"I told you, damn it, I thought it was a squirrel. Squirrels are good eating. You just got to get enough of them to make a good meal."

"It'd be a damn small squirrel you shot. It was about three inches long. Besides, a squirrel ain't nothing but a rat with a bushy tail. I ain't eating them. You need to earn your keep and get a deer this year, or the club may just toss your ass out," Paco said as he winked at Stems. "I got me three of them last season and didn't even need to use a gun for one of 'em," Paco said to Stems.

"What'd you do? Hit it with a car?" Stems asked.

"Naw man, I was sitting in the woods, and it came walking out to me and it came so close that I just hit it over the head with the barrel of my gun," Paco explained.

Brody interrupted and said, "That's bullshit, man."

"You saw the deer, didn't you?" Paco said to Brody.

"Yeah . . . I saw the deer, but I don't believe you hit it in the head with your gun."

"Did you see any bullet holes in that deer?"

"No, but . . . ."

"Well, alright then. Until you can explain how I ended up carrying a deer out of the woods without any bullet holes in it, you need to quit challenging my version of events!"

"I think the damn thing just died of natural causes. What do you think?" Brody asked Stems.

"I don't got no idea, chief, but sounds like the man's got a point if he had the deer," Stems said, trying to remember how they got on the topic. "So, what do you say? You gonna help me load up the boat?"

"A case each, and you got yourself a deal," Paco said.

Stems quickly did the math in his head and reluctantly agreed, having decided he'd still have enough beer left for several days. The three men then walked over to the trailer, and Stems rolled up its back door.

Seeing the odd assortment of goods, Brody asked, "What the hell you got furniture for?"

"Not your typical scalloping trip, fellas," Stems explained. "We're gonna do a bit of exploring, and I want to get her outfitted right for a comfortable trip."

"On a scallop boat?" Paco asked, looking perplexed.

"Yep."

"That's some crazy shit," Brody said, still staring at the goods in the trailer.

"Maybe," said Stems. "Tell you what. How about I get up on the boat and run the deck crane and you guys load up down here? I'll drag the stuff off when I get it up on the boat deck."

"Why not?" said Paco as he walked over to grab a wooden pallet from a stack off the side of the parking lot.

Stems boarded *Fat Lily* and swung the boom of the deck crane over the side of the boat and lowered its cable down just behind his truck and trailer while he watched Brody and Paco start to unload the hodgepodge of items from the trailer into the parking lot. Brody hoisted up the large recliner and carried it out of the trailer by himself. He carried it over to the pallet and set it down with a grunt.

"Careful there, chief," Paco commented. "You ain't that young anymore."

"I'm in my prime," Brody responded as he stood up straight, puffed out his chest, and pulled in his belly.

"That's right, suck in that gut!" Paco said.

"Watch it," Brody said. "Don't even think about it!"

Paco let out a full-throated yell, "SOOOOOEY!!" He ended the hog call with a high pitch that carried across the water and echoed.

"You're about to open up a can of whoop-ass," Brody said, angrily taking a step toward his friend.

"Alright, alright, big boy. Take it easy. Just having some fun," Paco said, quickly taking several steps backward.

"That's what I thought," Brody mumbled under his breath.

The men secured the recliner with tie-down straps, and Paco gave a whistle up to Stems along with a thumbs-up, indicating the chair was ready to go.

"You got her hooked up good?" Stems yelled down. "I don't want to lose none of this stuff."

"Don't worry, Chief, we do this all the time. Never lost a load yet—well, almost never!" Brody yelled back.

The deck crane, which was designed to unload the boat's catch, had a capacity of over six tons and made easy work of the pallet and chair. Once Stems maneuvered the pallet over the boat and down to the deck, he quickly dragged it off and then lowered the pallet again to the two waiting men. They loaded the remaining furniture and television in successive loads. With the furniture loaded, Brody and Paco could see more clearly the remaining items in the trailer.

"Is that a ping-pong table in there?" Paco yelled up to Rye.

"Yep," Stems replied.

"What are you, some kind of ping-pong fanatic? Never leave home without it?" he ribbed Stems.

Stems didn't respond.

The men started loading the smaller items and were successful in completely unloading the trailer over the next half an hour.

"Anything in the truck you want us to get?" Brody yelled up.

"No, I'll get that myself," Stems replied, deciding it would be better for him to handle the multiple loose wine bottles that were in the truck floorboard and seat in addition to the expensive shotguns that were laying on top of them. He retreated off the boat and headed back down to where the other two men were now milling around by the trailer.

"We loaded up our two cases of beer in my car," Paco said. "Pleasure doing business with ya. So, where you going, exactly?"

"Down to the Bahamas to do some island-hopping."

"You planning to go ashore on any of these islands?" Paco asked.

"I reckon," Stems said.

"You a good swimmer?" Paco asked.

"Not bad. Why you ask?"

"I'm just wondering how you're gonna get off the boat and onshore down there?" Paco asked. "You know, a lot of those islands don't have piers for boats this big. Ya got to anchor out and run in on something smaller and I don't see no tender on *Fat Lily* there."

Stems walked over to the edge of the pier and looked up to the deck of *Fat Lily*, making note of the overall size of the vessel and the distance from the deck down to the water and said, "Damn, you got a point there, man."

Stems leaned back and rubbed his chin for a moment, then said to Paco, "I got an idea. You guys still aren't locking up the gate at the end of the day, are you?"

"Naw, buddy. It's always open," Paco said.

"I got to go get me something," Stems said as he hurried to his truck and drove off with the trailer in tow.

A couple of hours later, Stems pulled back into the boatyard without his work trailer. Instead, he was pulling his eighteen-foot, bright metallic-blue bass fishing boat, *Bassassin*.

Chapter Nine

I had something to do with Stem's acquisition of *Bassassin*. He came in to see me a short time after he lost his job down at the docks. Stems walked into my office carrying what appeared to be an assault rifle, complete with a large magazine clip. Seeing this, my receptionist let out a panicked scream and jumped under her desk, guessing that I had pushed a soon-to-be ex-husband over the brink. By the time I got out to the front room, Stems had already calmed her down and explained he was just carrying a paintball gun. Even though he didn't have an appointment, I made time for him and invited him into my office.

He told me his name was Samuel, but everybody called him Stems. He was easygoing, and I immediately liked him. He asked me a few questions about my connections to the area and told me about his roots as well. It quickly became clear to me that Stems knew nearly everybody in Yorktown, and we had a lot of mutual acquaintances. I was surprised we hadn't met growing up. It was probably because I'd gone to the rival high school at the other end of Yorktown.

"So, what's the gun for?" I asked.

"I want to sue the manufacturer of this here contraption," Stems explained.

"For what?"

"For this," he said as he made an exaggerated smile and turned his head to the side to reveal a few missing teeth on the upper left side of his jaw. "The damn thing knocked out two of my teeth, and the dentist tells me it's gonna cost me a fortune to fix 'em."

"Why don't you tell me what happened," I said.

"Sure thing, Counselor. Me and my buddy Jason were heading to the paintball course up in Gloucester, and we stopped to get a couple of foot-longs on the way at Dad's Dogs just down the road here. This here is Jason's gun," Stems explained, holding up the rifle he had carried in. "We get our food and sit down, and he pulls this thing out and shows it to me. It was brand-new and ain't never been shot."

"He carried the gun in the restaurant and nobody said anything?" I asked.

"Naw, man. We were in full camos for the course, and they probably just figured we were going hunting or something. People carry guns into Dad's all the time. Besides, there's always so many cops in there you'd have to be nuts to try and pull something."

I was very familiar with Dad's Dogs. They were always busy at breakfast and lunch. In fact, there were usually a handful of construction workers already waiting outside in the parking lot when the cook arrived at quarter to five in the morning. Eggs, bacon, sausage, and grits were staples for the morning crew. The building didn't have a great exhaust system, and even entering the restaurant for a few minutes could impregnate your clothes with a diner smell that would linger for most of the day. Stems was right that police also tended to hang out there. Many of the restaurants in Yorktown still gave a 50% discount to police officers. I never asked the owner at Dad's whether they followed this policy, but based on the heavy presence of officers in the place, I always assumed they did.

"So, Jason loads up the hopper of the gun with a bunch of paintballs from one of his coat pockets, showing me how much the damn thing will hold," Stems continued. "Then he decided to go ahead and put in the CO_2 cartridge so it would be ready for the paintball course. He'd never used the gun before, and he couldn't figure out where to put in the cartridge at first. I started to laugh because he was getting aggravated. I'd just smoked a fat one before we walked in and thought it was funny as shit. He finally figured it out, and when he put it in, it started shooting all by itself. I was like a foot or two from the end of the barrel and I caught three paintballs in the face, including one right here in the side of my mouth," Stems explained as he showed me the gap in his teeth again.

"That sounds painful."

"Damn right," Stems said. "Counselor, do you know what blue and red make?"

"Purple, I think," I responded.

"That's right! I think they taught me that at Seaford Elementary, but I'd forgotten. Jason had loaded up blue paintballs, and I had a bunch of purple liquid dripping into my bacon and eggs. You can guess where the red came from."

I asked Stems if his friend had his finger on the trigger when it went off.

"Nope, not even near it. I went and saw the dentist, and he told me that it was going to cost me near twenty grand to get implants and it would take a year or so to heal to do it right. He said something about posts or stumps or something and maybe like some kind of bone grafts."

"Your friend was pointing the gun at you when he inserted the air cartridge, correct?"

"I know where you're going with that, and I ain't interested in suing my buddy. We've known each other too long. Besides, he didn't have any idea the damn gun was gonna start shooting all by itself. It's gonna have to be the company that makes the gun that pays out or nothing," Stems explained to me.

I ultimately told Stems that I would give it a shot and asked him to leave the paintball gun with me.

"It's all yours, Counselor," Stems said as he got up to leave. He gave me a handful of paintballs and a few CO_2 cartridges so I'd have the entire setup that resulted in his recently acquired gap-toothed grin.

"Don't let her get away from you. She's got a mind of her own, and, so you know, I ain't looking to get rich or nothing. If you can get me enough to fix my teeth, I'll be happy."

After a little digging the next day, I found a mechanical engineering professor at a nearby university who agreed to take a look at the paintball gun for me to see if there were any design or manufacturing flaws. A stamp on the bottom of the gun showed that it was made by "Pain with Prejudice Ballistics Inc. (PPB)," headquartered in Illinois. I loved the name, and my mind immediately jumped to how I might use it in closing arguments if the case ever went to trial. I called and left a few messages over the next week at their corporate office, but nobody bothered to return my call. As a result, I sent a letter to their legal department, putting them on notice of a possible claim and telling them I would follow up with a settlement demand soon. This got their attention, and an attorney from a law firm in Chicago called me a few days later.

The lawyer was more than a bit condescending and was quick to tell me that the paintball company received specious claims all the time and, in the many years his law firm had represented the manufacturer, he had yet to see any design or manufacturing errors related to their products. Still, out of an abundance of caution, he suggested I send them the gun so they could have it inspected to confirm it was properly operating. I felt confident that if I sent it to them, they would quickly assure me the gun was in working order and we would never see it again. I explained I had hired our own engineering expert to investigate the malfunction and invited them to be present when he did so. He reluctantly agreed, and two weeks later, two lawyers from a large Chicago law firm, in-house counsel for PPB, and one of their design engineers all flew into Yorktown.

The law firm hired by PPB was a large, well-known national firm. I was initially surprised that the paintball gun manufacturer hired such a prestigious firm. When I dug a little deeper, I discovered that PPB was a subsidiary of a much larger conglomerate whose primary businesses were related to the manufacturing of *real* guns. The Chicago law firm involved in the matter was what lawyers sometimes refer to as a "white-shoe law firm." Not that any of the lawyers in such a firm would be caught dead actually wearing white shoes, except perhaps on a golf course. Instead, the term is thought to have originated from a certain trendy "white buck" shoe that was popular in the 1950s among young, male Ivy League students. The white buck shoes were made of a fuzzy suede material that was easily scuffed. As a result, the impressionable young men wearing these shoes quickly learned the life lesson that it was preferable to step on someone else instead of being stepped on.

The white-shoe firms only recruit top students from the top universities in the United States. This equates almost exclusively to Harvard and Yale Law School graduates, with just a sprinkling of Columbia students mixed in. All the hires were expected to graduate *Phi Beta Kappa* and to have served on the boards of their respective law reviews.

This elite hiring model was started by a lawyer named Paul Cravath, who practiced law in the late 1800s and early 1900s. Mr. Cravath first made his name defending Westinghouse in numerous patent infringement suits brought by Thomas Edison, where Edison claimed that Westinghouse was infringing on Edison's 1894 patent for the incandescent light bulb. Mr. Cravath was apparently instrumental in stalling and dragging out the suits until after the expiration date, thereby setting the standard for his future young hires.

I met the PPB group at the engineering professor's laboratory. He was my expert on the case. By the time we arrived, the professor had already set up a video camera to record his inspection. He had also invited a handful of his undergraduate students to observe, having concluded that his forensic work might provide an illuminating teaching moment.

Everyone gathered around the professor as he started the videotape and began his inspection. After memorializing the date, time, and people in attendance, he noted that the hopper for the paintballs was disconnected. He then proceeded to install a CO2 cartridge to pressurize the gun. As soon as the compressed air was attached, the gun immediately ejected a paintball that was lodged in the gun's barrel that was not readily observable to the engineer. The professor's hands were nowhere near the trigger of the gun when it fired. The paintball slammed into the chest of one of the Chicago lawyer's $3,000 Oxxford suits with a splat, and the lawyer yelped with surprise. One student in the room snickered as the thick blue liquid oozed down the lawyer's chest and dripped onto his shoes. To make matters worse, the PPB design engineer blurted out on camera, "It's not supposed to do that."

Stems was excited when I delivered the settlement check to him soon afterward. I mentioned that he could now get his teeth fixed and have some money to spare. In response, he told me he had a new plan.

Chapter Ten

When Stems arrived back at Yorktown Scallop with *Bassassin*, he pulled up alongside *Fat Lily* and then carefully loaded the wine bottles and shotguns from the cab of his truck into the bass boat. He then disconnected the boat trailer from his truck and used several heavy-duty tie-down straps he had brought with him to attach the trailer and bass boat directly to the cable of the deck crane. After a few adjustments, Stems was able to lift the boat and trailer and maneuver them together onto the deck of the scallop boat. He then used the same tie-down straps to secure the trailer and boat to the deck of *Fat Lily*. The entire process took over an hour. When *Bassassin* was locked down good and tight, Stems popped open a beer to celebrate his success. He then unloaded the wine and shotguns and carried them to one bunkroom below deck and stowed the remaining gear. The sun was getting lower in the sky, but Stems still managed to arrange the outdoor furniture into a cozy seating area on the rear deck. He also mounted the television before he left and headed to Club 17 for one last visit.

In contrast to Stems's busy schedule, Rye began his morning at a much more leisurely pace. Rye's first task was to decide what was truly essential for the trip. In tune with his minimalistic intent, Rye ultimately chose to bring only two sets of clothes, consisting of two pairs of shorts, two T-shirts, and two pairs of underwear. He removed the clothing from his bedroom dresser and put one set in a duffel bag and laid the other out on a chair for him to wear on the day of departure. He then walked down the hallway to the extra bedroom. Rye instinctually bowed before he stepped through the threshold of the room. This was the only room in the house with hardwood flooring. There were mirrors that completely covered one wall, with the other three walls finished in a rough-grained dark wood. There was a slew of weapons mounted along the wall opposite the windows in the room that gave the room the appearance of a three-hundred-year-old Japanese armory. Three samurai swords that dated back to the seventeenth century were prominently displayed in sword racks mounted at eye level. Below them were more rudimentary weapons, including several sets of traditional nunchakus, wooden tonfas, and three-pronged steel sais. There was also a wooden barrel in the corner of the room with several wooden bows stacked inside.

Rye surveyed the wall carefully. He then gently picked up a pair of flip-flops that were placed neatly on the floor and exited the room, once again bowing. He slipped on the footwear and then proceeded to pack his toiletries and a single towel. He then searched through several drawers until he found a large flashlight. Testing it, he was pleased to discover that it still worked. He packed the flashlight and an extra set of batteries in the duffel bag and then left his house to complete his preparations.

Next, he went to the local bank and emptied his checking account, where he had just over $8,000 deposited, having decided that some compromises to his ascetic existence may be necessary—at least in the short-term. He rationalized the use of these funds as a necessary but unsavory means of support until he could reach his destination and live in a fully sustainable means in accordance with nature. He felt that this amount of money should be more than enough to get him settled at his still-to-be-determined destination. As a result, he did not touch the savings account where the bulk of his life money sat. Rye then proceeded to the local drugstore, where he bought a half-dozen spiral-bound notebooks and a package of three black ink pens, with which he intended to take notes and ultimately create his masterpiece. Next, he proceeded to the grocery store and purchased the provisions for the trip, and finally to a local hardware store, where he purchased a paintbrush and a quart of white paint. He then returned to his home to relax for the rest of the day. He went to bed early, dreaming of the journey upon which he was about to embark.

Chapter Eleven

Rye left his house early the next morning. Deep in thought about all the great things he planned to write, he inadvertently cut off a vehicle while pulling out of his driveway. The driver of the small, beat-up car laid on his horn and flashed his lights spasmodically. Rye jumped and then immediately pulled forward and off the side of the road so the vehicle could pass.

The black Ford Escort, which had been retrofitted with flashy, green wheels, a spoiler, and a fart-cannon muffler, shot by— or at least passed by—a rate slightly faster than an elderly power walker. Its young male driver with long, frizzy hair rolled down his window and yelled something indiscernible but clearly threatening. He was gesticulating wildly in his seat, yet somehow managed to shoot both his hands out the window while maintaining forward momentum just so that he could flip Rye a double bird at close range. Rye just shrugged as he watched the vehicle pull away.

The noisy, sputtering box of a car had an intricate vinyl design across its rear window. The artwork depicted a serene hillside setting with a plethora of animals, including deer, bunnies, and doves taking flight. The centerpiece of the wildlife scene was a massive cross with angel wings that spanned the entire width of the window. Rye also spotted a red bumper sticker on the retreating vehicle. It said something about Jesus that he couldn't quite make out.

Rye had recovered from the road rage incident by the time he arrived at the scallop company. He pulled up by the dock to unload the few items he had brought. It was a Saturday, so nobody was around when he arrived. It shocked Rye when he stepped out of the car and spotted the furniture and bass boat sitting on the rear deck of the *Miss Elizabeth*. The leather couch and recliner chairs, along with a throw rug that Stems had appropriated, were arranged into a makeshift outdoor seating area under a large overhang that extended behind the wheelhouse. Stems was nowhere to be found, so Rye unloaded the provisions for the trip. As he entered the galley and spotted the fine dinnerware and silverware, his agitation grew.

Rye was still ruminating when Stems finally arrived around a quarter to ten. Stems, who had had a late-night sendoff with several of the regulars at Bar 17, was nursing a serious hangover. He had convinced one of his friends to drop him off so that he could leave his truck parked safely at home.

Stems thanked his friend for the ride as he climbed out of the old Jeep Cherokee and grabbed a large black garbage bag from the rear seat. As he walked to the boat, Rye yelled down to him, "By the dog, what are all of these excesses scattered about this vessel?"

"Mornin', Doc. Can you keep it down a bit? My head is killing me."

Rye relaxed a bit. "I'm sorry to hear that, Samuel. Are you ill?"

"No more than most mornings, Doc," Stems replied. "Good news is that it always gets better as the day goes on. I feel sorry for people who don't drink. When they get up, that's as good as it gets for them all day. It's the opposite for me."

As Stems climbed up on the boat, Rye explained more calmly, "Samuel, I wanted to minimize our possessions on this trip. I'm concerned these frivolities I see might be a distraction for me."

"Sorry, Doc, maybe I got a bit carried away. I just want to be comfortable."

"I don't even understand why we have some of these things. For example, why do we have a boat on our boat?" Rye inquired.

"You mean *Bassassin?*"

"What is an *ass . . . baskin?*" Rye asked, struggling to repeat what Stems had said.

"*Bassassin*, Doc! Shit, 'Assbaskin' sounds like some hippy nudist! *Bassassin* is my bass boat. I figured if we're gonna be going ashore, we need a way to get there. You know, a lot of them places down in the tropics don't got no dockage, so we'll need to anchor off and have to use a tender to go to shore. I figured I already got this boat, so may as well use her. We can lower her down to the water with the deck crane and there you go."

Rye had not contemplated this issue and had to agree that it made sense. "Okay, perhaps it is a useful tool for our trip. It appears to be a bit overly dressed for our endeavor, though."

"She's something, ain't she! I got the money for her from a malfunctioning paintball gun."

"What about the television and furniture?" Rye asked.

"I was trying to make a nice outdoor living space. You know, they're all the rage now, Doc. That's what they say on that house fixer-up channel, anyway."

"This is exactly what I am trying to escape," Rye said pleadingly.

"Look here, Doc, I'm not gonna distract you from your mission. I'm just asking you to do the same for me."

"What is your mission?" Rye asked, looking perplexed.

"Same one every day—just to get through it. Besides, I've been thinking. This really is better for you, too."

"How do you mean?"

"You said that you wanted to reject the modern comforts and stuff and live this minimal lifestyle, right?"

"Yes, that's correct."

"Well, it's one thing to do that when you ain't got nothing to start with. Hell, that's what a good chunk of the people on this planet do already. But I figure that if you got the stuff in front of you and don't use it, now that's doing it at a whole 'nother level."

Rye paused, considering his friend's logic. "Perhaps this is a positive development after all," he said finally. "To exercise the willpower to resist temptations immediately available certainly is an accomplishment of greater import."

"That's the spirit, Doc! You're welcome! I can give you plenty of temptation if that's what you're looking for. Shoot, this whole trash bag right here is full of weed. I harvested my entire crop for this trip!"

Chapter Twelve

Rye sat on the front deck as Stems went below to stow away his weed, along with a few other things he had forgotten to bring the day before. When Stems re-emerged topside, Rye saw him toting a large cardboard box. Stems carried it to the railing at the side of the boat and promptly dumped the contents of the box overboard into the creek.

As Rye walked over to investigate, Stems said, "First things first, Doc. You brought a bunch of bananas."

"Actually, both bananas and plantains," Rye corrected him.

"They all looked like bananas to me."

"They are closely related, of course. Cousins, if you will," Rye explained. "These fruits are thought to be among the earliest crops cultivated on this planet by our species. You know, Alexander the Great was so taken by the taste of this unique food source that he is the one that transported it from India to the Middle East, where it eventually spread across the world. 'Banan' is actually the Arabic word for 'finger.' The fruit is thought to have spiritual attributes in parts of the world, and, more fundamentally, they have many health benefits. I bought them in various stages of ripeness so they will last. I intend to utilize them as one of the main staples for sustenance on this journey."

"That's all interesting stuff, Doc, but I threw 'em all overboard."

"Why on earth would you do that?" Rye asked with his brow furrowed, as he looked over the side of the boat and saw his entire stash of yellow fruits bobbing up and down in the water.

"Can't have no damn bananas on a boat. It's bad luck."

"How do you know this?" asked Rye.

"Every sailor around these parts knows this. Goes back to when they were using galleons, I think. They started noticing that the ships carrying bananas were sinking. Ask any sailor worth his salt and he'll tell you—you don't want a single one of those yellow bastards on the boat," Stems explained, looking serious.

"I never heard the Maori say anything about this when we sailed across the Pacific," Rye muttered dejectedly as he continued staring at the jettisoned bananas.

"Also, Doc, when I was looking around the galley, I saw a good bit of other fruits and vegetables, but I didn't see any meat!"

"Oh yes . . . that. I'm a pescatarian," stammered Rye.

"I'm a Methodist. Ain't that pretty much the same thing?" asked Stems, scratching the side of his head. "They're both Catholic Light—half the tradition and none of the guilt. The minister ain't said nothing to me about not eating meat."

"I think you're thinking of Presbyterian. Pescatarian means that the only meat I eat is fish and other seafood."

"Out of choice?"

"Yes, that's correct."

"Okay," Stems said tentatively. "Why not?"

"I generally ascribe to the theory of panpsychism. I say 'generally' as I do, at present, place some limits on this designation. If I were to fully subscribe to it, ethically, I would be vegan, I believe."

"Hey, Doc, you know how to tell if someone's a vegan?"

"How?"

"Just talk to them. They'll tell you in the first thirty seconds," Stems said, smiling.

"I see," Rye responded, not catching the joke. "I'll make a note of that."

"What'd you call it—pan *what*?" Stems asked.

"Panpsychism. It can broadly be described as the idea that consciousness is not restricted to organisms with the highest levels of intelligence. Instead, consciousness is ubiquitous in the universe and present in all objects. As a consequence of this, it means that animals likely have levels of consciousness, albeit perhaps not to the same extent as humans. Still, their level of consciousness and intelligence gives me pause to consume them as a meal. Although fish may also have some level of consciousness, I have drawn a line—admittedly a somewhat arbitrary one—to permit myself to eat the less-evolved sea life."

"So, just so I understand, you only eat dumb animals?"

"That's a close approximation of my position, yes."

"You know, I've seen a few pigs in my day. Didn't seem too damn smart to me. They like to spend a lot of time in their own shit, you know. Chickens ain't no better, seen them eat a lot of their own crap along with their feed."

"I was not aware," Rye replied.

"Now, if you're talking about cows, I've had some dealing with them and have to say that them bastards are smart as hell."

"Interesting. What did you see?"

"You know where our house is way down at the end of Seaford, right?"

"Yes, I recall."

"One of our neighbors down there had a small farm. I think just twenty acres or so. It used to be called Bay Tree Farm. Remember, they'd chase us out when we were little."

"Yes, I recall that place. They raised bees back there, correct?"

"Yep, that's right. After you left, they got themselves some cows for some reason. They had a fence but didn't keep it closed up half the time. Dangerous as hell, by the way. I was driving home once right after I got my license and came around the corner, and one was standing right in the middle of the damn road. I nearly hit the thing. I don't expect either of us would've fared too well if I hadn't stopped. I ended up just giving him a little bump instead of a wallop, and he just looked at me and walked off."

"You're saying they're smart because they stand in the middle of roads? I don't think I see the connection."

"I'm getting there. Just hold your horses. So, like I said, these cows would wander around but would usually come back home at feeding time. Well, there was a group of about a half-dozen one day that decided not to come back home. People don't think about cows as being wild animals, but on occasion, they decide they want to live on their own in the wild. That's what this group did. They went feral. I guess that's kinda what *you're* doing, now that I think about it," Stems said, grinning. "Your goin' feral, ain't ya?"

"Perhaps," Rye replied. "So, how did the cows fare in the wild?"

"Pretty good, actually. They could survive off the stuff growing in the marsh. When they get wild like that, the group will take off and run whenever they see people. I tell ya what, catching a wild cow in a swamp ain't no easy task. Those suckers can swim good—better than people. You can't catch 'em by chasing 'em in a truck because they'll run into the marsh and water, and you can't catch 'em in a boat 'cause then they'll just run back up on the land and run through the woods. You were right about what you said earlier—cows are a lot smarter than people give 'em credit for."

"I will make a note of that for future consideration."

"Still, Doc, I don't get it. If you're pisca—"

"Pescatarian."

"Yeah, that. Well then, you still eat fish, and I didn't see none of them down there, either."

"With the fishing gear that you have secured from my father, surely we can catch enough food to sustain us," Rye said confidently.

"This really ain't a fishing boat, so not sure how well that will work. I guess we can give it a try. If it don't work, I reckon we can jump into a port as we're heading down the coast and make a food run."

"Yes, that's agreeable," Rye replied.

"How about we run 'til dark and anchor up, and I'll make us some grub and we'll run in and grab a few more supplies in a day or two?"

"An excellent plan. I have one more request, Samuel."

"Sure thing, Doc. Whatchu want?"

"Wait here one moment, please," Rye said as he disappeared below deck and soon returned with the paints and brush he had purchased. "I thought about changing the name to the boat, but I have decided we can just add a second AKA instead."

"Three names, huh?"

"Correct."

"Alright, I'll bite. What's the new name?"

"*My Barrel*

."

Stems managed to add the new name and get everything situated on the boat over the next hour, and the *Miss Elizabeth* aka *Fat Lily* aka *My Barrel*, with its crew of two and an odd assortment of gear, was off by early afternoon.

They had not departed for long when Stems received a cell phone call from an unknown number. Assuming it was a telemarketer, he didn't answer. However, he picked up when they immediately called back a second time.

"Hello?"

"Is this Samuel Keene?"

Stems was immediately suspicious of the person using his proper name. "Who's this?" he asked.

"This is Ernie Harker."

"Who?"

"I'm an attorney. I was able to get your phone number from your prior employment records at the scallop company. I am attempting to contact Rye Smyth. Does he happen to be with you?"

"I can get him for ya."

"Before you do, can you tell me if what I have heard is correct?"

"What'd ya hear?"

"I was told that you and Mr. Smyth have taken the *Miss Elizabeth* from the harbor."

"Yep, that's right."

"Where are you going?"

"Not sure yet. Heading south at the moment," Stems answered, deciding it might be best to keep his answers vague until he had more information about why this lawyer was asking questions about their trip.

"And why on earth would you be doing such a thing?"

"What's it to you?" Stems asked as his suspicion changed to annoyance.

"Let me speak to Mr. Smyth."

Stems cracked open the outside door to the wheelhouse and yelled down to Rye, who was sitting cross-legged on the front deck writing in one of the notebooks he had brought.

"Rye, you got a call!"

Rye walked up to the wheelhouse and Stems handed him the phone, commenting loud enough for Ernie Harker to hear him, "Some damn lawyer on the phone. Seems like a nosy son of a bitch."

"Hello," Rye said as he took the phone.

Obviously flustered by Stem's comment, Ernie Harker said, "Eh . . . hello, Rye, this is Ernie Harker. I want to talk to you about that offer to buy your boat."

"Thank you, but I have decided that I have no interest in such a deal at this time. You see, I am off on an existential journey to discover my true nature and live in accordance with nature."

"What are you talking about? Have you lost your damn mind?" Ernie blurted out.

"Coming from someone so enmeshed in the trappings of modern society, that is a compliment I accept with some enthusiasm! Suffice to say, I have no interest in selling this vessel. Without it, it would be much more difficult for me to travel to the southern latitudes to find like-minded souls."

"Rye, I've been talking to the buyers, and they are very insistent. They thought the deal was effectively done with your father before he passed away. He just hadn't put pen to paper. If you don't go through with it, I think they may sue."

"So be it. Whatever use they may have for this craft, it is certainly less important than the mission upon which I have embarked, and I am confident that any learned jurist would recognize this logic and truth."

"Mr. Smyth, I strongly suggest you reconsider your position on this. Legally speaking, you are in a vulnerable . . . ."

Rye hung up the phone while Ernie Harker was in mid-sentence. "I have no more time for such nonsense," Rye said as he handed the phone back to Stems.

"What did he want?"

"Something about my father agreeing to sell the boat to someone. He threatened a lawsuit, and I explained to him the importance of this trip. I would expect that, with additional consideration, he will recognize the superiority of my position."

"I don't know, Doc. Maybe we should get a little backup."

"Backup? What do you mean?"

"I got the guy to call," Stems explained.

I was just walking out of court after representing a guy who had been charged with a DUI when I saw Stems calling me on my cell phone. I didn't have him in my contacts but recognized the number—he'd managed to score a great phone number that ended in 7000. I think he knew the woman that worked at the Verizon store. I hadn't heard from Stems in over a year, and when I answered the call, I wished him well and asked if he was still playing paintball.

"Hell no, Counselor, I gave that shit up! No, I'm calling 'cause I need a little advice. I got you on speaker phone because I got a buddy of mine with me who's got a scallop boat and we got a couple of questions for you," Stems explained.

"I know very little about scallop boats, but go ahead and ask."

"Are you familiar with Mr. Earnest Harker?" Rye asked.

"Oh yes. I know Ernie," I said.

"Well, you see, I have inherited a scallop boat from my father and I am currently using the vessel, but Mr. Harker has told me that my father apparently made some commitment related to the sale of the boat before his death and that it is necessary that I follow-through on that transfer," Rye explained.

"So, did your father sign a contract to sell the boat before he died?" I asked.

"That's not entirely clear to me," Rye explained. "Mr. Harker seemed to suggest that he had committed to sell the vessel but had not yet signed the contract."

"Is the boat in Virginia?"

"Not at the moment," Rye responded.

"I mean, is the boat generally kept in Virginia?

"Yes, I believe so," Rye said.

"In that case, I think Ernie has a problem," I explained. "Under the Statute of Frauds, any contract to sell the boat would need to be in writing to be enforceable. I tell you what, let me call Ernie and see what he's got to say about it. Hopefully, I'll be able to get a better feel for what's going on."

"Sound good, Rye?" Stems asked.

"Yes, that would be appreciated," Rye responded.

"I'll be back in touch soon," I said as I hung up the phone.

Just as they were getting off the call, an alarm went off on Stem's cell phone and he quickly glanced at it and turned it off. "4:20, Doc," Stems explained as he pulled out a small bowl and bag of weed from his pants pocket. "You care if I grab myself a beer? I usually don't drink until 5:00, but what the hell, close enough, I'm thinking."

"A man at all times can only do what he wills himself to do, and he does this because he already is what he wills," Rye replied.

"Does that mean okay?" Stems asked, looking confused.

"Yes, it does," Rye responded flatly.

"Amen, brother," Stems replied as he lit his bowl and grabbed a beer from a cooler he had stashed under the captain's seat.

Chapter Thirteen

I was wrapping up with a client and walking him back through the reception area of my office when my legal assistant told me that Ernie Harker was on the phone. I told her to let Ernie know I'd be with him in just a moment as I retreated into my office and closed the door. I sat down, picked up the phone, and said hello. In response, Ernie said," Hello, Mr. Forelle, this is Ernest Harker returning your call. What can I help you with?"

Ernie was one of those guys who would often refer to another person by their family name not out of respect for that person but rather a none-too-subtle hint that they should address *him* by *his* family name.

"Hi, Ernie. I got a call yesterday from a Rye Smyth. Does that name sound familiar?"

"Yes, of course. I know Rye. I represented his father for years before his business went to hell. What did he want from you?"

"Just to get a better handle on his current situation. Rye said you have a client who has an interest in buying the scallop boat Rye inherited, and—"

"It's more than an interest. It was more like a commitment," Ernie interrupted.

"So, there's a contract in place?"

"Well . . . not exactly. I brought a buyer to Rye's father and he basically accepted an offer to buy, but they didn't get around to signing anything before he died."

"Ernie, maybe I'm not grasping something here, but without a signed agreement, I don't believe there is an enforceable contract."

Ernie was silent for a moment and then said, "Look, Jackson. Technically, there may be a few issues, but he agreed to sell it.

Besides, selling the boat is what's best for everyone. Rye Smyth knows nothing about the scallop industry. Why don't you talk to him and explain why he should sell it?"

"Who is it that wants to buy it?" I asked.

"I'm not at liberty to say," Ernie said defensively.

This caught me off guard. "You're not going to tell me who wants to buy the boat?"

"No, and I don't have to."

"Fair enough, and Rye Smyth doesn't have to sell it to them, either."

Ernie was quiet again. "Jackson, maybe you should just steer clear of this one. I think your guy may be nuts, anyway."

Once again, this surprised me. Nothing had stood out in my recent call with Rye that suggested he had any competency issues.

"Why do you say that?" I asked.

"For starters, I think he may have a head injury. When I first tried to track him down, I called the college, and they told me he knocked himself out somehow and then suddenly took off. Next thing I hear is that he's taken the scallop boat out on some extended pleasure cruise with his only crew being some pothead that got fired from the scallop company a few years back."

I was still trying to process this information but told Ernie that I had spoken to Rye and he seemed fine to me. I also told him that it was his boat and he could do whatever he wanted with it, as far as I was concerned.

"It's a total goddamn waste! Do you know the money that boat can make?" Ernie nearly shouted.

"No, I don't. But I don't see how that's relevant. It's his boat," I reiterated.

"I think it's relevant. It's like burning cash in a fireplace to heat a house. Just talk to him, Jackson. My client's not walking away from this."

"If you decide you're going to take legal action, send it to me. He's traveling, and I expect I'll be representing him," I explained.

Ernie said nothing else and hung up the phone.

Chapter Fourteen

Stems found a spot not far offshore in around a hundred feet of water to anchor up for the evening, just off the Virginia and North Carolina border. After a less-than-hearty meal composed of a hodgepodge of cooked vegetables, Rye turned in early, leaving Stems on the back deck drinking beer. Rye was still sound asleep the following morning when a Navy cruiser that was heading out for early drills passed by the *Miss Elizabeth*, leaving a large wake and causing her to suddenly sway back and forth. Rye, who had decided to use the top bunk in his quarters, was lying on his back when this occurred, and the sudden movement startled him awake. Rye tried to sit up quickly with his eyes still closed and immediately slammed his head into the steel ceiling. The boat rolled again from the wake, causing Rye to fall out of the bed and plummet to the floor below.

Still dazed, Rye sat on the floor with his legs sprawled out and slowly looked around the small room, feeling the boat sway back and forth. Briefly, excitement and anticipation surged within him as he thought a storm was brewing, but as the rocking subsided, he realized that his hopes of glimpsing the sublime so quickly after their departure were dashed. As a result, Rye crawled back into his bed and slept a few more hours.

When Rye finally crawled out of bed and worked his way down the corridor in the direction of the stairwell, he passed Stems, who was in the galley sitting on a stool at the counter and rubbing his head.

"Good morning, Stems. How are you this morning?" Rye asked.

"I'll be doing great as soon as I light one up," Stems said. "How 'bout you, Doc?"

"I am a rich man today as contentment is natural wealth," Rye said.

"Glad to hear it," Stems said, rubbing his temples. "I was thinking about making some breakfast, but I couldn't find any eggs."

"I brought almond milk and granola if you would like some."

"Maybe I'll just have some toast," Stems said as he stood up and opened one of the overhead cabinets and pulled out a bottle of vodka. "This is the best hangover cure I've found, except weed, maybe."

"I thought you said you did not, as a rule, consume alcohol before five?"

"Hell, Doc, this ain't drinking. It's medicinal," Stems said as he unscrewed the cap from the vodka and poured a good amount into the coffee he had just made. He then pulled out a recently rolled joint from his shirt pocket.

"I see. I'm off to start my morning routine. Let us continue this conversation afterward," Rye said as he exited the room and headed up to the deck.

Stems went topside shortly after Rye, having decided that some fresh air might also do him some good. As he came out on deck, he spotted Rye up on one of the open areas of the front deck. Stems leaned against the exterior wall of the wheelhouse, discreetly watching Rye from a distance. Rye appeared to be practicing some type of martial arts. At least that was Stem's best guess as to what Rye was up to. Stems couldn't decide whether Rye was following some memorized pattern of moves or simply making it up as he was going along. Rye was punching and kicking as if fighting an invisible opponent and occasionally jumping up into the air. Stems also noticed that Rye was wearing a flip-flop on his right foot, but he had apparently taken off his left flip-flop and placed it on his right hand with the sole pointed away from him. Rye would occasionally jut out the footwear as if he were trying to step on an invisible bug flying through the air.

Stems quietly worked his way up to the wheelhouse and watched Rye from the better vantage point of the captain's chair, fascinated by the show. A half-hour later, Rye finished up and bowed to the open sea. Rye walked inside and located Stems in the wheelhouse.

"What were you doing out there?" Stems asked as Rye walked in. "That some type of martial arts?"

"Yes, Samuel, that is exactly what it is. It is called *Nojo Ryu kara-tae*," Rye responded, using the traditional Japanese pronunciation for "karate" and emphasizing the final syllable.

"Takes a long time to learn?"

"I studied daily for several years in Okinawa, actually. Were you not aware of this?"

"No, I had no idea."

"Yes, it was a small dojo up in a remote mountain farming community. I stumbled across it while seeking refuge in the forest. Only a handful of foreigners are even aware of the school, and I was the first one permitted to practice there. Their most effective techniques are closely guarded. You see, *Nojo Ryu*, which basically means 'farm school,' is a style of martial arts that teaches open-hand combat and the use of farm and household implements as weapons. It's quite fascinating. Its innovative style was necessitated because of a long-ago ban by the Japanese ruling class that prohibited Okinawans from carrying swords. The Okinawans, being a rather imaginative lot, figured out how to use all kinds of everyday items as very effective weaponry. They've mastered the use of walking sticks, hoes, shovels, towels, chopsticks, garlic presses, and even dental floss."

"Towels?" Stems asked.

"Absolutely. There was a time I taught a group of CIA operatives up at Langley how to kill silently with a towel. Mark my words, Stems, a towel is a deadly weapon."

"They also teach you to use shoes as weapons? I saw you with your flip-flop on your hand out there a little earlier."

"Of course," Rye explained. "A sandal or flip-flop can be a very effective means of blocking knife attacks. It can also be deployed aerially in an offensive manner."

"You mean, throwin' a shoe at someone?" Stems asked.

"Yes."

"I'm not sure that would work for me. I suspect if I was about to get in a bar fight and bent over to untie my shoe, I'd get knocked over the head."

"Yes, I believe slip-ons would perform better," Rye commented.

"Now, a shovel, I get. I reckon I could knock someone upside the head pretty good with one of them."

"Oh yes, the art of the shovel is quite elegant. I had to fight with one during my black belt test. It is all a bit of a blur now. You see, it went on for several days without sleep and only brief breaks for food and water. Five of us were testing for our black belts. I remember our group running barefoot for hours up and down the mountain terrain while reciting ancient Japanese poetry. If you neglected a certain intonation in your recitation or, God forbid, forgot a line, you'd be beaten with bamboo sticks around the ankles.

"We then ran to a secluded beach and swam for miles in the cold ocean water with our thick uniforms weighing us down. We were all exhausted by the time we crawled back up on the black volcanic sand. Our instructors were, of course, overseeing all of this. As we dragged ourselves back up on dry land, they told us that we must fight each other as part of the final test. Only the last person standing would be awarded his belt. Twenty minutes later, it was just one other student and me who remained. The instructors, who had been drinking sake for three days straight, livened things up by throwing a shovel to me and a hoe to the other student.

"The poor guy looked as if he had lost his mind when he came charging at me, swinging the hoe wildly. I glanced at the instructors, who suddenly looked nervous. You see, although minor injuries during the test were encouraged and rewarded, the maiming or murder of other students was generally frowned upon. I retreated to a small outcropping that protruded into the water and climbed up on it, thereby gaining the advantage of higher ground. As he shot toward me, spinning his hoe like a helicopter, I gave him a good little tap on the head with the shovel, which calmed him down considerably. A gentle kick is all that was required for him to fall over. I was awarded my black belt and bestowed with the honorary title of *Kurutta Bakujin*."

"What's that mean?" Stems asked.

"I'm not sure, but it was a very proud moment for me. Picture it, Stems: me, standing there, victorious . . . like a crane . . . on a rock."

"Yep, I learned a long time ago, don't fuck with no cranes. I've seen them kick the ass of many of a pelican fighting over scraps on the boats. But damn, Doc, that whole thing sounds pretty dangerous."

"Of course it was dangerous. Otherwise, what would be the point?" Rye said with a shrug.

Stems just shook his head. "To each their own, Doc. Anyway, I'm thinking we should get underway and head down farther south. Sound good to you?"

"By all means."

Rye went below to rinse off in the small shower as Stems got the boat underway. When Rye came back above and stepped outside, he noticed that the day was warming up already. He went into the wheelhouse to find Stems with a beer in hand already, and it was only midmorning.

"Doc, I was thinking maybe we should try to do some fishing today as we head farther down the coast. You up for giving it a shot?" Stems asked.

"Certainly. I do like the idea of living off the land, or, in our case, more accurately, the sea," Rye said, correcting himself.

"Damn right, Doc. Tell you what, we're not gonna catch anything great in this close to shore. How about I work offshore a bit as we head south? I can probably get us out close to the Gulf Stream by early afternoon. We can fish a few hours and then head back in closer to the coast for the night."

"If you feel that's appropriate, then please proceed. I know little of these matters."

Stems set a southeast course as Rye went out on the back deck and began to write again in his notebook.

A few hours later, Stems backed off the throttle, opened the side door of the wheelhouse, and yelled down to Rye, "I think I found us a good spot!"

Rye appeared to be furiously writing in deep concentration and did not respond to Stems.

"Hey, Doc!"

Rye finally looked up.

"What you writing there?"

"I am drafting this important treatise that I mentioned to you previously. It is in its very early stages but is beginning to take form."

"I spotted us a nice weed line up ahead!" Stems yelled back with some excitement.

"I thought we were looking for fish, not weeds?"

"We are, Doc," Stems said as he scurried down from the wheelhouse. "You know the little fish sometimes like to hide up under them weeds, and when you have little fish, that can bring in the bigger fish," Stems explained.

"Oh yes, I see. It's much like the small fish that would conglomerate under our craft in the South Pacific. Although our fishing techniques were much more rudimentary with hooks made from shells or bones. Interestingly, did you know that in the Maori culture, human bones were considered the most superior material out of which to make a fishhook, particularly if the bones were from a defeated enemy?" Rye replied.

"Can't say I did. I prefer steel myself."

"Of course, Samuel. Let's proceed, then."

"I stowed them rods and reels from your dad's house in the locker on the back deck," Stems explained as he led Rye to the locker.

Stems pulled out the gear and spread it around the deck as he examined the various rigs he had brought. He laid out four large rods and reels and explained to Rye that they would likely work for tuna. "I heard that the charter boats from Oregon Inlet have been catching some Blackfin out here." He rigged up the four lines and then gestured for Rye to follow him to the rear of the boat.

"I'll need to run the boat, and ain't no way you're gonna be able to handle four lines by yourself," Stems said, leaning back and rubbing his chin in deep thought. "Hold on a minute," he added as he spun around and shot into the cabin. He re-emerged on deck a few moments later with what appeared to be an armful of colorful ropes.

"Check it out," Stems said as he approached, holding up what Rye could now tell were various bungee cords. "We always keep a stash of these things on here. You got to watch out for these suckers, though. They'll take out an eye if you ain't careful."

Stems used multiple bungee cords to fasten the four fishing poles to the railing encircling the back deck. "This ought to work," he explained cheerfully. "I'm going back up and run the boat, and we're gonna troll along that weed line, and hopefully, a fish will hit. I'll leave the door open. If we get a fish on, yell up to me and I'll stop."

Rye sat observantly, and a few minutes later, he saw one of the rod tips jerk suddenly and sporadically. "By the dog, something is happening down here!" Rye shouted up to Stems. Stems put the boat in neutral to drift and then quickly exited the wheelhouse and ran to the rear of the boat. He quickly untethered the fishing pole and handed the rod to Rye and said, "Time to get to work."

Rye took the rod and reeled the fish up toward the back of the boat. After a few minutes, the fish became visible and Stems said, "Looks like a tuna, alright. Nice one, too! I bet she's fifteen or twenty pounds."

Rye continued to reel the fish to the stern and then felt its full weight as he attempted to lift it out of the water. He had to brace the rod up against the boat railing as he continued to reel the fish up, but it was slow going. It was about halfway up the stern when the fish gave a sudden shake and freed itself, falling back into the ocean and disappearing.

"I was afraid of that," said Stems. "It's gonna be hard to get 'em up here. Lower your line back in, and we'll try again. The quicker you can get it up, the better—less chance he'll spit the hook."

Stems refastened the poll to the rear railing and then went back up to the wheelhouse and began trolling again along the same weed line. Another fish hit almost immediately. Rye untied the fishing pole and was steadily reeling the fish by the time Stems arrived back at the rear deck. The fish was another tuna that shook free when it was lifted only a few feet out of the water.

"Damn," Stems said, disappointed. "Tell you what—let's try it one more time. Got me an idea."

Stems got underway again, and after around ten minutes, a third fish hit one of the lines and Rye again yelled up to Stems. Rye detached the rod and began to work the reel. Although it had not yet surfaced, Rye could tell the fish was large from the heavy tug on the line. He continued to fight the fish for several minutes, but Stems was nowhere to be found.

"Samuel, I could use some assistance!" Rye yelled as the fish approached the stern of the boat.

Stems suddenly appeared, running with a shotgun in hand. "Reel him up to just the back of the boat. I got something to calm him down!"

Chapter Fifteen

Stems quickly packed away the fishing gear and prepared to head back to shore. He was disappointed that they hadn't landed any fish. Rye wouldn't allow Stems to shoot the fish while they were on the line, declaring that it would have exhibited poor sportsmanship to do so. Without the aid of the firearm, each fish shook free and disappeared into the ocean before they could wrestle it to the deck.

Stems had just finished getting everything stowed for the ride in and was heading to the wheelhouse when I called him to give an update on my conversation with Ernie Harker.

"What's going on, Counselor?" Stems asked.

I told Stems I had some news and that it might be best to get Rye on the phone so that I could give them both an update. Stems found Rye on the front deck working on his notes and put me on speakerphone.

"Rye, I just got off the phone with Ernie Harker," I explained.

"I assume he understands that whatever his intent was with this vessel, my mission is more important," Rye replied.

"Not exactly," I said. "He claims your father committed to the sale of the boat and suggested he'd take legal action to force you to sell it to his client if necessary."

"So, what does this mean?" Rye asked.

I explained to Rye that I felt he had a very strong case. "Ernie as much as admitted he didn't have any written document to memorialize a contract, but he said he's not going away or giving up."

"I see," Rye replied. "What do you recommend?"

"He may be bluffing. It bothers me that I asked him who the potential buyer was and he wouldn't tell me. He also brought up your state of mind. He said something about a head injury and going to the hospital. Do you know what he is talking about?" I asked.

"Well, I did strike my head rather hard, resulting in a visit to a young physician who, by the way, had never undergone any serious trauma in his life. He was really of no assistance."

"Damn, Doc, when did this happen?" Stems asked.

"Just before I came to see you at the bar."

"You sure you're okay?" Stems added, looking worried.

"I couldn't be better, Samuel."

"Mr. Forelle, I can assure you my mental clarity has never been better in my life," Rye said to me.

"Rye, I don't really think there is anything for us to do other than wait at this point. The ball is really in Ernie's court, assuming you don't want to sell the boat," I said.

"I do not," Rye answered.

"You could always counteroffer what they offered you, although I have no idea what the boat is worth," I mentioned.

"It is not about currency. At least not the monetary type," Rye said.

"It's your boat," I conceded.

"Thank you, Mr. Forelle. If you hear more from Mr. Harker, please let us know. In the interim, we will continue on our journey," Rye explained.

After our phone call, Stems ran *Fat Lily* back into shallow waters and found a good anchorage for the evening. It was dusk by the time he had the boat secure. He then walked to the back deck where he found Rye lying on his back, looking up at the stars that were just emerging in the sky.

"I didn't want to dock up too close to the shoreline 'cause there's a lot of marsh over there," Stems explained, pointing to the expansive wetlands along the coast. "Figured we'd stay offshore so the mosquitos couldn't make it out to us. They can't fly but so far from shore, ya know."

"I have never considered that. That's very thoughtful of you, Samuel."

"Being from Seaford, you know mosquitos as good as me. Some of them bastards back home are tall enough to stand flatfooted and fuck a goose."

Rye laughed. "I really should take a drive back down there. I haven't been there in years. Has it changed much?"

"It's pretty much the same. A few new places, but not much changes down there. I like it that way. The little house I rent ain't too far from my mom's. Even if I'm gone for a long stretch like this, nobody's gonna mess with my stuff. People down there will look out for ya. At least half of them, anyway. The other half, they don't want to mess with me because they think I'm crazy. I got a reputation of sorts. Hell, the whole family does, but maybe me more than others. They think we're all nuts, which ain't the case. We're just a little on the wild side, maybe like them feral cows. I had my share of trouble, you know."

"I don't really recall that from back then, Samuel."

"Hell, Rye, near all the trouble I got into was a little later in life. It was after you left."

"So, you were not one to always follow the strict dictates of societal law. This can be a good thing sometimes."

"The local cops didn't think so."

"I imagine you're correct there. What types of things did you do?"

"Nothing too bad. Like, back in the late '80s, they put in the first stoplight in the town, and most of us locals didn't like it none too much. Hell, we didn't need no stoplight. There was a stop sign before, and nobody was gettin' in wrecks," Stems explained. "So, late at night, after we had ourselves a few drinks, me and a buddy of mine would go and steal that stoplight. The locals loved it—they didn't like the damn thing, either."

"You'd steal the stoplight?"

"Yep."

"How would you do that?"

"It was easy. My buddy worked for Virginia Power, and they let him drive a bucket truck home after work. We'd just take that truck up there and he'd cut the lines, and we'd lower the light down. A cop drove by one night when we were doin' it and just kept goin'. I reckon he saw the truck and figured we were doin' maintenance or something."

"What would you do with the stoplights afterwards?"

"Hell, that was the best part. I was wiring them up in the barn at the back of our property in Seaford. I was making myself a disco and had five of them stoplights hanging up back there before the cops finally caught on to what we were doin.'"

"Did you get in much trouble?" asked Rye.

"I had to spend a couple of weekends in jail, but it won't no big deal. The local jail was down by the waterfront in Yorktown back then. Actually, it had a nice view of the York River. The food was somethin' else, too. They had a damn good cook. I'd show up on a Friday night and leave on Sunday afternoon. We'd have us some *serious* poker games too. I was makin' a killing!"

"You were playing for money?"

"Is there another way to play? Hell, I was makin' more on the weekend poker games than I was during the week—most of it from the deputies. The problem those guys had was that they didn't know how to bluff worth a shit. Take it from me, Doc, you don't want to play cards with a bunch of convicts. You'll get your ass handed to ya. By the time I was done serving my sentence, I was thinking of doing some more stupid shit just to get sent back. I figured if I served a month or two, I'd have been able to pay off all my bills and have a little money saved. Never did it though. I guess I got a little lazy. Still, all in all, it was a pretty good investment."

"Samuel, nearly all men are prisoners who think they are free only because they refrain from touching the jail walls."

"The walls there weren't really too bad, but I tried not to touch the floors too much. They could get a bit nasty. You know, they closed that jail up probably fifteen or twenty years ago. If you get in trouble now and have to serve some time, they send you to some big corporate-run thing up by Williamsburg. Some people say it's nice, but that's 'cause they don't know no better. A guy I hang out with at Bar 17 was tellin' me that when he got locked up there, they were serving a slice of baloney and a piece of bread for breakfast. That was all they gave them! That ain't no way to start your day."

"Indeed, I would certainly struggle with that diet."

"Damn right! That's the problem with this country right now—big business is takin' over everything. The old jail had good service and generally satisfied customers, but I guess they weren't making enough money. That's why you gotta support local business."

"A poignant observation, Samuel."

After a meal composed of different varietals of squash and broccoli, Stems settled down in the outdoor entertainment area with a cooler of beer and a bag of weed. With some effort, Stems figured out how he could stream his cell phone to the large-screen television. They were close enough to shore that he could pick up a cell phone signal and ended up watching porn late into the evening before falling asleep on the couch.

By around 7 a.m. the next morning, Rye was drifting in and out of sleep and had the vague sense he was not feeling well. When he finally opened his eyes around 7:30, he realized that the seas had picked up just a little. He rubbed his eyes and climbed down from his bed, and discovered that he was slightly seasick. The room was stuffy, so he made his way to the deck to get some fresh air.

When he walked outside, a gray sky and cool breeze greeted him. He took a few deep breaths, and within a few minutes, his stomach settled. Seeing Stems still sleeping on the couch, Rye headed to the front deck and worked for a bit on his writing. Nearly two hours later, he decided he would rouse his travel companion. He walked over and cleared his throat and quietly said Stems's name. Stems didn't stir. He looked more closely at Stems's heavily tattooed arms and weathered face. Even though he knew they were around the same age, he thought Stems looked much older than him.

"Samuel!" Rye repeated, this time louder than he had intended as he hovered over his friend.

Stems startled awake and had a panicked look in his eyes. "Damn, Doc, you scared the hell out of me."

"My apologies, but I would like to continue our trek if you are agreeable."

"Sure, why not," Stems said as he sat up, rubbing his eyes, which were very bloodshot.

Stems scanned the horizon and noticed the dark sky for the first time. "Looks like it might be a little choppy today," he commented. "Based on what I saw last night, I think the weather is gonna continue to build a little today. Nothing scary, just a little rough."

"If that's the case, I better get through my kata sooner than later. I saw an old pair of rubber work boots in one of the rooms below. I was thinking about incorporating them into my weapons routine. The combination of elastic properties and solid sole could be quite lethal if properly employed."

"Knock yourself out, Doc."

"No, that's not my intent at all."

"I mean, have fun."

Rye excused himself and went below to find the pair of boots, then came up again to the back deck to go through his morning routine while Stems prepared to get *Fat Lily* underway. Rye tried to employ the boot but was finding it difficult to execute for two reasons. First, jamming his hand into a boot was more awkward than he expected. Second, the rocking boat kept throwing him off-balance. After around twenty minutes, he gave up and went to find Stems, who was now on the bridge.

"Done already?" Stems asked.

"Yes, I am struggling to determine the best way to use the boot as an effective means of self-defense."

"You could try it on your foot," Stems volunteered.

"Perhaps," Rye responded, intrigued.

"What do ya think about us taking a break around lunchtime and shooting a little skeet?" Stems asked.

"I would prefer to spend the day writing, Samuel. I am close to working out some particularly enlightening aspects concerning the illicit lure of consumerism."

"Oh, come on, Doc. Just for a bit. It'll be fun."

"I suppose there is no harm in it."

"Great, Doc. I'll run down the coastline, and we can try to find a good spot to lay up and do some shooting."

Rye went back outside and wrote on the back deck while Stems motored south. Rye refused to use the furniture Stems had brought but sat on the deck with his legs crossed and watched the scenery go by. A few hours later, Stems dropped the engines down to an idle and popped his head out of the cabin to yell down to Rye, "You ready to do some shootin', Doc?"

"Yes, let us proceed," Rye responded.

Fat Lily was about a mile offshore, and not seeing any other boat traffic around, Stems let the boat drift as he went below and then re-emerged on the front deck a few minutes later, carrying a shotgun and a box of shells. He handed them to Rye and then quickly shot back below to retrieve the box of skeet, skeet thrower, and a beer.

"I tell you what," Stems said to Rye. "Let's head to the bow, and we can shoot out over the water. I'll throw 'em first and you shoot, and then we can switch."

"That's agreeable," Rye responded, actually beginning to feel a little excited about the activity as he walked to the very front of the boat.

"You ever shot one of these before?" Stems asked, holding up the shotgun.

"This particular type of gun, no, but I have extensive experience with rifles. I was a Marine sniper, you know."

"When the hell did you do that?"

"Several years ago. I went into boot camp after spending a few years living in a commune down in Mexico. The sergeant didn't know what to do with me at first, but then somehow decided that I would have a natural affinity for this task."

126

"You ever shot anyone?"

"Luckily, no. I was deployed several times, but orders were never given to proceed. Frankly, despite my deadly accuracy, I don't know if I would have actually pulled the trigger. I did enjoy the desert training very much, though. In fact, I enjoyed it so much that one year, I went and ran the Marathon des Sables."

"What the hell is that?" Stems asked.

"It is a 155-mile foot race across the Sahara Desert that is completed in six days. Basically, it is running six marathons in a six-day period across the desert. Things did not go quite as planned, though. You see, on the fourth day of the race, I got myself turned around in a sudden sandstorm and wandered off the course. I was stranded for quite some time and don't think I would have survived if I hadn't constructed a solar still out of my rain jacket and plastic cup. This allowed me to purify my urine for consumption."

"I drank a cup of my own piss one time," Stems replied.

"Really?"

"Yep, did it on a bet. I was leaving Bar 17 and got into an argument with some dude. I was telling him that urine was sterile and it wouldn't hurt ya if you drank it. He said I was full of shit and told me he'd give me a hundred bucks to drink a glass. I pulled a plastic cup out of the back of my truck and filled it up and drank it on the spot. I was fine afterward. No more of a hangover the next morning than any other."

"Interesting. Evidence of one more thing we have in common," Rye commented.

"You ready to shoot some skeet, Doc?"

"Absolutely."

The skeet thrower was a simple device made from a single piece of stiff plastic that was thin and around eighteen inches long. It looked a little like a plastic rod or stick that had a handle at one end and a place to hold the disk-shaped skeet at the other. The design allowed for the user to slide a single skeet into the head of the thrower by squeezing it between two flanges that gripped it in place. The person using the thrower would then throw it with a snapping motion to accelerate the skeet forward and out of the thrower.

Rye loaded the shotgun and stood at the front rail, and Stems was off around ten feet to one side.

"When you're ready, just yell *pull*," Stems said as he loaded one of the skeet targets into the thrower. "I'll fling this thing out and you shoot it. That's all there is to it."

Rye took a deep breath and then exhaled and yelled, "Pull!"

Stems decided he wanted to really have some power on his first throw and did a quick, strong backswing as a windup. Unfortunately, he pulled back a little too fast, resulting in the skeet flying backward out of the thrower and behind Stems and Rye.

Rye, assuming the throw as intentional and employed as a means for Stems to test Rye's skills and reflexes, quickly spun around on his feet, raised the shotgun to his shoulder and shot the skeet out of the sky, pulverizing the small disk. However, in doing this, he also blew out the front window of the wheelhouse that was located directly behind the skeet he had shot.

"Holy shit!" yelled Stems, ducking down.

"Success!" Rye yelled, referring to the strike on the skeet.

"*Success?* What do you mean *success?* You blew out the damn window, Doc!"

"Perhaps you shouldn't have thrown the skeet in front of it then," Rye said calmly.

"It won't intentional!"

"Oh, I see. I had not considered that."

"What are we gonna do now?" Stems asked, eyeing the gaping hole in the wheelhouse window and the shattered glass scattered around the deck.

Rye surveyed the damage and then pontificated, "Do we really need a window up there, anyway? It seems to me that the view is clearer without it. Just think, we won't have to worry about cleaning it the rest of the trip."

"That's really great until it rains, Doc!"

"A valid point," Rye conceded. "What do you propose we do?"

"I reckon we can get it taken care of when we head into port. I think we can make it into the harbor outside of Charleston by this evening if we get moving."

Stems, still a little worked up, went below deck and dug out a bottle of wine from the trove he had pilfered from Rye's father's home, deciding at the moment that it might be a pleasant change from beer. He pulled out an old-looking bottle with writing that he assumed was French. He then went to the galley looking for a corkscrew when he realized that the bottle didn't have a twist-off cap. Stems rummaged through several drawers with no success, so he pulled out a steak knife and started whittling the cork out. He couldn't get the last bit out, so instead, he jammed it into the bottle with the sharp end of the knife. This caused some of the wine to shoot out of the neck of the bottle and spray him in the face and chest.

"Damn it!" Stems said as he wiped his face with his forearm. He skipped the cup and headed to the bridge, drinking from the bottle. When he got to the helm, he rolled a joint and took another swig of wine and then fired up the engines. By midafternoon, Stems was doing much better and had a cool buzz going. Rye had been hanging out on the rear deck, having decided it would be best to give Stems a little space.

An hour later, Stems was thinking about the food he planned to purchase in Charleston to stock the boat and was mentally in a good place when his cell phone rang. He recognized the number this time and considered not answering but decided perhaps it was better that he did.

Stems answered the phone and Ernie Harker's voice suddenly bellowed out loudly, "Hello, is this Mr. Keene? This is Ernest Harker."

"Yep, what'd you want, Mr. Harker?"

"I have a prepared statement I am going to read to you."

"A what?"

"A statement I have prepared in advance that I am going to read to you now."

"Okay," said Stems, a little confused as to what was happening.

"You should also be aware that I have a stenographer here in the room with me who will be transcribing my statement and your response."

"A what?"

"A stenographer. She's typing everything we are saying to properly memorialize our conversation," Ernie said, sounding annoyed by the questions.

"Alright, Chief, what do ya got?"

"Mr. Keene, my name is Ernest Harker, and—"

"You already said that," Stems interjected.

"Please let me finish and don't interrupt. It's for the recording. I am going to start over."

"Excuse the hell out of me. Go for it," Stems said.

Ernie tried again, sounding flustered. "Mr. Keene, my name is Ernest Harker, and I am a licensed Virginia attorney. It has come to my attention that you have aided and abetted a Mr. Rye Smyth in his misappropriation and conversion of personal property that has been committed for sale to another party in contract. Be advised that Mr. Rye Smyth puts such property at risk in his current unproductive endeavors and that he has further refused to honor the contractual obligations and commitments of the prior owner of the property. If said endeavors were to cause damage to or destruction of said property—to wit, the *Miss Elizabeth*—Mr. Smyth could potentially be found in breach of said contract and be found personally liable for any loss in value of said vessel or other damages, related or unrelated. Also, be advised that your assistance in these actions could give rise to separate causes of action under Virginia law, including tortious interference with contract and civil conspiracy under Virginia's Unfair Business Practices Act. As a result, I hereby demand that you immediately abandon your current reckless and wrongful undertaking and take any and all actions necessary to return the *Miss Elizabeth* back to port—"

"Port don't own the damn boat, Doc does!"

"What?"

"I said Port don't own the damn boat. The owner of *Fat Lily* is here on the boat with me."

"Mr. Keene, I have no idea what you are saying."

"You're talkin' about Port—the guy that runs the docks at the scallop company, right?"

"No, I am not. I'm talking about *the port*. The place where the boat is kept!" Ernie nearly shouted.

"How the hell was I supposed to know that? You should be more clear in what you're sayin' seeing as you're recording it and all."

"Mr. Keene, you really need to stop interrupting me!"

Stems did not respond.

"So, where was I? Yes . . . here we go. As a result, I hereby demand that you immediately abandon your current reckless and wrongful undertaking and take any and all actions necessary to return the Miss Elizabeth back to . . . *its harbor* in Yorktown, Virginia."

Stems still did not respond.

"Mr. Keene, are you still there?"

"Yep, I'm here. You all done now?"

"Yes, I am finished. What is your response?"

"'Cause I wouldn't want to interrupt you again if you ain't done yet."

"Yes, I have completed my statement. How do you respond?"

"Look here, Mr. Harker. I don't understand half of what you just said, but we talked with Jackson Forelle and he said you ain't got jack shit of a case."

"Mr. Keene, I don't have time for this! You should—you ought to—you *need* to be careful! I reserve the right to take any legal action I feel is appropriate. I may have you both charged with theft, as a matter of fact. I may also take this matter up with the United States Coast Guard to inquire as to how it may impact your captain's license. If they take your license, you realize you may never be able to work in the scallop industry again."

"Well, joke's on you. I ain't got no damn captain's license. I never did. I was a deckhand on these boats, and you don't need a license for that. Still, I spent enough time on 'em to know how to run one."

"You realize you need a license to take a party on a charter. You have now admitted to illegal activity," Ernie Harker said.

"If I'm not mistaken, that don't apply unless you're getting paid. I ain't getting paid for shit! We're just a couple of buddies taking a little ride together."

"Is that all you have to say in response to my inquiry?"

"Actually, no. You still got that steno—person there?"

"The stenographer, yes, that's correct. She's still here."

"Good, I'm going to say this nice and slow so they can take it down correctly."

"Yes, we are ready," replied Ernie Harker.

"My response is . . . go fuck yourself!" Stems shouted as he hung up.

Chapter Sixteen

Stems was still a little agitated as he pulled into the dockage outside of Charleston. He had told Rye about the phone call with Ernie Harker and had to smoke another joint to settle himself. After they arrived and got the boat secured, he made a few calls and located someone who could come out and replace the glass window the next day.

"Doc, you got some money to pay for this window and get us some food?"

"Yes, I believe so."

"Okay, good. Let's go ahead and run into town and stock up on some provisions, so we're set for a few weeks. I'll show you how to food shop for a trip like this!" Stems said, feeling a bit more cheerful.

The Uber XL arrived twenty minutes later, and the two men walked out to meet the driver, who was driving an extended-length minivan. The man rolled down the window and yelled out, "Are one of you Stems?"

"Yes sir, that's me," Stems yelled back. "You Baris?"

"Yes, correct," the man said with an accent Stems didn't recognize. "Hop in."

Stems and Rye climbed into the vehicle. Stems was carrying his now half-empty bottle of wine, and Rye had one of his notebooks in hand.

"Are you commercial fishermen?" the driver asked.

"Currently, no," said Stems, taking a swig of wine. "We're on a field trip," he explained.

"Field study," Rye corrected.

"What does that mean?" the driver asked.

"I am on a mission to reject social and societal constraints and live in accordance with nature."

Baris did not understand and changed the subject. "Is that your boat?" he asked, pointing back toward the *Miss Elizabeth*.

"It's Doc's boat," Stems said, nodding at Rye. "We're taking her on a little trip."

"Seems like a funny boat for a pleasure cruise," Baris said as he pulled away from the docks.

"She ain't so bad. I got her outfitted pretty good," Stems said.

"Is that a bass fishing boat I see on top?"

"Yep, that's our tender," Stems explained.

"Seems like a strange choice," Baris commented with a shrug.

"It is functional," Rye answered.

"How long you been driving?" Stems asked the driver.

"You mean for money?"

"Yeah, for Uber."

"Couple of years now. It's not bad. I can set my own hours."

"Where you from, Baris?" asked Stems.

"I'm Turkish, but I've been here for a very long time."

"Maybe that explains it—the accent, I mean. You got a little southern twang mixed in with your Turkish accent there, I think," said Stems.

"Could be," said Baris. "I learned my English here."

"How you like Charleston?" asked Stems.

"Great weather and great people. What's not to like?" responded the driver.

"Mr. Baris, I have a question for you," Rye said, seeing an opportunity to gain insight from a traveler from a foreign land.

"Just Baris," the driver corrected.

"Baris, do you see a more oppressive consumer-driven society here as compared to Turkey?"

"I don't understand this question," Baris replied.

"How do you feel about the capitalism here?" Rye tried again.

"Maybe better than Turkey," Baris said.

"Interesting. Why do you say this?" Rye asked.

"In Turkey, there is still a class system. There, even if I saved my money and dressed very nicely and went to an expensive restaurant for a special occasion, they would not treat me very well if they knew what I did for a living. Here, it doesn't matter. If you can pay, they will treat you nice. Money makes everybody the same."

Rye quickly pulled out his notebook and scribbled down several sentences. "An interesting perspective," Rye commented.

It took around fifteen minutes to get to the grocery store. Baris pulled up and dropped the two men off directly up front.

"Baris, you mind waiting for us? We'll pay you some extra cash," Stems said.

"Fine by me," Baris responded, shrugging his shoulders.

As they walked in, Stems grabbed a cart and told Rye to also get one so that they could load up. "I'll show you how it's done, Doc."

"I'll bring my notebook in the event I decide to take some notes," Rye responded.

It was at this point that Stems explained he didn't like to go aisle by aisle, working his way from one end of the store to the other, but liked to shop meal by meal. He explained it could result in some backtracking but that he was less likely to forget something. Stems suggested they start in the breakfast aisle, where he grabbed multiple boxes of cereal, several pounds of oatmeal, an assortment of breakfast bars, and twenty boxes of chocolate Pop-Tarts. He also grabbed a half-dozen boxes of pancake/waffle mix. They then went to the dairy section, where he grabbed five cartons of eggs and three gallons of milk.

Moving on to lunch, Stems went to the bread aisle and got a half-dozen loaves of bread and a few packets of hamburger buns, and then the deli section, where he grabbed an armful of pre-packaged containers of ham and turkey and various condiments, along with multiple packages of cheese. They then proceeded to the aisle with chips and dips, where he promptly filled up Rye's cart.

Finally, stocking up for dinners, they proceeded to the meat section, where Stems cleaned out all the ground beef on display and then likewise grabbed all the steaks. Stems explained they could freeze some of the meat and bread to save it for the trip. He also grabbed several pounds of chicken breasts and pork chops. They next went to the canned vegetable aisle, and Stems loaded up with canned beans and corn. Then they moved to the fresh vegetable aisle, where Stems just grabbed several bags of potatoes. They then proceeded to the frozen food section, where Stems loaded up on frozen pizzas and other frozen meals along with several gallons of various types of ice cream. He grabbed another twenty pounds of frozen tuna and salmon fillets for Rye. Just to be safe, Stems then decided to get an extra cart and loaded it with four cases of beer. It took some effort for Stems to handle two carts, but he managed to push one and pull the other.

"This should hold us for a bit," Stems said as they rolled the packed grocery carts to one of the checkout aisles where Rye paid for everything, which came to well over a thousand dollars.

Baris saw the men walking out of the store struggling to handle the three carts, so he pulled up to the curb and helped them load everything into the rear of the minivan. It was getting dark by the time they pulled out of the shopping center.

"I have to say that it is interesting to shop with you, Stems. I usually stay primarily to the outside perimeter where the fresh fruit and vegetables are located, and you apparently thrive on the inner aisles," Rye mused.

Stems reached back and pulled out a cold beer from one of the cases they had just purchased and popped it open. It was also at this point that Stems got the idea of hitting a strip club on the way back to the boat. When he first asked Baris whether there were any of these clubs nearby, Baris didn't understand what Stems was talking about.

"You know, the sexy, dancing women," Stems explained.

"You mean the go-go?" Baris asked.

"Damn right, the go-go! Let's *go* to the go-go!" Stems said.

"There is one about a mile from the waterfront. I have driven past it many times but have never gone inside," Baris explained.

"There you go. I say let's check it out. Sounds like it's on the way," said Stems. "Rye, what do you think?"

"I've never been to one," said Rye. "Tell me about these places."

"Hell of a lot easier to show ya than tell ya, but the general idea is near-naked women dancin' on a stage," Stems explained.

"And they get paid for this, presumably."

"If they're good, they sure do."

"Stems, I have some concerns that this might promote the sexual objectification of women. I wonder if these women are being taken advantage of."

"Hell, Doc, if anybody's being taken advantage of, it's me. They got a lot of money from me over the years."

"It certainly is an interesting proposition. They may have some valuable observations and insights regarding working in a service industry in a consumer-driven society. It may provide comparative data to contrast with those who have rejected and left behind this type of society. Obviously, every scientific study requires a baseline, you understand."

"No, Doc, sorry. I don't understand."

"Allow me to explain further. If they are selling a product that only leads to a greater desire for more of that product, they may also be the perfect embodiment of capitalism and consumerism."

"I'm not sure I'm following you, Doc."

"I presume that you have historically gone to these establishments based upon sexual desire, correct?"

"Well . . . sure."

"When you leave, if the dancers have done their job well, you have given them a considerable amount of money and they have only increased those desires, leaving you wanting more."

"I reckon. But putting it that way kinda takes the fun out of it, don't you think?"

"It's really quite brilliant, Stems. It's like a restaurant that charges top dollar to go in and just look at the food, and then you must leave."

"Huh, never really thought about it that way, but I get your point. Kinda like getting a really good tastin' drink, swishing it around in your mouth, and then spittin' it out."

"Actually, Stems, I understand that there are many wine aficionados who do exactly that."

"I love your sense of humor, Doc. We should probably get these groceries back to the boat pretty soon, but I say we make a quick stop. Baris, you want to take a break and come in with us?"

"Fine with me," the driver replied.

Baris pulled into a nearly empty parking lot of a rundown strip shopping center. He grabbed an open spot directly in front of a nondescript business with a generic red neon sign that simply said, "Gentlemen's Club." Rye was thoroughly confused as the place looked nothing like the exclusive eighteenth-century "gentlemen's clubs of London." Those clubs, which catered strictly to upper-class men of the era, were often known for their grand architecture. In contrast, there wasn't a single Doric portico with matching columns that Rye could see anywhere in the shopping center. Instead, there were only the surrounding businesses, consisting of a tattoo parlor, a check cashing business, and a hot wings restaurant.

The three men entered the club, and Rye paid a $10 cover for all of them to a large bouncer with a tight T-shirt and shaved head. The room had no windows. It was dark inside, with a scattering of a few overhead lights and a disco ball straight out of the '70s. The men scanned the room and observed a full bar along one length of the room and two stage areas—one to the left and one to the right. Each stage had a center pole for the dancers to exhibit their skills. There were also high-top tables with barstools dotted around the room. There were only a half-dozen other patrons in the establishment, so most of the tables were open. No women were currently dancing, so Stems led the group over to one of the open tables in the center of the room, strategically located between the two stages. There was also a thin DJ wearing a Guns N' Roses T-shirt set up at the end of the room opposite the bar. The DJ had not yet started his set, resulting in an uncomfortable silence. A few minutes later, a skimpily dressed waitress came from behind the bar and over to the table where Rye and the others sat.

"What can I get y'all?" she asked, smiling.

"A round of bourbons for everyone," responded Stems.

"None for me," Rye interjected.

"Bring three anyways," Stems said. "I'll drink two. Where's the girls, anyways?"

"They're on break, but they'll be up there in a bit. You know, it's still early. We don't *really* get going until late in the evening," the waitress explained.

The server returned shortly with the drinks and distributed them to the group. "You guys from around here?" she asked.

"Nope, came in on a scallop boat," Stems said.

The server smiled a little broader upon hearing this, likely being familiar with the free flow of cash that often comes when scallopers return to shore from a trip. "Great, I'll try to hurry things along. Anything else I can get you in the meantime?"

"Another round," said Stems.

"You got it, honey," said the waitress.

Shortly afterward, two attractive women emerged from a door located at the rear of the room. Both women appeared to be in their early to mid-twenties. One of them had blonde hair and was wearing some kind of corset. The other woman was darker-skinned and was wearing a black miniskirt and matching halter top. The women stayed in the back of the room performing various stretches, apparently warming up before their sets.

Rye noticed that their waitress went to the back of the room to talk to the two dancers before she returned with the round of drinks.

"Here you go!" the waitress said enthusiastically as she set the drinks on the table. "You gentlemen all set?"

"I have a question for you, young lady," Rye said.

"What do you need, sweetie?"

"I have a question regarding the protocol here regarding tipping?"

"What do you want to know?"

"As I understand it, the general rule is that the dancers are given money by the patrons, but is that process ever reversed whereby the dancers tip the patrons?"

"Why the hell would the girls be tipping the customers?" the waitress asked.

"Perhaps based upon the benefits they confer upon the dancers by increasing their prestige and reputation. For instance, in my particular case, considering the importance of the task that I undertake, one could argue that my attendance here could bring considerable fame and fortune for years to come for these performers. As a result, a small gratuity could be in order. Mind you, I am not actively seeking remuneration."

"And just what *task* would that be that you are doing?" the server asked.

"I am seeking to live in accordance with nature and writing a book that is designed to broadly address the human condition."

"So, you're a writer?"

"I suppose that's accurate, although it sounds quite understated when you put it in those terms," Rye replied.

"I'll give you credit, honey. We've had a few famous people in here over the years, including a couple of professional athletes and actors, but I never had anyone with the balls to think they ought to get the tips!"

"With your description of these prior patrons, that certainly makes sense. I am not involved in such frivolity as sports or entertainment. I'm on a spiritual quest."

"I don't know what the hell you're talking about, but just to be clear, if you want the girls to dance for you, then you tip them. It isn't the other way around."

"Actually, I'm primarily interested in obtaining inspiration."

"Aren't we all," the server quipped.

One of the two dancers, likely having been already tipped off by the waitress that the men at the center table just got off a fishing boat and might have a lot of cash to burn, decided to do a quick drop-in before getting on stage.

"This gentleman here is looking for inspiration," the server said, nodding in Rye's direction as the dancer approached.

"I can inspire," the young woman said with a smile.

"Be careful, he might want a tip," the server said as she walked away.

"*You* might want a tip? It doesn't usually work that way, honey," the dancer said.

"Yes, that has already been explained to me. Do not worry yourself. I'll forgo any gratuity. I am looking for insights, and I am hoping that you may be able to help."

"I got to get dancing in a minute. What do you want?"

"You see, I am investigating our current capitalistic society and contrasting it with the consumerism it has spawned with a more simplistic lifestyle of living in accordance with nature. Right now, I am trying to consider how your profession fits into this analysis." Rye opened his notebook and prepared to memorialize the woman's responses, adding, "You know, it is a great honor that I am prepared to give you. This could be your chance to contribute to the creation of a great literary masterpiece that will almost certainly provide guidance for generations to come."

Obviously amused but not fully sure what to make of Rye, the woman responded, "You know, if you really want to write about how capitalism affects an exotic dancer, you should be asking about how the bouncers, managers, DJs, and owners take part of our tips. We're the ones doing the hard work, and when we complain about them getting a cut of our money, they say, 'Well, that's capitalism' or 'That's how it works,'" the woman explained.

"Fascinating! That has never crossed my mind," Rye responded as he continued to swiftly take notes. "Perhaps you should unionize."

The DJ hadn't started the music yet, and the club was still quiet—quiet enough that their conversation apparently caught the attention of a man with some authority sitting at the bar. Rye noticed the man, who was wearing a dark, shiny button-down shirt, suddenly sit up straight on his bar stool and make several sharp jerking motions with his thumb towards the front door. Rye wasn't sure what was going on, but almost immediately afterwards, the bouncer appeared at their table.

"Gentlemen, it's time for you to leave," he said in an authoritative voice.

"What for?" asked Stems, very surprised.

The bouncer stammered for a moment, clearly not knowing the reason for the eviction. Then, taking note of the baseball cap Stems was wearing, said, "Because you're wearing a hat inside sitting at the table, that's why."

"What the hell! You think this is my dad's dinner table or something?" Stems asked, very agitated.

"This is a respectable place, and we have a dress code," the bouncer responded.

"Are you shittin' me? It's a strip club. It ain't no goddamn opera house!" Stems shot back, thoroughly confused.

"Excuse me, sir, I have just started on my interview, and we are making exceptional progress," Rye added. "This is a very important undertaking—"

The bouncer cut him off and said loudly, "All of you are gone! Time to leave! That's all you need to know!"

The dancer standing nearby objected, but the bouncer told her this was beyond her pay grade and that she needed to stay out of it. Not wanting to see things escalate further, Baris assured the bouncer that they were not looking for trouble and he ushered Stems and Rye to the door. Stems cursed under his breath as they exited the building.

"Maybe it's for the best," Baris said as they walked out. "You got to get these groceries back to the boat, and I need to get home soon."

"Aw, bullshit. We weren't doing nothing wrong," Stems complained with slurred speech as the continuous drinking throughout the day had caught up to him.

As they approached the car, Baris felt the phone in his front pocket vibrating and pulled it out. He saw it was his wife calling to check on him, and he instinctively answered. As he paused outside the vehicle to talk, he put his index finger up to his puckered lips, directing the others to keep their voices down. The volume on Baris's phone was turned up high so Stems, who was standing next to him, could hear both sides of the conversation taking place.

"Hello," Baris said nonchalantly.

"How is your shift going?" the female voice at the other end of the phone said.

"It's going well. I am wrapping up the last call now. Can I call you back in a little bit? I'm right in the middle of something."

"No problem—love you."

"You too—talk to you soon."

Baris quickly jammed the phone in his pocket and said, "Okay, let's go."

As they climbed back into the van, Stems noticed Baris fishing his wedding ring out of his shirt pocket and putting it back on. "What'd you take your ring off for? You think them girls aren't gonna dance for you if they know you're married?" Stems asked, ribbing Baris.

"I don't know. It's none of your business, anyway," Baris said defensively.

"Sir, I apologize, but I only give lap dances to single men," Stems continued, imitating the dancers using a high-pitched voice.

Baris thought he heard a distant woman's voice shouting his name. He looked around, confused, and then realized it was coming from his pocket. He quickly pulled out his phone and, to his chagrin, realized that he had never hung up with his wife. He tentatively put the phone to his ear. "Ah . . . hello," he stammered.

The volume was still up on his phone, and both Stems and Rye could clearly hear Baris's wife.

"Baris! What are you doing blowing our money in a strip club, and why the hell are you taking your ring off?"

"I didn't mean anything by it, sweetheart. I'm sorry."

"Yes, you are very sorry! I agree with you in this respect. I don't even want to talk to you right now. I'm trying to decide if I'm going to pack up your things and put them outside."

"Honey . . . " Baris continued as she hung up.

Baris was distraught. He looked up at Stems, who was sitting in the front passenger's seat, and yelled, "Now look what you did!"

"Me? You're the one that forgot to hang up the phone," Stems said.

"Things would have been much easier for me in Turkey," Baris lamented. "She's been here a long time now, and I can't get away with anything." Clearly flustered, he attempted to put the van in reverse with the shifter on the steering column but went past reverse and into neutral because of his agitation. The van rolled back a bit as it was on a slope, but Baris kept pushing the accelerator down more, trying to speed up. He then glanced down and realized he was in neutral and slammed the shifter up into reverse. The engine was still revved up, and the van lurched back suddenly, causing Stems to hit his head on the dash. Baris immediately slammed on the brakes, throwing him and everyone else to the back of their seats.

"Damn, Baris, you trying to kill us?" asked Stems.

"Oh no, sorry. My fault," Baris said as he looked around the parking lot, trying to get his bearings. The van was pulled far enough back that he could now turn and exit, but as Baris tried to put the van into drive, he realized that his sudden maneuver had damaged the transmission and that it was stuck in reverse. He tried to pull down the shifter a few more times to no avail and then announced, "We have a problem. I think the transmission is broken."

"It won't drive?" asked Stems.

"It's stuck in reverse," Baris responded.

"Well, shit!" Stems said.

After a few additional failed attempts to get the van out of reverse, he explained to Stems and Rye that he had a friend who drove a tow truck and he would call him. Unfortunately, the friend was across town towing another vehicle, and it would take him well over an hour to get there.

"Damn, Baris, I got meat in here I need to get on ice," Stems explained.

Baris scanned the seedy industrial area. There was no traffic on the road. He sighed and then said, "No problem, I'll take care of you. It's not that far to the boat," he added as he spun the van around in reverse and maneuvered through the parking lot and onto the road, driving backward.

"Damn, Baris, I like your style," said Stems.

Baris nearly made the mile-long trip back to the boat in reverse without issue, but when he was only two blocks away from the docks, he drove past a police car sitting on a side street with its lights off. Stems spotted the vehicle and told Baris, but there was really nothing they could do by then. Baris kept driving, hoping that there was no one in the car, or if there was, that the officer didn't see the vehicle drive past in reverse. Ten seconds later, the police car pulled out behind them with its lights on.

Baris pulled over and started sweating profusely. The officer pulled up behind the van and, because Baris had been driving in reverse, this resulted in the vehicles facing each other with each vehicle's headlights shining at the other's. The police officer was driving an SUV, and the men in the van could clearly make out "K-9" in large letters on the hood.

Seeing this, Stems immediately asked if anyone else had any weed on them as he hastily pulled two joints out of his front pocket and then chewed and swallowed them.

The officer got on his vehicle's loudspeaker and instructed Baris to turn off his vehicle and his headlights, which he immediately did.

The young-looking police officer continued to sit in his vehicle, and Stems could tell that the policeman was talking on his radio. He then climbed out, holding a large German Shepherd by the leash, and shouted for all the men to exit the van slowly with their arms raised above their heads.

Everyone exited the van as instructed. They were all feeling more than a little nervous, considering the circumstances. Stems, having had a few run-ins with the law, was resigned to the fact that they were all likely to end up spending the night in jail. Rye, on the other hand, was feeling confident that once he explained the importance of their journey, the officer was certain to leave them be.

Officer Rich stood next to his vehicle with his dog on a leash at his side. "Anyone have any weapons?" he asked.

"What's that, sir?" asked Stems.

"Any of you guys packing?" the officer yelled back more aggressively.

For some unexplained reason, when the officer shouted back, the German Shepherd must have misinterpreted what the officer said as a command to attack. The animal suddenly ripped its leash free from the officer and shot at the three men standing next to the minivan.

Rye was the closest to the dog, and it looked like the animal had homed in on him for its first victim. The German Shepherd was in a full sprint, and Rye, somehow misinterpreting the dog's intent, was welcoming him with open arms and said, "Look, he's coming to play!"

When he was around six feet out from Rye, the dog launched into the air with bared teeth, determined to latch onto Rye's nearest appendage. Rye suddenly realized that the dog's intentions were less than friendly. Worse yet, he no longer had time to deploy a flip-flop.

Baris was horrorstruck as he watched the events unfold in front of him in slow motion. He yelled out at the dog when it was in midair, "Bad! Bad dog! Bad dog!" This must have caught the dog's attention as the animal turned its head toward Baris, looking almost confused.

At the same moment, Stems, feeling well-lubricated from the alcohol pumping through his veins, decided to intervene for his friend. He stepped in front of Rye and took a wild haymaker swing at the dog with his eyes nearly closed. By chance, the right hook connected squarely with the jaw of the briefly distracted dog. The German Shepherd hit the ground with a thud.

The police officer, who was clearly stunned by the unexpected turn of events, was beside himself. He quickly pulled his service weapon, pointed it at Stems, and yelled, "What the hell did you do to my dog?"

Stems, more than a little surprised that he had hit the leaping animal, responded, "I punched the son of a bitch. Why'd you sic him on me?"

"All of you on the ground! Now!" yelled the officer.

The three men complied, and as they were lying down, the dog stood up, shaking its head.

"Calm down there, Chief. He just got a little shook up. He's fine, see?" said Stems.

The dog retreated to the police officer, a little dazed and unsteady on its feet. The policeman attempted to pet it, but the dog growled at him and jumped in the still-open door of the officer's SUV. The officer then turned back to the men who were still lying down on the pavement. After a brief pause, he asked, "Why the hell were you guys driving backward?"

"The car is broken," Baris explained.

"Where are you guys going?" the policeman asked.

"Right down the street to our scallop boat," Stems replied. "We're just tryin' to get our provisions back to the boat and then head out of town."

"Is your boat within walking distance?"

"Yes, sir," said Stems. "It's right down at the docks."

"Tell you what. If you get your asses up and walk down there pronto, I'll let you off with a warning."

"Yes, sir, you got it," said Stems.

"What about me?" asked Baris.

"Call a ride."

"Okay, fine by me," replied Baris. "What about the van?"

"You can't leave it in the road, and you can't drive it backward. Call a tow truck," said the officer.

"Hey, Baris, we'll carry the meat. Have your buddy tow the van by the boat first so we can unload the rest of the groceries, if you don't mind," Stems said as he grabbed a few bags out of the back of the vehicle.

"Fine," Baris said as he looked at his phone to call his buddy with the tow truck and ask him to hurry up.

Part II

Chapter Seventeen

It was a little past 10 a.m. when Kaia walked down one of the side streets in George Town, heading to the weekly flea market. There was nothing particular she was looking to buy, but she was hoping to find something small to memorialize her time on the island.

Kaia had a little extra spring in her step. The sun was already high in the sky with just a bit of cloud cover, but the island breeze kept the temperature in check. She was actually a little chilly in her T-shirt, which was pulled over a bathing suit that hadn't fully dried out from the day before. Kaia smiled and waved to a shopkeeper who was in the process of opening a small grocery store Kaia frequented.

"Hey Mama, how you doing this morning?" Kaia shouted in a chipper voice.

"I'm good, Kaia! How about you?" the Bahamian woman yelled back.

"I'm lovin' it!" Kaia responded enthusiastically. Having been on the island for nearly three months, Kaia was enjoying being part of a community again. Still, she was also getting that nagging feeling that it was time to move on. At thirty-four, Kaia hadn't spent over six months in any location for the last six years of her life.

She rounded a corner and walked into a field by the waterfront where they had set up the flea market. It was busier than she expected. The peak season for George Town—the capital of the Exumas—was during the winter when the town was flooded with tourists who were there to escape the cold from North America and

Europe alike. Summers were usually more chill and relaxed, but a few locals had told her that things were changing and that George Town had been "found."

There were several aisles of makeshift tables at the market with an odd assortment of goods, including some fresh fruits and vegetables, as well as T-shirts, sunglasses, and various trinkets for the tourists. Kaia knew many of the merchants were selling cheap, gimmicky stuff made overseas, but there were also a handful of local artisans mixed in. Kaia was trying to figure out why the market was so busy when she spotted two massive tour buses in the parking lot from Slip Shoes Oasis, the large, mostly self-contained resort on the other side of the island.

Kaia cruised down one aisle and paused at a table set up by an older Bahamian man she had not noticed before. The man was selling an assortment of exotic-looking beaded bracelets and necklaces. As she stopped at the table, she also spotted a small but prominently displayed plaque with a fish on it propped up against a conch shell on the corner of the display. The man didn't notice Kaia at first, as he was in deep concentration, stitching together some of the beads.

Curiosity got the better of Kaia, and she asked the man, "Hey, what's the plaque for?"

The man looked up with a smile. "That's a world record I got around ten years ago," he explained.

"For what?"

"I caught the biggest palometa fish at the time."

"Palmetto, like the cheese?"

"Close, but no. Pal-o-meta," the man said more slowly.

"Cool. How big was it?"

"One pound and three ounces," the man said. "The record stood for a few years before someone caught a bigger one. I think it was up in Bermuda."

Kaia looked more closely at the bracelets and necklaces. The beads were black and appeared almost furry. "What kind of beads do you use?"

"They're a type of seed that grows on some small trees in the area."

"Seeds, huh? How do they hold up?"

"Good, just don't get them wet."

"What happens if you're wearing them and it rains?"

"Maybe they sprout, and you end up with some tiny tree on your wrist," the man said, grinning.

"That's probably not going to work for me. I'm in the water all the time—like a fish. Congrats on the world record, though."

The man just smiled and nodded.

Kaia continued down the aisle and paused at another table that was selling an odd assortment of nautical-themed souvenirs when she glanced up and spotted a middle-aged man farther down the aisle who was walking around with a flashlight. He was shining the light at various people, although it was very bright outside with only a few clouds in the sky. Everyone in the crowd was doing their best to pretend the odd man was not there. The man was working his way down in Kaia's direction, and she purposely averted her eyes back to the table as he got closer. He paused next to her and shined the light squarely at her face. Kaia couldn't help but see the light out of the corner of her eye, and after what felt like an eternity, she glanced up.

The man stared at her in a serious fashion and announced, "I am looking for an honest man."

This caught Kaia off guard for just a moment, but she quickly recovered and asked, "Why not an honest woman?"

The man's serious look softened, and he said, "That is a very fair question. I was referring to the term *man* in a broader sense, as it is sometimes applied to our entire species, regardless of gender. But your point is well taken, and I certainly don't want to limit my inquiry to half the human population. With that being said, allow me to amend my statement to 'I am looking for an honest human.'"

"Any luck finding one?"

"Not as yet, but I just arrived yesterday, and this is my first excursion. Perhaps I am talking to one now."

"I think I'm pretty honest."

"Do you happen to be traveling on one of the vessels in the harbor?" the man asked.

"No, me and a friend are living in a house here on the island."

"I see," the man said.

"What's the deal with the flashlight, anyway?"

"Illumination."

"Alright . . . yeah, that's usually what they're used for," Kaia said tentatively.

"I came ashore to this location in the hope that it might be frequented by those who have managed to throw off the shackles of modern life and live in accordance with nature. I noticed several boats in the harbor, but I have not yet had the opportunity to converse with any of my fellow travelers. You may call me Rye."

"Hi Rye, I'm Kaia. Yep, the folks on the boats are around. You just got to know where to look. You might find a few stragglers here coming in for some fresh fruit or something, but if you really want to meet the ones staying on the boats, head to the sandbar where they meet up. They're there pretty much every evening."

"This is excellent news! Now I know where I must go! In the interim, Kaia, perhaps I could ask you some questions for my research and ascertain the level of your honesty," Rye said, holding up one of the notebooks he had been carrying, along with the flashlight.

"Hmm, I don't know. Me and a friend were hoping to do some surfing today, and I should probably get back to get her moving. We're thinking about renting a small boat and heading to a little reef break down the coast. A friend of ours told us about it, and you can only get to it by boat."

"Surfing, you say. That's interesting." He paused for a moment. "Do you know where this sandbar is located—where the boat people commune?"

"Yeah, sure. I've been there a few times."

"I have a proposition for you, then. I happen to have my tender here at the dock. How about I take you and your friend surfing so that you don't need to rent a boat, and then later, you take me to the sandbar?"

"Alright, alright, maybe," Kaia said, thinking about how expensive boat rentals were on the island. "You could surf with us. You got a board?"

"No, I have tried not to burden myself with excessive possessions."

"Nothing excessive about a surfboard. It's essential," Kaia said. "Have you ever surfed before?"

"I have not, but it sounds intriguing."

"Tell you what. I think I can borrow a board for you. We'll

give it a go. Let's meet in an hour down at the little beach by the boat docks."

"Excellent," Rye responded.

Chapter Eighteen

Kaia walked back to George Town Kiteboarding, a local business where she had been giving lessons the last few months. She had taken the day off because there was no wind. The local owner, Javon, who had been born and raised on the island, was behind the counter looking bored.

"Hey Javon, I'm thinking about trying out that surf spot you told me about."

"Which one?"

"The little reef break you mentioned."

"You renting a boat?"

"Was planning on it but met someone who's going to take us."

"Of course you did," Javon said, smiling. "You got a knack for making friends."

"What can I say. That's me. Can you show me on the map how to get there?"

"It's no problem," said Javon, pulling out the map of the Exumas from under the counter and laying it out. "You just head east from the marina to get outside the reef and sandbars and then work north around the edge of the island to this cove." He pointed to a small inlet. "You'll see the break, and you can anchor off twenty or thirty yards to the east and swim over to it. It's very gentle. Where is Nori, anyway?"

"Nothing on the books, so she slept in and is relaxing a bit," said Kaia. "You got a surfboard around we can borrow for the dude with the boat?"

"I just bought a new one, but I'm not letting anyone ride that but me. But I got an old longboard at the house in the back shed.

You can swing by and grab it on the way. Should be some wax in there somewhere, too. It's been a while since it's been used, so you may want to take the old stuff off and re-wax it. There's some snorkel gear in there if you want to take that too. There are some pretty cool coral formations in the area and maybe a few lobsters also."

"Thanks, Javon. You're the best!"

"Wake up, *mon amour*," yelled Kaia as she opened the screen door and walked into the little house the two women had been renting. "We got to get moving!"

The home was on the beach and owned by a retired race car driver from the UK whom the women had met in the spring in the Turks and Caicos. The three had spent a night partying together at a beach bar, and the man had told them he had a place in the Bahamas that he hardly ever used. He told them he would cut them a sweet deal if they wanted to spend some time there. The two women packed their bags a week later and headed out.

Nori was in the kitchen drinking tea and eating a sandwich. "I'm up, *mi amor*. You get the boat?"

"Even better. I found a dude with a tender that's going to take us."

"Hell yeah! We just got to go by Javon's house and pick up a board for the guy to use. He also wants us to take him to the sandbar this evening to meet some of the folks on the liveaboards."

"Sounds good. They're usually good for a laugh."

Nori quickly put on her bathing suit and grabbed a couple of towels. The two women then strapped their surfboards to the top of their rental car and headed to Javon's house.

"So, who's the guy with the boat?" Nori asked.

"Don't know much about him. He came in by boat yesterday. He's . . . a little different but seems basically harmless."

"That describes about ninety percent of the liveaboards. *Basically* harmless, huh?"

After a short drive, the women pulled into the gravel driveway of Javon's house. It was a typical Bahamian home built out of concrete blocks and situated on a small beach. The pale blue-painted house was well-kept.

"Where's the shed?" Nori asked.

"Around back, I think. Let's take a look."

As they walked around to the back of the home, they spotted a thick patch of trees and vines growing over a rusty metal shed.

"That it?" asked Nori.

"I think so," Kaia said as they walked back to the heavily overgrown structure.

"The surfboard in there?" asked Nori.

"I think."

Nori tried to slide back the door of the shed, but it wouldn't budge. She gave it a hard jerk. The door popped open with a loud screech, and a small brown snake darted out toward them. Spotting the women, it spun around and shot back into the depths of the shed.

"Damn!" yelled Nori, jumping back. "Well, I guess we're not getting the surfboard."

"Oh, come on. Let's get the board and get out of here," said Kaia.

Nori gazed back into the dark shed. "The snake is in there."

"It was little. Probably just one of those Brown Racers."

"Are they poisonous?"

"Maybe, but someone told me they have venom, but they're not poisonous to humans."

"What the hell does that mean? That makes no damn sense at all."

"I don't know. Just go in there and get the board."

"Why don't *you* go in and get it?" asked Nori.

"Hell no," Kaia said while laughing. "Use your phone and shine a light in there."

Nori cautiously stepped closer to the open shed and stretched her hand inside, holding the phone. She spotted the surfboard in the back corner. "I see it!"

"The board or the snake?" Kaia asked.

"The board."

"Cool. Now go get it."

"Damn it," Nori said as she gingerly walked into the shed, scanning the light of the phone all around. She made her way to the board and handed it out to Kaia without spotting the snake.

"See any wax in there?" Kaia asked.

"Nope. How's the wax on the board look?"

Kaia inspected the board in the sunlight. "I think it's manageable. Don't worry about it. You see any snorkel equipment in there?" asked Kaia.

Nori looked around a little more and saw several pairs of fins, along with a few masks and snorkels, on a shelf. "I see some stuff. Want me to grab it?"

"Go ahead and—"

"Holy shit!" yelled Nori, interrupting Kaia.

"What is it? The snake?" asked Kaia.

"No, a spear gun thingy! You know—a Hawaiian sling. Can we take it?"

"Sure, why not? Go ahead and grab it," said Kaia.

Nori tossed the snorkeling gear out of the shed and grabbed the Hawaiian sling. She slowly exited the shed, gripping the weapon tightly. "Come at me now, bitch."

"Leave that poor snake alone and get out of there!"

"Not so tough now, are you?" Nori said as she exited the shed more confidently.

The ladies quickly strapped the third surfboard on top of the other two that were already on their vehicle and then threw the other gear in the back seat. They then headed off to meet Rye.

Around twenty minutes later, they pulled up in front of the marina and parked. The ladies walked around the back of the building and headed to the single pier extending out into the blue water.

"What's this dude look like?" asked Nori.

"Middle-aged. Kinda thin."

Kaia spotted Rye sitting on the beach cross-legged, writing in his notebook. As they approached, they saw he was in deep concentration, and he didn't notice them at first. He was writing away feverishly.

"Hey, Rye," Kaia finally said.

Rye glanced up and smiled.

"This is Nori," Kaia added. "You ready to do some surfing?"

"By the Dog Star, yes! However, I would like to ask you some questions first. Is that agreeable?"

"Sure, why not," Kaia said.

"Hey, I really have a craving for some switcha," Nori said. "How about we grab a glass before we leave? We can go to MJ Cays."

"What is a *switcha*?" Rye asked.

"It's like this really tart local lemonade," Nori explained.

"Yes, yes. Let's proceed," Rye responded.

They walked down the street to a small, bright yellow building with the words "MoJack Cays" painted in pink next to the front door.

"Have you visited this establishment before?" asked Rye.

"Absolutely," said Nori with a smile.

As the three walked into the bar, Rye saw that there was a large open room with a smattering of wooden tables and chairs, along with a bar on the opposite wall. There were a few tourists grabbing an early lunch, but the place was quiet. As Rye's eyes adjusted to the light, he noticed that the walls and ceiling were covered in dollar bills. They stepped farther in, and a Bahamian woman working behind the bar spotted them. She was wearing a bright floral dress, and her hair was wrapped up in the same fabric. She beamed and said, "Hey girls, you working today?"

"Not today, Celeste. We're going to do some surfing," explained Nori.

"Then, what you are doing *here*?" asked the woman in her rich Bahamian accent.

"We thought we'd grab some switchas before we headed out," Nori said.

"A great idea," the bartender said. "Who's your friend?"

"This is Rye," Kaia said.

"Nice to meet you, sir."

"You as well," Rye replied. "Tell me, why do you have all the currency hanging throughout this establishment?"

"Oh, that's something they've been doing for years. Tourists like to staple them up on the wall. They'll color them with different Sharpies, put dates and names on them. Things like that. People are always wanting to put their mark on things. Just like a dog peeing on a bush. I guess it makes them feel good when they have to go back to work to know that their money is still hanging out at some fun place. I don't get it myself, but if it makes them happy to leave extra money here, fine by me."

"How much you think you got up on the walls right now?" asked Nori.

"Not sure, probably five thousand dollars. About every six months, we'll pull down five hundred dollars or so to free up some wall space. The local bank didn't want to take it at first because they're so marked up sometimes, but they gave in. We told the bank manager he couldn't drink here anymore if they didn't deposit the money!"

"Nice," said Nori.

Celeste set up three glasses of ice and then filled them with the yellow-colored beverage from a pitcher behind the bar. Kaia paid the bill and then Rye, Kaia, and Nori took the drinks and migrated to a booth in the back of the small restaurant.

"So, you are both surfers, correct?" Rye asked as they settled in.

"Damn right," Kaia said.

"And do you travel a great deal in pursuit of this endeavor?"

"You could say that," Kaia said.

"Excellent. I had hoped to run into some vagabonds on my journey."

"Vagabonds. Humm, doesn't that have kind of a negative meaning?" Nori asked.

"Perhaps, but that really gets to the heart of what I am investigating. 'Vagabond' is from the Greek word *vagari*, which means inclined to wander," Rye explained. "Would you agree that you are inclined to wander?"

"Yep, I guess so," Nori said.

"Okay, we are definitely vagabonds, then," Kaia added.

"How long have you been here?" Rye asked.

"Maybe three months," Nori answered.

"And do you either of you have a job?"

"Sure," said Kaia. "We are both working with a local company giving kiteboarding lessons."

"Well, that's certainly disappointing," Rye said as he opened a notebook and took notes of the conversation.

"What's disappointing? Kiteboarding?" asked Nori.

"No, working," Rye clarified.

"Gotta eat, you know," Kaia said.

"Yes, this is a potential issue, isn't it? I've been trying to work this out myself," Rye commented as he continued to write in his notebook. "Still, I would have preferred that you didn't work. I'm afraid that may necessitate that I exclude you from my field study."

Kaia and Nori just looked at each other.

"Still, I have a few questions about surfing. You see, there could be some aspects of this activity that warrant further investigation," Rye continued. "Tell me, what are your central philosophical tenets concerning the modern surf culture as it more broadly relates to our current societal norms and priorities, including the concepts of capitalism and consumerism?"

"Damn, Rye, that's a little much, don't you think?" Kaia replied.

Nori laughed.

"I see," Rye responded with a shrug. "Perhaps I am getting a little ahead of myself. Can you tell me why you find this endeavor enjoyable?"

"Sure thing! It's all about the vibe, really," Nori explained. "I love everything about it. You're out there surrounded by nature, and when you catch a wave and feel the power propel you forward, you get this big rush. You can't control it or force it, but you can still learn to go with it. It's incredible!"

"Fascinating," Rye said. "Perhaps this would be a good experience for me. Immersion therapy, if you will. I likely can get a better understanding *of* nature by undertaking more activities *within* nature. Also, some nature-based leisure activities would likely give me some mental breaks from my writings."

"There's a lot to it, you know. Every break is different, and every wave is different. You have to consider the tide, the wind, and the weather. You need to study all this stuff."

"Excellent, excellent," Rye said.

"When everything works and you get into the zone, that's when it gets real," Kaia said.

Rye responded, "Yes, being immersed in the flow of learning a complex task is a concept that I am familiar with."

"Let me ask you a question," Kaia said.

"Certainly," Rye replied.

"I don't really understand the thing with the flashlight. What was that all about?"

"Flashlight?" Nori asked.

"Rye here was walking around with a flashlight at the market and shining it on people," Kaia explained.

"During the day?" Nori asked.

"Yeah, when I met him a little earlier today."

"Okay, that's a little . . . different," Nori said. "Anything else you neglected to mention to me?" she asked, looking at Kaia.

"Ahh, my flashlight," Rye responded. "It is my attempt to find an honest man *or woman*," Rye explained. "In full disclosure, I did not invent this particular technique but borrowed it from someone who lived a very long time ago. The premise is that there are so few honest people in the world that you can't find one even in broad daylight without shedding further light upon them."

"You'll definitely find your share of scammers and pirates down here," Kaia commented.

"I have little doubt, but that's not what I am referring to. I mean honesty in the much broader sense. A person who is willing to shake off all the falsities society imposes upon them and live honestly and with integrity in accordance with nature. To live a much simpler life closer to the natural world. Like the life of a dog, if you will."

"I love dogs!" Nori commented.

"Yes, as do I," Rye continued. "You see, I intend to reject the facades that are so deeply ingrained in society that they create a prison in which we all live."

"A prison, huh," Kaia said, taking a sip from her drink.

"Yes, it is the most dangerous and effective type of prison as well. It is one that is invisible, and we act as our own guards. We toil away and spend. The more of both, the better. We all keep each other in line as well. We reject and ostracize anyone who strays too far from these norms," Rye continued.

"And someone is supposed to get all this from a flashlight in the face?" Kaia asked.

"Of course not," Rye said. "The light is just designed to get someone's attention. To get them to think outside their daily routine and stop for a moment. The flashlight is a metaphorical *hook*, in a way."

As the group finished their drinks, Kaia asked, "So, what do you think? Ready to hit the surf?"

"Certainly," said Rye.

The trio left the little restaurant and headed to Kaia and Nori's rental vehicle to retrieve the surfboards and other gear for their boat trip. As they approached a narrow street corner, they walked up to a small plastic table with two chairs set up on the sidewalk in front of one of the local souvenir shops. A simple chess set was set up on the table, along with a timer. It initially appeared that there were no players around to man the table, but as they reached the corner, Rye spotted a young Bahamian boy, perhaps ten or twelve years old, crouched next to the little shop, cupping his hands to slurp water out of a water spigot.

Spotting the group, the kid popped up quickly and said, "Hey, one of you play me in a game of chess."

"Thanks, but we're in a hurry trying to catch some waves," Kaia said.

Rye paused for just a moment and eyed the board.

Apparently picking up on the hesitation, the kid homed in on Rye. "Come on, mister. One game."

"I'm tempted, but my friend is right; we already have plans," Rye explained.

"Tell you what," the kid said, glancing at Rye's feet. "If I can tell you where you got those flip-flops, you play me in one game of chess."

Rye stopped and thought about the custom footwear he had acquired from an artisan in Okinawa.

Noticing Rye had engaged with the young boy, Nori said, "Come on, Rye . . . don't do it."

Her warning was too late, and Rye was convinced that there was no way this kid on the street could determine the origin of his flip-flops.

"Yes, I'll agree," Rye said to the boy.

Nori and Kaia, who were now several steps ahead, came to a full stop, and Nori let out a groan.

"Let me take a closer look," the kid said as he stooped down and eyed the flip-flops more closely."

"Stumped?" Rye asked.

"No," the boy said with some hesitation. "You got them shoes . . . on your feet," he added, grinning and looking up at Rye.

Realizing he had been outsmarted, Rye agreed to play and sat down at the board.

"Twenty bucks a game," the kid said, smiling as he took the other seat.

"I'll play you, but I don't think it would be fair to take your money. You know, in my youth, I played several highly competitive games against a certain well-known Soviet chess master. Of course, the games could take months due to the delay in making moves through the international post."

"It won't take that long for us," the kid explained. "We're playing Bullet Chess. One minute per player," he added as he moved out one of his knights and hit the timer.

Rye's time ran out before he made his third move, having mistakenly believed that he had one minute per move instead of one minute for him to make *all* of his moves in the game. He paid the young chess player and departed with his new friends to the rental car.

"You should have listened," Nori said as they walked off.

"Bullet Chess—whoever heard of such a thing!" Rye responded.

"He's really good. All the locals know not to play against him," Kaia said.

"I didn't foresee his play on words on where I got my shoes," Rye lamented.

"Of course you didn't. It's how he gets people to stop and play him. That's *his* hook!" Nori explained.

"By the Dog Star, I see it now! I've been outdone by a child!"

Once they retrieved all the gear, the group headed down to the sandy beach area near the boat dock. Kaia stopped and dug a small hole in the sand and then took Rye's board and laid it down on the beach with the fins down in the hole. "Okay, time for a quick lesson. Get on the board and show us what you got!"

"I don't understand," Rye said.

"Let's see your form. First, lay down on the board on your stomach."

Rye hesitantly did as he was instructed.

"Now pretend you're catching a wave. Paddle hard with your arms and then jump up on the board."

Rye did a few half-hearted paddles and then slowly climbed to his knees and then stood up one leg at a time.

"That was actually quite easy," Rye said.

"We need to do a little work," Kaia explained.

Kaia and Nori spent the next thirty minutes showing Rye proper surfing techniques. They showed him how to paddle hard to catch a wave and how to quickly jump to his feet on the surfboard in the proper stance. They also explained how to swim back out through breaking waves from the beach. Afterward, they took the boards and equipment down the dock to load into Rye's boat.

As they approached the end of the pier, Nori spotted the bass boat.

"Damn, is that your tender?"

"Yes, my friend Samuel owns it, but he assured me that *Assbassin* is an excellent craft. Earlier this morning, he took a little time and showed me how to operate it."

"*Assbassin?*" Kaia asked.

"Something to that effect," Rye said.

"Never seen anyone use a bass boat as a tender," Kaia commented. "What do you think, Nori?"

"I don't see any reason it won't work," she answered.

Chapter Nineteen

There was a gentle breeze and small rolling waves on the ride down the coast to the surf break. Rye was driving *Bassassin,* and Kaia and Nori were sitting toward the front of the boat in the two swivel chairs. Rye was eager to memorialize his thoughts and preliminary analysis from his earlier discussion with Kaia and Nori at the bar. He kept pulling out his notebook from underneath his seat and scribbling down thoughts as he drove.

Kaia had told Rye to keep offshore a few hundred yards and stay clear of any obstacles. She had been keeping an eye out for the cove, but thirty minutes into the trip, she pointed out a beach bar on the shoreline to Nori and the two started to debate how to get to the bar by car. Rye suddenly had a thought about the metaphorical meaning of a surfboard and once again pulled out his notebook and started writing frantically when, suddenly, he found himself jolted back to reality as the boat shot up onto a sandbar. His notebook went flying, but he managed to grab the steering wheel to brace himself. Kaia and Nori had nothing to grab and flew out of the boat as the vessel skidded to a stop. Rye heard the outboard engine screaming in a high pitch with its propeller out of the water. He quickly shut it off. When he looked up, he saw that Kaia and Nori had flown over the narrow sandbar and landed in several feet of water on the other side.

They were about 150 yards offshore and had run up on the sandbar that was several inches above the surface of the water. The boat had been cruising at around twenty knots at the time of impact, resulting in it sliding up on the sand and leaving a trail of neatly cut grooves behind it.

Kaia and Nori sat in the water, stunned.

"What the hell happened?" Kaia asked.

"Looks like we hit a sandbar," Nori responded, looking at the boat behind them.

"Everyone alright?" Kaia asked.

"I'm fine," said Nori.

"I am as well," Rye added.

"How the hell did you miss that thing?" Nori asked Rye as she stood up to inspect the clearly visible white sandy patch of land the boat was sitting on.

"I have no idea. It suddenly appeared out of nowhere. By the time . . . ." Rye stopped midsentence and had a panicked look in his eyes. He scanned the area and then jumped out of the boat and ran to his waterlogged notebook that was floating in a few inches of water just off the edge of the sandbar. He quickly opened it and confirmed that, although smeared, his notes were still legible. He sighed with relief.

"A little time in the sun and everything should be recoverable," Rye said, gingerly carrying the notebook back to the boat and laying it out on the rear seat to dry.

Rye stretched and felt a slight pain in his lower back. "I believe I have sustained a minor injury after all," Rye said.

"Is it bad?" asked Kaia.

"No, I believe I can manage. Just a minor muscle pull."

"Okay, cool. Let's see how stuck we are," Kaia suggested.

The three tried to push the boat back to the water, but they could not budge the craft.

"Is it low tide?" Kaia asked, looking around.

"Yeah, I think it is coming up, but it may be a few hours before we can get off this thing," said Nori.

Nori looked around again. "You know, I think that's the surf break over there," she said, pointing farther north.

Kaia looked and was able to make out the small breaking waves. "Yep, I think that's it."

"How far you think that is?" asked Nori.

"Maybe a quarter of a mile," Kaia replied.

"We could paddle the boards over there and surf while we're waiting for the tide to come up," Nori suggested.

"Maybe," said Kaia. "Rye, you up for that? Looks like a nice gentle break from here, anyway. Should be good to learn on."

"I suppose," Rye said, eyeing his soaked notebook. "Do you think it will be okay to leave my book here?"

"It'll be fine," Kaia said.

"Then, let us proceed," Rye said.

Nori handed Rye his surfboard, which had managed to stay in the boat. He took it and waded out into the cool water.

Kaia and Nori grabbed their boards, and Kaia also grabbed a mask and snorkel to scope out the bottom of the surf break. The trio paddled off in the direction of the surf break. Twenty minutes later, the group approached the mouth of the small cove where the waves were breaking. Nori had taken the lead, and Kaia and Rye were around twenty yards behind her.

"Stay a little outside, Nori!" Kaia yelled as all three approached the break. "Let's take a closer look before you go."

"Got it!" Nori yelled back as she sat up and straddled her board.

Kaia and Rye quickly caught up. The break was clean and between two and three feet high. From their vantage points on the boards and the glare of the sun, nobody could see below the surface of the water, so Kaia slipped on the mask and disappeared underwater to take a better look. She popped back up quickly and said, "It's maybe six or seven feet deep here so probably okay, but we need to be careful."

"What do you mean?" asked Rye.

"It's a reef break, so you definitely don't want to hit bottom," explained Kaia.

Rye still looked a bit confused.

"I tell you what, hop off the board and put on this mask and you'll see what I'm talking about," she said.

Rye rolled off the board and took the mask from Kaia. He was having a hard time trying to hold the board with one hand and put the mask on at the same time as the other.

Observing him struggle, Kaia said, "I'll hold the board for you."

Rye put on the mask and looked down and was immediately surprised by what he saw. First, the bottom was closer than he thought, and second, it consisted of jagged rocks and coral formations with what looked like clumps of large black needles jutting out in various locations.

Rye lifted his head up and said to Kaia excitedly, "By the Dog Star, what it is that I see under there? It looks like the ground is covered with some kind of submersible porcupines!"

"Are you talking about the urchins?" asked Kaia.

"I am referring to the small, black, inhospitable-looking clumps of spiny quills sticking out!"

"Ha, yeah, those are sea urchins."

"Are they alive?"

"Yep."

"Do they move around?"

"They can move around, but they're pretty slow. They mostly stay put," Kaia explained. "Are they dangerous?"

"Only if you touch them," said Nori, smiling.

Rye sat on his board in deep thought for a moment and said, "You know, I feel that living in accordance with nature means following the rules of nature, and when nature shows you a landscaped covered with an abundance of living migratory weapons, it is telling you to stay clear."

"If you fall, just don't fall headfirst. You want to fall off backward and away from the board like we explained on the beach," Kaia explained.

"Young lady, I am not sure you fully understand the concept of falling. I feel that, by definition, falling constitutes some lack of control. Your advice is akin to telling someone that if you wreck their automobile, just steer away from the trees."

Nori was listening to the discussion with some amusement and chimed in, "How about I give it a go and test it out?"

"Sounds good," said Kaia.

Nori paddled in, timed her wave, and effortlessly jumped up on the board and rode in for around twenty yards, then gently fell off to the side before paddling back out again.

"I think it's okay," she said when she got back out to Kaia and Rye.

"It's your call, but I think it's okay," Kaia said to Rye. "Just do what we showed you on the beach."

"No, I think I will decline the opportunity at the moment. When I observed the surfers in Polynesia, they were riding waves in the vicinity of nice sandy beaches. I feel that such an atmosphere is much more in harmony with nature than what you propose I undertake here," Rye explained, still thinking of the rocky bottom littered with sea urchins lurking below.

"Okay, I got it," Kaia said. "There are a few beaches like that not too far from us, but we'd really need to do some island-hopping to get there. You cool with just hanging out on your board for a bit and letting Nori and me catch a few waves?"

"Of course, I am more than content relaxing in the sun. Do as you wish."

Kaia and Nori surfed for around half an hour, but as the tide came in, the break subsided, and they paddled back out to Rye, who had been sitting on his board watching them.

"Let's head back to the boat," Nori said. "On the way over here, I think I saw some holes in the bottom. We may see some fish there."

"Yes, this is agreeable," Rye replied. "I can make sure my notebook is okay."

"Okay, cool. Maybe we can try out the Hawaiian sling," Nori suggested.

The three made their way back to the boat. Kaia arrived first and waded up to the sandbar. The tide had come in a little and the sandbar was no longer visible above the surface of the water, but the water was still only an inch or two deep where the boat sat. Just to be sure it was still stuck, she attempted to give the boat a good shove, but the boat remained in place and was solidly grounded. "Still going to be a bit before we can get out of here," she said. "Nori, you guys want to take the equipment and snorkel?"

"Hell yeah!" Nori responded. "I saw those holes again swimming back. Let's check them out."

"Could you tell if anything was in them?" Kaia asked.

"Not sure. Didn't really have time to check them out."

"What is your interest in these holes?" asked Rye.

"When you get holes in the ocean floor, fish and lobsters sometimes like to get in them for protection," Nori explained.

"Ingenious," said Rye.

Kaia handed Nori the mask and fins, and Rye put on the other set that was in the boat. Nori also grabbed the Hawaiian sling. The spear consisted of a five-foot-long thin yellow fiberglass pole with a rubber bungee cord that looked like surgical tubing at one end and several menacing stainless-steel barbs at the other.

"I assume that weapon is to get these fish or lobsters," Rye said to Nori.

"Yep. That's the idea. You want to try it first?"

"Well, if I am going to live in a self-sustained fashion, I suppose I should try to diversify and improve my fishing methods, as I have had little success thus far. Please give me some instructions," said Rye.

"Okay, great. So, we'll swim over first and see if we can find the holes. If we do, we can swim down together and look for lobsters or maybe a grouper. If I spot something we can shoot, I'll point him out. You'll swim down and spear him. Just take the spear in your hand and put the bungee loop between your thumb and pointer finger," Nori explained as she demonstrated for Rye. "Then pull the rod back hard so that it stretches the band tight—maybe a foot or so. Then grab hold of the rod and hold it tight," she added, turning her wrist over so Rye could clearly see how she was holding the apparatus. "It should have a good amount of tension and be hard to hold. You'll just swim down and put the barbs real close to what you're going to shoot and let go of the shaft. The elastic will shoot the spear forward."

"I believe I understand," Rye said.

"Here, try it," Nori said, handing Rye the spear.

"Like this?" Rye asked as he held the spear with an outstretched arm and pulled back the elastic band as instructed.

"That's right, but don't point it at Kaia," Nori said as she watched Rye experiment with the sling.

Kaia stayed with the boat, and Nori and Rye swam out in search of the holes Nori had seen earlier. They worked their way back toward the surf break with their masks in the water, looking in all directions as they swam. Around forty yards behind the boat, Nori spotted several holes in the seabed's bottom. They were in around ten feet of water. There was one large hole that was around two feet wide and nearly six feet long and a half dozen irregular-shaped smaller holes with diameters ranging from six inches to two feet.

Nori and Rye were swimming side by side along the surface of the water when she spotted the holes. She tapped Rye on the shoulder and pointed them out. The water was clear, and Rye nodded his head when he saw them. Nori then motioned with her thumb for them to lift their heads above the water so they could talk.

As both raised their heads above the surface, Nori took the snorkel out of her mouth and said, "See the holes, right?"

"Yes, I did."

"Okay, cool. Let's swim down and take a closer look."

Nori put her snorkel back in her mouth, took a deep breath, and dove to the bottom, near the largest hole. Rye followed. She swam up to within a couple of feet of the hole and peered inside while Rye hovered a few feet above. After Nori had a good look, they both re-surfaced.

As the two popped up above the surface, Nori asked, "You see them?"

"What, the holes?"

"No. The lobsters. There are several in the big hole. Maybe a dozen."

"No, I didn't see them," Rye said.

Kaia yelled over from the boat, "You see something?"

"Yep, we got some lobsters below us!" yelled Nori.

"Nice, what are you waiting for?" said Kaia.

"Just chill! We're working on it!" Nori yelled back.

Nori placed her mask back down in the water for another look. As she lifted her head again, she said, "Look down from here, and you can just make them out."

Rye placed his mask down into the water and scanned the bottom until he located the holes again, but he did not see anything in them.

"I don't see any lobsters," Rye said as he lifted his head.

"You see the little antenna sticking out?"

"The what?" asked Rye.

"The antenna—they stick out the top of their heads. You can just make them out from here, but they're pretty small."

"You're making this up, aren't you?" Rye asked.

"No, I'm serious—look again."

Rye put his face back down in the water and indeed noticed what looked like several brown-colored prickly sticks poking out from the underside of a ledge in the largest hole.

"I believe I see them," said Rye as he raised his head.

"So, I'll swim down with you, and you spear one."

"After I spear one, what do I do? Do I grab it with my hands and swim up with it? And what about its claws?"

"These don't have claws. That's a different type of lobster. These are called spiny lobsters. Just impale it on the barbs and swim up with it on the end of the spear."

"No claws? Really?"

"Yep, get the barbs really close to it before you let go of the sling," explained Nori.

"Okay, I believe I understand."

Rye swam down to the hole, and Nori followed. The hole had a ledge around the top that opened up into a larger cavern below it. A few of the lobsters were hanging upside down on the underside of the ledge with only their antennas sticking out. As he got closer, he could also see the sandy bottom of the hole a few feet deeper and noticed a few more lobsters scurrying about. Rye stuck the end of the spear into the mouth of the hole and attempted to put the barbs close to one lobster traversing the bottom. The lobster quickly retreated to the deeper confines of the hole upon seeing the strange object approach.

Nori was swimming a few feet above, watching the events unfold. Rye was trying to locate another lobster but was also feeling the need to surface and take a breath. Seeing no other obvious prey from his vantage point, he took one more look before he surfaced. He swam closer to the opening of the hole and stuck his head partially inside to have a better look around.

Nori saw Rye maneuver his head inside the hole and then saw him exhale quickly, jettisoning bubbles from his mouth and nose and simultaneously shooting to the surface. Nori didn't have time to get out of the way and Rye's face slammed into Nori's stomach, knocking Rye's mask down around his neck. It also knocked the wind out of Nori, causing her to swim to the surface quickly for a breath.

The two surfaced, and each took a deep breath. Looking confused, Nori asked, "What happened?"

Rye, wiping the water from his eyes as he tried to catch his breath, said, "There's a shark in the hole."

"No shit?" Nori asked. "How big?"

"I'm uncertain. A couple of feet, perhaps," said Rye, still excited.

"Hold on a minute. I'll look." Nori took a deep breath and swam back down. She returned after about thirty seconds and, after popping back above the surface, said to Rye, "Not a big deal. I think it's a nurse shark."

"So, what do we do?" asked Rye.

"Just ignore it. I doubt it will mess with us."

"Do they bite?" asked Rye.

"Not usually. I don't think so, anyway. It has a kind of round pucker mouth. They remind me of those suckerfish in aquariums. Never heard of one biting someone. We see them lobstering all the time. They're lazy and don't move around much."

"I'll give it another try," Rye said. "Any suggestions on how to get a good shot at one of the lobsters? I don't know if I can get the spear up close to one. It's a difficult angle."

"It's tough to get them when they're deep in a hole like that. Try sticking in the end of the pole and flip one out of the hole and then shoot it."

"Okay, if you say so," said Rye.

Rye took another deep breath and dove. Nori stayed at the surface this time and floated with her face down in the water so that she could get a view from above but reduce the chances of another collision.

Rye reached the hole and looked around as best he could from the outside. He didn't see any lobsters and reluctantly got closer, still worried about the shark inside. As he looked to one side, he saw an enormous lobster hovering near the nurse shark. The shark wasn't moving but was just lying on its stomach at the bottom of the hole. Already getting low on air again, Rye quickly stuck his spear into the hole near the large lobster and thrashed it around violently to get it to leave. In doing so, he inadvertently struck the lounging nurse shark in the side with the sharp barbs, resulting in it quickly shooting around the hole in a circle and then jetting out directly at Rye. Rye frantically paddled his arms backward as he tried to retreat, but the shark, which was between two and three feet long, shot up and quickly latched onto Rye's bare chest with its mouth. Rye screamed, panic-stricken, while still underwater and darted for the surface with the shark still attached. Nori watched in astonishment. Rye quickly broke the surface and yelled, "Get it off! Get it off!" The fish flailed around but refused to let go. Finally, Nori grabbed the shark's tail with both hands and pried it loose, at which point it quickly swam back down to the ocean floor and then disappeared.

Rye was still stunned as he peered down at his chest, expecting to see blood pouring into the open water. Instead, he saw a perfectly circular reddish-purple hickey on his chest about the size of a tennis ball.

"I thought I may have sustained a mortal injury," Rye said excitedly.

Nori looked at the hickey and burst out laughing. "Holy shit, I never thought *that* would happen! I *thought* they were docile. You alright?"

"I believe so," Rye said, struggling to regain his composure and get a better look at the circle on his chest. "How does it look to you?"

Nori swam closer and laughed harder and even snorted. "Looks like you had a crazy night on the town."

"I'm inclined to swim back down there and return the favor," Rye said indignantly.

"What, give that shark a hickey?"

"No, give him a good thrashing!"

"Tell you what, how about you take a break and give me a shot at the lobsters?"

Beginning to calm down, Rye said, "Fine, suit yourself, but if that little beast approaches me again, I reserve the right to fully defend myself by any means possible."

"Fair enough," Nori said. Nori swam down and peered into the hole. She spotted the large lobster Rye had been eyeing earlier that was hiding in one of the corners. Seeing no signs of the nurse shark, she flipped it out with the spear. She lowered the spear so that the barbs were inches away from the retreating crustacean and released the sling. The barbs immediately penetrated the back of the lobster, and it began kicking its tail furiously. Nori swam to the surface and raised the lobster, still impaled on the barbs, out of the water. She was smiling broadly as Rye congratulated her.

Rye then observed the lobster wildly slapping his tail to his body and making a strange grunting noise that reminded him of the sound a piglet makes when it is rutting in the mud. He distinctly remembered hearing a similar noise when he visited the petting zoo as a child with his family.

"By the Dog Star, what is that creature doing?" Rye blurted out.

"It's freaking out a little, I think," said Nori. "Can you blame it?"

"I mean the noise—it's grunting or something!"

"It's something they do by rubbing their antennas together," explained Nori.

"What do we do?"

"We'll take it back to the boat and kill it and then eat it."

"I see," said Rye, feeling some regret as he thought that crustaceans may soon also be off his list of acceptable food choices.

The two swam back, and as they neared the boat, Kaia yelled out, "What the hell was all that screaming about?"

"Rye had a date," Nori yelled back.

"Say what?" Kaia shot back.

"Hold on a second, we'll show you when we get there," Nori yelled, trying not to suck in water as she swam, still holding the impaled lobster out of the water with one hand.

Rye and Nori swam up to the sandbar and then waded to the boat that was now sitting in ankle-deep water.

"Show her, Rye," Nori said.

Rye turned slightly to the side so that Kaia could see his large purple hickey.

"What were you guys doing under there?" Kaia asked, grinning.

"It wasn't me," said Nori.

"Horny mermaid?" asked Kaia with a laugh.

"It was a shark, I'll have you know," Rye responded as he eyed the hickey on his chest.

"That must have been one horny shark," said Kaia, still smiling.

"It was crazy, Kaia—it was one of those nurse sharks. The damn thing got aggravated and latched onto Rye," Nori said.

"No shit?" asked Kaia.

"I shit you not. I had to pull the thing off him," Nori said.

"The deranged beast is lucky that I didn't recover from the initial shock sooner," Rye added.

"Wild," Kaia said, shaking her head, "but I'm still suspicious of what really happened."

Nori walked over to the boat and handed Kaia the lobster that was still in the sling. Kaia quickly took it from her, severed the head and body from the tail, tossed the tail into a five-gallon bucket, and threw the rest back into the water.

"Nice job. Going back for more?" asked Kaia.

"I don't believe so," Rye said as he walked back to check on his soggy notebook.

"I'll go back and see if I can get a couple more," Nori said excitedly.

Rye climbed in and sat in the grounded boat and watched Nori swim back to the hole. Over the next twenty minutes, she swam back a half dozen more times, each time with a lobster on the end of the sling, and each time, Rye watched Kaia quickly decapitate it and discard the carcass in the water. They then watched Nori dive several times underwater, coming up empty-handed. Finally, she surfaced with a large thrashing fish at the end of the spear. Nori swam back, holding up a large grouper that had apparently been hiding deep in the hole. Kaia pulled it off the prongs and tossed it in the bucket with the lobster tails, where it flopped around violently.

The sun was now getting lower in the sky and the tide had come up more, so the water was now six inches deep where the boat sat.

"Let's try to push her off again," Kaia suggested.

"Sure thing," Nori said. "Hopefully, we can get her off now and get back to the marina by dark."

Rye climbed back out of the boat and went to push from the bow while Nori and Kaia got on opposite sides.

"On the count of three, let's push," said Kaia. "One, two . . . three!"

The boat was still sitting on the bottom but was significantly lighter because of its buoyancy from the rising water. With some effort, they were finally able to push it free of the sandbar. It took them around thirty minutes to return to the harbor.

By the time they were back at the marina, Rye's notebook had dried, and he was in much better spirits. As soon as he could obtain another pen from the *Miss Elizabeth*, he could re-commence work on his masterpiece. He was also very excited about the prospect of going to the sandbar, where the people traveling and living on the boats in the harbor met in the evenings.

"I have another idea," said Rye as they pulled up to the pier. "Before we depart for the social gathering at the sandbar, would you ladies like to see *My Barrel?*"

"Will there be room for all of us?" Kaia asked?

Rye said, "It's bigger than you think. Let me show you," as he spun *Bassassin* around and headed to the *Miss Elizabeth* anchored out in the harbor.

Chapter Twenty

"A bass boat for a tender and a fishing trawler for a mother ship. You're full of surprises," Nori said as they pulled up alongside the boat.

"Thank you, although it's actually a scallop boat," Rye explained.

"I love scallops. You have any on board?" Kaia asked.

"Unfortunately, no. I believe that the scalloping equipment is non-functional at the moment," Rye explained.

Rye pulled out the portable air horn he had gotten from Stems before he left earlier in the day and gave it a quick blow. A few minutes later, Stems's face peered down over the side of the deck.

"Hey, Doc, how's it going?"

"Doc? Are you a doctor?" Kaia asked Rye.

"No, the designation is academic, not medical, and I have repeatedly suggested that Samuel just call me Rye, but he seems insistent on using the more formal nomenclature."

"I'll throw you a line," Stems said. "I see we have company. Hello, ladies."

"Hi," said Kaia.

"Hello, there," Nori yelled up.

Rye crawled up front, working his way around Kaia and Nori, and threw the bow line up to Stems, who secured it on one of the large deck cleats.

Stems threw a rope ladder down from the deck.

"Thank you, Samuel," Rye yelled up to him. "I spent the day with these two wayfarers. This is Kaia, and this is Nori," Rye explained as he pointed to the two women. "The gentleman on the boat is Samuel. He is a very long-time acquaintance."

"Ladies, come on aboard and call me Stems. Everybody does except Doc here."

"You mind throwing me another line down for this first?" Nori asked, holding up the bucket that contained the lobster tails and grouper for Stems to see.

"Get it right to you," said Stems as he tossed another line down to Nori. Nori tied the line to the handle of the bucket, and Stems promptly hauled it up to the deck.

"Nice! I didn't realize we were doing takeout this evening!"

"I got an early start on you guys," Stems said, holding up a beer as Rye, Kaia, and Nori climbed up the ladder and onto the deck of the trawler. "Either of you ladies like a drink? I can grab you a couple of nice cold beers. We had a bunch of wine but lost pretty much all of it on the crossing from Lauderdale to the Bahamas."

"Was it rough coming across?" Kaia asked.

"No, not really. Just a few swells, but I had all the wine stacked up in a bunk and it just rolled off and broke on the floor. Reckon I should have brought a wine rack or something."

"Beers would be great, Stems," Nori said.

"Comin' right up! Doc, you got a second?" Stems asked as he motioned for Rye to follow him.

"Of course, Samuel."

"Ladies, I'll be right back with those beers, and then maybe we can play a little beer pong," Stems suggested as he pointed to the ping-pong table tied up against a post on the back deck.

As Rye and Stems stepped away, Stems explained to him that I had called while Rye was out and had asked that they call me back once he returned. They managed to reach me at the office, and Rye asked if there had been any developments. I explained that earlier in the day, I had received a copy of a lawsuit in the mail from Ernie

Harker. Ernie had sued Rye and his father's estate for breach of contract and a handful of other causes of action, including detrimental reliance and unjust enrichment.

"What does that mean?" Rye asked me.

"It means his client really wants your boat."

"I see. Out of curiosity, who is his client?" Rye asked.

"I'm still not sure," I answered. "He filed suit on behalf of some corporation that I've never heard of. I looked it up on the Virginia State Corporation Commission website, and it just shows some other shell company as its owner. The buyer is clearly trying to keep a low profile."

"What do you propose we do?"

"I assume you still don't want to sell the boat?"

"That's correct," Rye said.

I explained to Rye that it bothered me that Ernie had sued his father's estate, considering Ernie had previously represented his dad. It made me wonder if he really had been looking out for the best interests of Rye's father over the last few years. I told Rye that I still believed the lawsuit itself to be weak. Ernie had made no mention of a written contract in it. As a result, I thought it might have been a bluff.

"It won't take much time for me to file an answer and shoot some holes in it," I said. "Still, he could drag things out for a long time and potentially try to make you run up a big tab. Maybe he's thinking you'll give up and sell the boat. Hard to say for sure at this point. How about I file an answer for you and see what he does? It will cost you a couple of grand to do that. Let's call his bluff and see what he does."

Rye agreed and explained that it might be some time before he returned. He also asked if I needed payment immediately, to which I responded we could square up later. I then signed off and got to work.

Stems had been standing next to Rye and heard the conversation. "Ernie Harker is a real prick," he said.

"I try to not concern myself with such matters as best I can, but it appears that it may be necessary here if I want to continue my journey unobstructed. Let us get back to more important matters," Rye said with a shrug. "First, Samuel, I have to tell you we had a minor accident with *Bass . . . assin*," Rye said, still struggling to properly pronounce the name of the tender.

"What happened?"

"A sandbar suddenly arose in front of me, and I somehow ran up upon it."

"Is she okay?"

"Yes, I believe she is fine, but I wanted to apologize for the error."

"It's alright, Doc. Shit happens."

"Also, I wanted to tell you that we have an amazing opportunity this evening, Samuel. The ladies have informed me that there is a small nightly gathering not far from here that is frequented by many of our co-travelers. I believe this may be my first opportunity to finally meet others who share my views. Kaia and Nori have agreed to take us to make introductions. I have to say that I am quite excited. We have journeyed far, but I think we are on the cusp of something amazing. I am quite certain that my conversations this evening could lead to some of the most important chapters of my book."

"That's great news, Doc. You know *I'm* down for a party," Stems said. "Come on. Let's get back to the ladies."

"Quite the setup you got here," Kaia commented as the two men rejoined them on the back deck.

"Thank you. I'm the decorator," Stems said with a grin. "So, what's this I hear about some meetup tonight?"

"A lot of the boat people meet up every evening, weather permitting, for drinks at a sandbar near here. Rye wants to check it out," Kaia explained.

"Sounds good. Should we eat first?" Stems asked.

"Tell you what. How about we boil up the lobsters and eat those, and if you got some lemons or limes and salt and pepper, I can make some ceviche with the fish and we can take that with us," Kaia suggested.

"I'm sure we got some lemons and limes down there. We got pretty much every fruit and vegetable known to man in the galley," Stems said.

"Perfect," Kaia said. "These things are BYOB, but it doesn't hurt to bring a little food to share also, especially if you're new to the group."

"Excellent!" Rye said. "I need to get me a new notebook from below and start drafting some questions," he added as he quickly disappeared below deck.

Chapter Twenty-One

An hour later, Rye, Stems, Nori, and Kaia headed out for the sandbar for the nightly gathering. Stems had volunteered to drive the boat as he was still a little concerned about Rye's earlier confessed mishap. Meanwhile, Rye hunched over in his seat and busily wrote last-minute questions in his notebook. He felt like he was a student back in graduate school cramming for a final exam.

As they approached the rendezvous, Rye looked up and saw several tenders pulled up on an isolated sandbar that sat a few hundred yards offshore. The sandbar was around twenty yards across and at least two hundred yards long, creating a miniature island. The tenders were nothing like *Bassassin*. Instead, they were the traditional tenders found on large sailboats and yachts, consisting mostly of rigid hull inflatables with small outboard engines. Besides the tenders, there was an assortment of various coolers, lawn chairs, and even a few float toys.

As they pulled up, several of the people on the sandbar gave Rye and his crew a few odd looks, obviously surprised by the presence of a bass boat in the area. Nori jumped out as they got close and helped pull the bow of the boat up on the sandbar. The rest of the crew then disembarked, carrying the two coolers they had brought, one of which contained beer and the other the ceviche and a few other snacks.

As they walked toward the gathering, Rye noticed two distinct clusters of people, each with about a dozen members. The groups had arranged themselves in loose circles, seated like schoolchildren at storytime, each facing inward toward its own center. There were multiple conversations going on, and nobody initially spoke to Rye and the others as they tentatively approached.

"Where should we go?" Rye asked.

"Let's just set up outside the group closest to us," Kaia suggested.

The four paused on the outskirts of the nearest group. Not having brought chairs, they decided to just sit on the sand around the two coolers.

Stems popped open the cooler containing the beer and grabbed one for himself as well as two more for Nori and Kaia.

"Rye, you don't want one?" Nori asked.

"He don't drink," Stems volunteered. "It don't affect him, for some reason. I told him he oughta get that checked out."

"Is that right, Rye? You can't get drunk?" Nori asked.

"To the best of my knowledge, yes," Rye explained. "I would like to start my interviews as soon as possible. Oh, I left my flashlight in the tender," he added as he started to walk back over to *Bassassin*.

"Rye, how about you forget about the light for now? Some people may be a little put off by that," Kaia said.

"That's the entire point," Rye said.

"Trust me, Rye, you'll get more out of this encounter if you just chill a bit," Kaia explained.

Rye just sighed and came back over and sat down, clearly disappointed.

"Quite a group here," Stems said, scanning the small crowd.

"It's kind of an odd assortment, just like the boats in the harbor," Kaia said. "You get a little of everything. We met one kid out here a month ago who was eighteen and was living in this little twenty-one-foot boat that he sailed down from Savannah."

"I don't think the kid had ever sailed before his trip. He had saved up some money working at a burger joint and then just quit and bought the boat and took off the next day heading south," Nori added.

"I don't see him here. I wonder if he headed back?" Kaia asked Nori as she scanned the crowd.

"Rye, you also got some big money people here, too," Nori explained. "See that catamaran over there?" she asked, pointing to one of the larger boats anchored not far from the meetup. "We met her captain a few weeks back when he came ashore for supplies. That boat is almost seventy feet and costs close to ten million."

"You seem to know a lot about the people here," Stems commented.

"Small island," Nori said with a shrug. "You know, a few years back, Kaia and I signed up as crew on a sailboat bigger than that one. We sailed all over the Caribbean in it and even over to the South of France. The owner kept sending us to different places to meet up with him, but he'd never make it there in the end."

"How come?" Stems asked.

"Too busy working. He kept a permanent crew of four on the boat and we traveled all over for a year in that thing, and he ended up spending a grand total of two weeks on the boat during that time. We were getting a little stir-crazy, and that's one reason we decided we were ready to do something else for a while."

"Sounds like a damn waste. If I could afford a boat like that, I'd sure as shit use it," Stems said.

"Kaia and I came up with the tonnage to funnage inverse ratio rule."

"What rule is that?" Stems asked.

"The bigger the tonnage of the boat, the less funnage the people have on it," Nori explained.

Rye was only half paying attention. His patience was running low, and he was eager to start his research. The group sitting immediately next to them was still engaged in their own conversation, and nobody had yet acknowledged Rye and his friends.

"Shall we engage with them?" Rye asked.

"Tell you what. Let's push in," Kaia said. "Rye, bring the ceviche and leave the notebook."

"Oh, fine," Rye said as he gently laid his notebook on the sand and grabbed the ceviche from the cooler.

Kaia stepped in between two people in the group and said, "Hey, mind if we join you guys?"

"Of course not, young lady," answered a man with a Panama Jack hat who was sitting in a reclined beach chair. "The more the merrier. Everyone spread out a bit and make some room for these fine men and women."

The individuals in the group slid back, enlarging their circle and making a space for Rye, Stems, Kaia, and Nori to sit.

"That's some boat you have there," the same man said, nodding towards *Bassassin*.

"Thanks. She may be a little out of her element, but she gets the job done," Stems answered.

"Indeed," the man replied.

"We brought some ceviche with us," Kaia said as she motioned for Rye to set it down on one of the coolers in the center of the group. Rye unwrapped the bowl that contained the raw fish soaked in lemon and lime juice and set it out for everyone to enjoy.

"Oh, wait," Kaia added as she pulled from her pocket a box of toothpicks that she had grabbed from the galley and placed them down beside the fish. "We just caught that today," she said, smiling.

"Thank you, my dear," a woman sitting directly next to the man in the Panama Jack hat said. "What type of fish is it?"

"Grouper," Nori answered.

"Splendid," the man with the hat said as he reached for a toothpick and took a piece of the fish. "We just made ceviche last week from barracuda and it wasn't half bad, but I am sure it won't compare to this."

"Barracuda? They're dangerous, aren't they?" a skinny man wearing an unbuttoned, floral print Hawaiian shirt asked.

"Mostly when they're alive," the man with the hat answered.

"No, I mean, aren't they dangerous to eat? Don't they sometimes carry parasites or toxins or something?" the man in the Hawaiian shirt clarified.

"That's no problem," the man with the hat said. "We know how to deal with such a contingency. We just give some of the catch away and don't eat any of what we keep for a day or so. If nobody gets sick, we know it's safe for us to eat."

A woman sporting a bright green bathing suit who was sitting close to Rye whispered to the man next to her, "Didn't he give us fish last week?"

The man, who was wearing a faded blue T-shirt, just shrugged and shook his head.

Either not hearing or ignoring the comment, the man with the hat then asked Nori what had brought her and her friends to the island.

"We've been here a couple of months. Just hanging out and teaching kiteboarding."

"Kiteboarding! How fun!" the woman with the green bathing suit commented. "Perhaps we should give it a try," she said to the man in the blue T-shirt.

The man was about to respond but was interrupted by a loud fit of laughter from the second group of people who had set up a little farther down the sandbar.

"They're getting rowdy already," the man in the unbuttoned Hawaiian shirt commented.

"Yes, I think it is going to be one of those evenings," the man with the Panama Jack hat said. Turning to Rye, the man then asked, "And are you also here teaching kiteboarding?"

Rye responded, "No. Actually, I am on an exploratory mission to better comprehend how to live in accordance with nature. I recently met Kaia and Nori."

"What exactly does that mean—living in accordance with nature?" the man with the hat asked.

"It is a rejection of many of the social and societal constructs that prevent us from living how we were intended," Rye explained.

"Humm, sounds a little hippie-dippie, doesn't it?" the woman next to the man with the hat asked.

"What do you mean?" Rye asked her.

"I believe she means that it doesn't sound very practical," the man with the hat explained. "Just to make sure I understand you, do these social constructs include working?"

"Absolutely," Rye said.

"In that case, allow me to retort that I am personally quite happy with our societal constructs. I dare say that I wouldn't be down here lounging on this sandbar without them."

"How do you mean?" Rye asked.

"I fully support the concept of work as long as it's done by someone else," the man explained. "You see, I am very successful, mind you. I run a company that helps—or at least ostensibly helps—inventors patent products," he said with a grin. "We advertise on late-night cable television. You may have seen our ads if you have ever had insomnia. There isn't anything we can't patent. Where would I be if I didn't have all these people working for me and taking those phone calls? I don't pay them much, but—"

"You wanna see my tits! I'll show 'em to you!" a woman suddenly yelled loudly from the other group.

Rye looked over and saw a middle-aged woman standing up and pulling her bright pink tank top up over her ample belly.

"Nobody wants to see your damn tits, Tammy. Everybody here has already seen them plenty!" a man sitting next to her yelled back in response to the invitation.

The woman in the green bathing suit said, "Maybe we should find a different sandbar?"

"They can be entertaining in brief spurts," the man in the hat countered.

"What's the craziest thing that you've managed to patent?" the man in the Hawaiian shirt asked the man with the Panama Jack hat.

"That's difficult to say. There's been so many. One of my personal favorites was the Ugly Stick."

"What was that?" the man in the Hawaiian shirt asked.

"It was a stiff, waxy product housed in a little cylindrical tube, similar to the popular lip balms you can buy like Chapstick. However, in addition to beeswax and shea butter, the concoction also included extracts from five of the six most potent hot peppers currently known in the world. The idea behind the invention is that an attractive young lady could go out to enjoy a little alone time at a drinking establishment without the annoyance of unwanted suitors by applying the product liberally to her facial area. It was guaranteed to cause sufficient redness and blotchiness to dissuade the most determined drunkards," the man with the hat explained. "They actually made a few sales when customers noticed that if it was applied only to the lips, it added some sought-after puffiness, but that ended when lip-fillers became widely available."

"So, they went out of business?" the man in the Hawaiian shirt asked.

"Not right away," the man in the hat answered. "One of the founders had the brilliant idea to rebrand the product as the Fugley Stick and market it as a marital aid guaranteed to spice things up in the bedroom. I understand that the product caught on in the S&M circles and they once again were on the road to making a profit, but a string of lawsuits shut them down for good when some of those same customers later claimed the potency of the product was killing their nerve endings, resulting in permanent damage to their pain receptors. Apparently, this was considered counterproductive in those circles."

"That's great," the man in the Hawaiian shirt said. "Any other great ones?"

"Let's see . . . . There was also WineDye. This particular client recognized that the white wine was generally a bit cheaper than the red at his local convenience store and came up with the clever idea of dye drops that could be used to easily convert any white wine to a rosé or, with a few extra drops, to a red wine. It even came with a color chart for different varietals, such as Merlot or Cabernet."

The man continued, "Oh, and I shouldn't leave out the 'dornet.' A young anesthesiologist invented a cute little stuffed duck to assist in giving shots to uncooperative young children. The thing was only a few inches long and had an open sleeve through the middle where you could insert a hypodermic needle. You could slide in a syringe through the hole at the bottom of the tiny creature, and

the needle would poke out of the bill of the waterfowl. This allowed
the doctor to surreptitiously sneak up on the kiddos and stab them
when they weren't ready. I believe they call the technique 'darting.'
The problem was that the damn thing was scary as hell. The duck
looked like it had a giant plunger lodged in its ass and the needle
sticking out of its bill reminded me of some ungodly crossbreed
between a duck and hornet, hence the name 'dornet.' If there is ever
an apocalypse, it's not locusts I'm worried about. I'm convinced the
sky will be filled with dornets."

"And you got patents on all those things?" the man in the
Hawaiian shirt asked.

"Of course, we can patent anything. The trick is to apply for
a patent so ridiculous that no sane person would have thought of it
before. We've trained our phone operators well. We teach them to be
very creative. Most of the people who call in from our
advertisements don't have very original ideas, and they have almost
certainly been patented before. We train our employees to suggest
more original variations of their ideas. The more absurd, the better.
I've found that failed writers—particularly failed science fiction
writers—perform this task in excellent fashion."

"Any of these things make any big money?" the man in the Hawaiian shirt asked.

"You know that they do. You've seen my boat," the man with the hat said, pointing to one of the large sailboats in the harbor. "We charge a great deal of money to file the patents, obviously."

"No, I mean, do the inventors make any big money on those things?" the other man asked.

"Of course not! They're all ridiculous ideas. They are so ridiculous that you can get a patent on them and also so ridiculous that nobody would actually buy any of them. You need to understand that we are selling the *dream* of making money, not an actual way to make money," the hatted man said with a laugh.

Rye's heart sank as it became clear that the group of people with whom he was conversing were not the people he had hoped them to be. Unable to hold back any longer, he said to the man with the hat, "I am tempted to tell you all the reasons the conduct you just described is abhorrent and unethical, but I expect you already know them."

There was silence for a moment, and then the man in the hat laughed again. "You can't take these things too seriously. I'm just having some fun. I'm sure there are *a few* people who have made money from their inventions. Now, if you are one of the true believers in this . . . living according to nature, perhaps we should get some input from the other group adjoining us. You see, most of us here in this group come down for a few weeks to a few months in the winter, whereas the other group next to us is mostly made up of people who live on their boats full-time."

Rye got a new rush of excitement, realizing that perhaps his thousand-mile journey was not a bust and that they had just stumbled into the wrong group.

"Keep in mind that some of them have little water on their boats so they tend not to shower too often, and so we try to set up upwind when we can," the woman sitting next to the hatted man said.

"That's of no importance," Rye said. "Yes, I would very much like to talk with them."

"What's his name again?" the man with the hat asked the woman next to him. "Will or Bill? Oh yes, it's Willy."

"Oh God, don't call him over," the woman replied.

"It will be fine," the man in the hat replied comfortingly as he turned his head and yelled over to the other group, "Willy! Come join us for a moment. There is a gentleman here who would like to meet you."

Rye looked over and saw a lanky, shirtless man with a gray scruffy beard get up off a cooler and walk over. He was clearly stumbling. As he arrived, the man with the hat said, "Willy, this gentleman here—I'm sorry, what is your name?"

"Rye," Rye said.

"This gentleman here, Rye, appears to share some of your views with regard to the trappings of capitalism."

"What the hell ya talkin' 'bout?" the shirtless man asked with slurred speech.

"The problems with society back in the United States and everyone working all the time and whatnot," the man with the hat clarified.

"Goddamn righ'," the shirtless man said to Rye.

"Yes, I am on this voyage to live in accordance with nature and to find others who have followed this path," Rye explained. "You see—"

"Preachin' t' the choir!" the man interjected loudly.

"Yes, the artificial societal constraints—" Rye tried to continue.

"Damn right," the shirtless man interrupted again. "Singin' to the fire . . . the . . . the . . . choir," he slurred as he spotted the ceviche and stuck his hand deep into the bowl. The man grabbed a handful of the fish and jammed it roughly into his mouth. "Bunch of dumbasses up there, workin' their asses off while we're livin' it up. Livin' the dream—that's what I say! Sometimes though, I wish da hell somebody'd come an' wake me up!" the man said with a loud laugh as lemon juice ran down his chin. "Shiiit, jus' lookit this place."

"Yes, you know, I believe that the culture—" Rye tried again.

"I mean, jus' lookit this place," the drunk man interrupted again. "It's so damn beauta . . . so damn beauta . . . so damn pretty," he said as he swayed back and forth, pointing at the surrounding ocean.

The drunk man went to grab another handful of ceviche but fell over as he bent down and spilled the bowl into the sand. "Sorry 'bout that, Chief," he said to Rye as he stood up and brushed himself off and meandered back over to his group.

"Enlightening, isn't it?" the man with the Panama Jack hat asked.

Rye said nothing. Deflated, he sat quietly for the next half an hour as his group chatted with the others before they headed out. On the way back to his boat, Rye was still quiet while Kaia was talking on her phone to the tour company where she had been working. As she wrapped up her call, she said, "Nori, looks like we got a little better wind moving in tonight and still nothing on the books. Javon said things are slower than usual."

"Sounds like we got some free time to do some kiting and maybe some more surfing," Nori said.

"Yep, not great for making money, but we got a bit to hold us for a while," Kaia said. "Rye, I got an idea. There are some other spots Nori and I have been wanting to check out on some of the other islands close by. I know the people we met tonight were jerks, but there are other hangouts on other islands in the Bahamas and plenty more if you're willing to go farther. How about we take your boat around a bit, and we can scope out the local scene for you and we can do some kiting and surfing. We'll even throw in some lessons for you."

"Sounds fun," Nori added.

"What exactly is kiteboarding?" Rye asked.

"Just what it sounds like. You're flying a large kite as you ride across the water on a board," Nori explained.

Rye perked up a bit and said, "That sounds interesting. Exposure to multiple elements of nature all at once—wind and water. And I have traveled a long way. I would hate to give up my journey so quickly. I really need more research for my book. Perhaps some local guides would be of help. Samuel, what do you think?"

"Hell, Doc, that's what we came down here for, ain't it? Some adventure, I mean."

"Then, agreed, ladies," Rye said. "Let us continue this trek together."

Chapter Twenty-Two

It was a blustery day when Rye climbed out of bed the next morning, still feeling tired. Stems, Kaia, and Nori drank late into the night, and as a result, the two women ended up sleeping in the extra bunk room. Around 4:30 in the morning, the wind really started to blow, and between the noise and the rocking boat, Rye was in a broken sleep most of the night.

Rye dressed and worked his way up to the topside, where he found Kaia and Nori sitting on the edge of the rear deck with their feet dangling off the side, sipping coffee. The skies were overcast, but there was no rain.

"Hey, Sleeping Beauty," Nori said, spotting Rye.

"Good morning. How long have you been up?" Rye asked.

"Not long," said Nori. "Maybe thirty minutes."

"How is everyone feeling today?" Rye asked.

"We'll make it. We figured out some time ago that the sooner you get in the water, the better on mornings like these," Kaia said. Her eyes were clearly bloodshot. "In my case, that means we need to get moving. So, we've been talking. How about we take our car today and head up to the north end of the island? There's a good kiting spot up there we've only been to once. We can go up there and hang out and then come back and head out somewhere else on the boat tomorrow."

"That's agreeable," Rye said.

It was around 11:30 a.m. by the time Rye, Kaia, Nori, and Stems retrieved the kite gear from the girls' house and then started their drive up the coast of the island toward the northeast shore in Kaia's rental car. On the way, they drove through several small towns that hugged the coast of the island. As they passed through one town, Kaia made note of a group of people who appeared to be setting up for something. The town was more ornate than some others they had passed through. There were maybe thirty or forty homes built from concrete blocks, along with a church. The townspeople had painted many of the homes in pastel greens, blues, and pinks. The church stood out in contrast as it was painted bright white. It was also made of concrete block and had a single spire above the front entry with a cross at the top.

Several people were milling around in an open field that adjoined the church. They were setting up makeshift tables constructed of sawhorses and plywood. There were also several large coolers being carried out into the field by others from the nearby houses.

"What do you think is going on here?" Kaia asked.

"Don't know," Nori responded. "Looks like they're setting up for a party or something."

"Want to stop and check it out, *amore mio?*" Kaia asked Nori.

"Let's head to the kiting spot first. We can always check it out later, *meine liebe,*" Nori answered.

The group continued to the beach as Stems dozed in the car. When they arrived, the wind had died down but was still blowing a steady fifteen knots. Kaia pulled off the side of the road onto a small dirt path. There was an onshore breeze with only a few clouds in the sky.

"Perfect!" said Kaia, stepping out of the car. "Great day to teach," she continued, looking at the small whitecaps on the water.

The beach was narrow, and the sand was white and powdery. Because of the wind, the water had turned more of a turquoise shade than the deep blue the day before. Kaia and Nori unloaded the gear from the trunk of the car and the boards from the roof rack. Stems was still trying to clear his head as he stepped out of the car and promptly lit up a joint.

"So, Rye, we're going to take this nice and slow today," said Kaia.

"Okay, may I help set things up?" he asked.

"No, we got it. Come on down to the beach, and we'll get started."

Kaia and Nori toted the gear down to the beach. Once they got to the edge of the water and dropped the gear, Nori—still feeling the effects from the night before—told Kaia she needed to chill for a bit. Kaia could see Nori was looking a little green and told her to relax and she would get things started. Nori retrieved two towels from the car, and she and Stems went up and found a place to lie down in the sand under the shadow of a few palm trees.

In the meantime, Kaia began to prepare the kite gear. She unfurled one of the large, colorful kites from its bag and laid it out in the sand. The bow-shaped kite was over ten feet long and several feet wide. She then laid out and attached the lines that tied the kite to the control bar and made certain everything was secure.

"So, Rye, first things first. Do you see how the wind is blowing onshore? That's what you want for kiteboarding," Kaia explained. "That way, if something goes wrong, you're just going to blow to shore. Side-on wind is also great, meaning that it is blowing onshore but at an angle. Side-shore—when it's blowing parallel to the shore—isn't bad but not optimal when you are just learning because you can end up being blown along the shoreline if you're down in the water and can't get up. You rarely want to kite in offshore wind because you can get dragged out to sea. Now, one of the nice things about learning here is that the water is shallow running way out. We'll walk out a hundred yards, and it will still just be waist-deep. That's nice because I can show you everything standing up. It's much easier that way than floating in the water."

"Understood," Rye said.

"After I explain the gear to you, we'll have you just fly the kite some first and then try to figure out the board afterward," Kaia continued. "The kite is going to want to fly downwind, and so you will stand with the wind to your back. Flying the kite is really more about finesse than strength. It's like sailing a boat. If you try to force it, things will probably go wrong. There's too much power. Instead, think of having the kite work with the wind."

"Ah, yes," Rye said. "That sounds very familiar. It reminds me of when I ran the Iditarod dogsled race in Alaska. You know, it takes nearly two weeks to run the 1,000-mile race through rugged terrain. Sled dogs can't be forced, either. If you try, they'll resist you. You need to be gentle. When a driver and team are working together, it's as if the dogs can almost sense where you want to go. There were times I had no idea where I was, but I assumed the dogs knew where we were going. You see, you become very dependent upon each other. You know, there was one night when I had just dozed off to sleep and the dogs suddenly started barking. I suspected a bear might be close at hand. I jumped up, scrambling to find my towel so that I might protect myself as well as my loyal companions—"

"Rye, how about we talk about that later? Let's get you to focus on what we're doing here," Kaia said.

"Oh yes, of course."

Kaia explained the basics of kiteboarding technique to Rye and then called Nori, who was just settling down for a nap, over to help Kaia launch the kite. Nori reluctantly pulled the towel off her face and stood up and walked over with a sigh. After they got the kite flying in the air, Kaia and Rye waded out in the water with the kite while Nori went back to the shade near Stems. Stems was already out cold, and Nori heard him snoring as she plopped back down.

The water was still only waist-deep when Kaia said that they had gone out far enough. Kaia showed Rye how to fly and control the kite, which went well overall. Kaia also showed Rye how he could relaunch the kite by himself if it fell in the water and how to quickly detach himself from the kite if such a need arose. After a couple of hours of practice, Rye got comfortable flying and controlling the kite while standing in the waist-deep water. It was getting hot outside, so the pair decided to take a break. Kaia took the kite back from Rye and they walked back up to the beach and Kaia yelled up to Nori, who also now appeared to be sleeping.

"Hey, Nori!"

Nori popped her head up and saw Kaia tapping the top of her head with her palm, signaling that she wanted to land the kite. Nori jumped up and ran over to the edge of the water, and Kaia gently lowered the kite to her.

Hearing the commotion, Stems woke up, and he was feeling hungry. "How 'bout we recharge the batteries and get a bite to eat?" he suggested to the group.

"There's a little convenience store about a mile down the road—we passed it coming in," Kaia said. "Nori, do you want to go grab some water and snacks? The wind is picking up, and Rye and I can set up the smaller kite while you're gone. With the stronger wind, the smaller kite will be safer."

"Yes, that's agreeable to me," said Rye.

"You want to drive, Stems? I'm still struggling with the manual transmission," Nori said.

"No problem. I drove one for years. You just need to show me the way."

Stems was a little rusty shifting at first, but muscle memory quickly kicked in, and he drove them to the small local grocery store. The store had a gravel parking lot with enough room for several cars to pull up to the front of the building. Stems pulled into one of the open spots, and he and Nori proceeded into the store.

"Felt damn good to drive a stick again. Reminds me of my racing days when I was a kid," commented Stems as they walked in through the front door.

"Yes, marvelous job. Maybe you can give me some lessons. Kaia doesn't have any patience with me, surprisingly," said Nori.

"No problem. We just need a big open parking lot."

"How about a field? There are more fields around here than parking lots," Nori commented.

"Fields ain't as good. They're bumpy, and you can't always see holes and shit in them. I rolled my truck over in a field when I was doing some donuts a long time ago."

Nori snatched a few water bottles and dropped them into the handbasket she had grabbed when she entered the store. She then spotted the beer in the standup refrigerators against the back wall and asked, "Should we get some Kalik?"

"What the hell is Kalik?" asked Stems.

"It's a Bahamian beer," she explained, pointing to the blue-labeled beverage conspicuously stocked in a large section of the refrigerator.

"Any good?"

"Not bad," Nori said with a shrug.

"Ain't they got any 'Merican beer? I'm partial to High Life myself," Stems commented.

"You can get it, but it costs twice as much," Nori explained.

"Alright then, let's just go with the local stuff. Should we get a case?" Stems asked.

"Maybe just a twelve-pack?"

"Better safe than sorry," Stems replied as he grabbed two twelve-packs from the cooler.

"I'm not certain, but I think you might be a bad influence on me," Nori said.

On the way to the checkout counter of the little Bahamian convenience store, Nori noticed a small drop-in cooler with an assortment of food items. She pulled out a plastic container of conch salad. There was no list of ingredients nor was there an expiration date. She decided to live dangerously and grabbed it anyway, along with a box of saltine crackers from a shelf above the cooler. After paying for the items, Stems and Nori headed for the car. Stems jumped back in the driver's seat and quickly popped open a beer and drank down half the can. He then pulled a joint out of his shirt pocket and lit it up and took a deep drag and then handed it to Nori.

Nori looked around to see if anyone was watching them. "Probably should keep a low profile. I'm not sure that's legal here," she said as she took the joint and ducked her head low in the car to take a hit.

"That's me. I'm all about keeping a low profile," Stems said. Feeling more confident about his handling of the stick shift, he then threw it into reverse and popped the clutch. The car lurched backward a couple of feet and then came to an abrupt stop with a loud crunch. Stem's half-full beer spilled in his lap, and he dropped the joint on the floorboard. Stems and Nori spun around and realized that a police car had pulled up immediately behind them.

"Where the hell did he come from?" asked Nori.

"No idea," responded Stems as he tentatively pulled forward to the front of the parking spot.

They both looked back again, and it appeared that the vehicle was empty.

Nori and Stems climbed out of the car. Stems was simultaneously trying to find the joint he had dropped and wipe off the beer from the front of his pants.

Nori walked back to survey the damage to the vehicles. "Oh shit!" she said, seeing the front end of the police car. There appeared to be extensive damage to the car, with the bumper pushed in and the front of the hood crumpled. Despite this, there was almost no discernible damage to the rental vehicle driven by Stems. Nori looked closer at the rental and could only make out a few minor scratches on the bumper.

Stems was in full panic mode. He wasn't certain of the conditions at the local jail but imagined they weren't great.

There was an older Bahamian man with a straw hat who was sitting on a bench in front of the store, and he was watching everything. He could tell Stems was frantic and walked over to survey the damage to the cars. He bent down and inspected the police cruiser closely and then said to Stems, "You may have a problem with that beer spilled all over ya. The weed you got in the car could be a problem, too. If you ask me, the best thing you can do is get going."

Stems, who was still futilely attempting to dry his pants with his hands, said, "If I leave and they catch me, they'll lock me up for sure."

"Hey, let me tell you something. I know that boy who drives this car. Sure as shit, he's in there drinking coffee and eating cake in the little booth at the back of the store. That's what he does every day. We're all paying his salary, and he just sits on his ass all day. I'll tell you something else, that boy can't drive worth a damn. He ran that police car of his into palm trees, other cars, and even my neighbor's house. He then told the poor lady that it was her fault for building the house too close to the road. That damage you see on the front of his car was already there. They won't give him a new car 'cause they know he'll just wreck it again."

"Really?" asked Stems, feeling relieved. Stems looked closer at the front of the vehicle he had run into and noticed that the damaged areas were heavily rusted, clearly showing that the damage had been done long ago. "I see what you're saying, but maybe I should talk to the officer and explain to him what happened."

"And you going to do that smelling like weed and beer?" the Bahamian man asked. "Did you come to the Bahamas to have a good time, or are you just looking for trouble? I'm telling you, best you just go on about your business."

Stems paused and then said, "That sounds like a great idea."

Stems and Nori climbed back into their vehicle and Stems then managed to work their car around the police cruiser, at one point, almost hitting it again. As they were turning around in the parking lot, Nori looked back and saw a young Bahamian policeman exit the store, carrying a cup of coffee and a handful of snacks. It may have been her imagination, but she thought he was looking at the front of his vehicle. The officer glanced her way, and she instinctively ducked a little in the passenger's seat. As they drove off down the small road, she looked back again, and the officer got into his car. The old man, who was sitting on the bench again, smiled and nodded to the officer but appeared to say nothing.

Chapter Twenty-Three

Stems and Nori headed back to the beach, and on the way, Nori suggested that they not mention the incident to Kaia.

"I don't think it did any damage, but better not to make her nervous. It's a rental, and she'll be paranoid turning it back in if she knows. This thing is pretty old and beat-up, anyway. Actually, I have an idea. Pull over for a minute."

Stems pulled over on the side of the road, and Nori got out to inspect the rear bumper.

"Hey, Stems, come on back here for a minute."

"No problem," Stems responded as he turned off the vehicle.

"I think a little camouflage is in order," Nori said as she reached into the open window of the car and grabbed one of the beers they had just purchased. She popped it open and then splashed some of it on the back bumper of the vehicle where the scratches were located.

"What the hell are you doing?" Stems asked. "That's sacrilege!"

"Easy, partner. I just need a bit of moisture to get the dirt to stick."

"Hell, I could've peed on it for you!"

"No, I'll pass," Nori said.

"Well, at least it ain't Miller," Stems said, shaking his head.

Nori took a handful of the dry, powdery dirt from the side of the road and sprinkled it on the bumper. She then stepped back to inspect her handiwork and said with a smile, "There you go. Just like new!"

"You want to hand me the rest of that beer?" Stems asked.

The two climbed back in the car and started their way back to the beach.

"You know why I like Miller beer so much?" Stems asked as they got underway.

"No idea."

"'First and foremost, 'cause it tastes damn good. Beyond that, 'cause it's the Champagne of Beers."

"Is that right?"

"Yep, that's why they sell it in clear bottles that look just like little Champagne bottles. You know, when I picked up my settlement check I used to buy *Bassassin*, me and my lawyer went on down to Bar 17 to celebrate and I bought us a couple of Millers. Mr. Forelle told me that night they can't even sell Miller beer over there in Europe."

"How come?"

"He said it had something to do with a treaty signed way back over a hundred years ago at the end of World War I. The French put something in that treaty that said they were the only ones that could sell something named "Champagne." He said it never became official law here because it was back during prohibition. The congressmen didn't want to bother with it since you couldn't sell any booze then anyway. I reckon the French weren't too worried about it for the same reason."

"That's interesting," Nori commented.

"Yep, but that don't mean you can sell it in them European countries though. Mr. Forelle even told me that, a little while back, someone accidently shipped a few thousand cans of Miller to Belgium. The French made a big stink about it and made 'em open up every can by hand and poured 'em down the drain."

"Sounds like a damn waste to me."

"You ain't shittin'. When he told me that, it messed up my whole night. Pourin' out all that beer just won't right, you know. Hell, I was so pissed off about it, I went home early that night, and I *never* go home early."

By the time Stems and Nori made it back to the beach, Kaia had the smaller kite ready to go and was sitting in the sand with Rye, waiting for them to return. Nori carried the water along with the conch salad and crackers down to the beach, and Stems carried a twelve-pack of beer.

The four sat on the beach and quickly devoured the food while Kaia and Rye drank water and Stems and Nori drank beer. Kaia and Rye then headed back out to the water. Neither Nori nor Stems mentioned the events that had occurred at the market.

"So, I think we're ready to try the board," Kaia said to Rye as they made their way back out to waist-deep water.

"Excellent," Rye replied.

"So, what you want to do now is to sit down in the water and put your feet in the board straps. Point the board horizontal to the downwind direction where the kite is going to pull you. The kite will have a little pressure on it. First, keep the kite up high in the sky, like at twelve o'clock. What you are going to do is dive the kite hard to one side and let it pull you up out of the water and then stand up. When you're coming out of the water, you'll want to turn your board so that your front leg is in the same direction you are diving the kite. So, you should dive the kite to the left and head down the shoreline, so you'll want to put your left leg forward. Got it?" asked Kaia.

"I believe so," said Rye.

"I don't want you to go too far when you get up. Just go a hundred yards or so, and then let the kite float back straight up in the air and sit back down in the water. That's all you need to do to stop."

"Understood," Rye said.

Rye dove the kite hard and felt himself being lifted out of the water, followed by the exhilaration of shooting across the water's surface as he stood on the board. He heard Kaia yell a heartfelt "Wooo!" as he jetted away from her. He was enjoying himself so much that he forgot Kaia's advice not to go too far. Riding downwind and parallel to the beach, Rye skimmed across the top of the water. There were no obstacles around except a channel marker several hundred yards down from where Rye launched. The marker was set in the sand with a large creosote post that was a solid twelve inches in diameter. Six feet above the waterline, the post had a triangular faded-red metal sign with the channel marker number 42 painted in white letters.

Kaia's excitement quickly changed to concern as she watched Rye continue heading straight for the huge post. She started yelling at the top of her lungs for him to stop. But Rye couldn't hear her, and by the time Rye realized he was at risk of slamming into the channel marker, he was in a full panic and forgot how to slow down, let alone stop. Just short of impact, he purposely wiped out, just missing the post. The kite lines also just missed the channel marker as the kite fell from the sky and floated harmlessly off to the side.

Rye was able to stand up in the shallow water to survey how far he had traveled. He looked back and saw Kaia in a half-run, trudging through the water heading to him. She appeared to be quite pale despite her tan.

When she caught up to him, she said, "You gave me a scare there. You went a little farther than I wanted."

"Yes, I forgot how to stop," he explained.

"Just bring the kite straight up, and you can let go of the control bar," she reminded him. "You managed to nearly hit the only hazard out here. You remember when you were talking about how kiteboarding combines the elements of water and wind?"

"Yes," Rye answered.

"Let's just keep it to those two. You would have added wood and metal to the mix if you had hit that post, and I can say with certainty it wouldn't have been enjoyable. I think the fifth element is dirt or something, right?"

"Yes, earth, I believe," Rye corrected.

"Yep, so stay away from that one as well. Dirt, mud, sand, they all hurt if you run up on them on a kiteboard. Just stick with wind and water, and you'll be fine!"

Kaia took the kite and board from Rye and tacked back upwind with the equipment as Rye walked back. She landed the kite and decided she was ready for a drink. "There's a pretty cool bar on the northeast shore not too far from here. It's a little tacky, but they have some great fish tacos. What do you say we check it out?" Kaia asked Rye as they walked over to Stems and Nori. "We may run into a few of the boat people up there, too."

"Excellent," Rye said. "I have a notebook in the car."

Chapter Twenty-Four

Kaia pulled into the parking lot of the Paradise Bar and Restaurant, known as PBR by the locals. There was a large paved parking lot in front of the white building, and Rye could make out a pristine beach just behind it. There were several neon-lit palm trees around the perimeter of the parking lot, and Rye could already hear steel drums playing as he climbed out of the vehicle.

The four walked down a short path that led behind the building and observed an expansive view over the turquoise water. Besides a stage set up by the waterfront, there was a walk-up bar with a handful of people sitting at it and several round tables scattered around the patio. There were also a few tiki torches strategically placed throughout the premises, all of which were lit, even though the sun was still high in the sky. There were colorful tropical decorations everywhere, including a large pastel-green gecko sculpture in the center of a multi-colored dance floor.

"So, how did you find this place?" asked Rye.

"We met the bartender down at the marina one weekend and became friends. He's Bahamian, and his name is Christopher. His mother actually runs the place. It's really more of a locals' hangout. They overdid the decorations as an inside joke."

As they approached the bar, Kaia saw that Christopher was working and waved to him.

"Hey buddy!" she yelled.

"Kaia! Nori! Come over here, girls," he said, gesturing the group over.

Kaia and Nori walked ahead of Rye and Stems. Kaia leaned over the bar between two men drinking and gave Christopher a big hug.

"Doing great. Can you hook us up here?" Kaia asked.

"Of course. What do you want?"

"This is Rye and this is Stems. They're friends of ours," Kaia said, pointing back to the two men behind her and smiling.

"Hey, fellas, nice to meet you. What would everybody like?"

"Give us three beers," Kaia said. "Rye, how about you?"

"Just water, please," Rye said.

"Christopher, how about a couple of orders of fish tacos, too?" asked Kaia.

As Christopher was handing the drinks to the group, Nori looked over and saw a police officer in uniform at the end of the bar who was holding a beer. She nearly panicked, thinking that he looked very much like the same officer from the convenience store. But closer inspection revealed that the officer sitting at the bar was wearing a different type of uniform. She took a deep breath and relaxed a bit.

"He off-duty?" Nori asked Christopher, discretely pointing to the man. The police officer with the beer appeared to be in his early twenties, short and very thin. He was wearing a uniform that was a little too large for him and hung on his body. The uniform was black with a matching black hat with a red strip around the brim. The man also had a handful of medals tacked to his left breast pocket and what appeared to be a scabbard strapped to his right hip.

"He's down here a lot," said Christopher. "He's one of the new police officers. The locals don't think too much of him, but he likes to hang out with the tourists."

"Is that really a sword?" asked Nori.

"Yes, he likes to wear his dress uniform when he comes down here. He wears something more casual at the station and on patrol but dresses up when he heads this way. It makes him feel more important."

Upon hearing this, Nori broke out into a sweat.

"Want to meet him?" the bartender asked.

"No!" Nori blurted out too quickly.

"Relax, Nori," Kaia said. "It's never a bad thing to know the local cops."

Before Nori could respond, Christoper called out to the policeman, "Hey, Emmy, come down here and meet these folks."

The man approached the group, smiling. "Hello there, I'm Officer Emerson. Nice to meet you."

"Hi," said Kaia with a big smile. "I'm Kaia, this is Nori, and this is Rye and Stems."

"Nice to meet you all," Emmy responded. "I hope you are having a good time on my island."

"*Your* island?" Stems said with a chuckle.

Nori was nudging Stems and trying to figure out how to tell him that she thought it was the same officer from the store.

Officer Emmy ignored Stems's comment and asked, "How long have you all been here?"

"Nori and I have been here awhile, but Rye and Stems just got in a few days ago."

Officer Emmy looked at Nori and said, "You look familiar. Have we met before?"

"No!" Nori said, once again, too quickly.

The officer then turned to Rye and Stems and asked which airline they came in on.

"Stems and I arrived by boat, actually," Rye explained.

"Ah, very nice," said the officer. "What type of vessel, if I may ask? Is it a monohull or catamaran?" he said, assuming Rye had arrived by sailboat like most of the others traversing the Caribbean.

"Monohull," Rye replied.

"Ah, yes. I do like the lines on the monohulls better. You wouldn't happen to be traveling on the schooner that arrived in the harbor earlier this week?" the police officer asked.

"No. Our boat is more of a trawler," Rye explained.

"Oh, the fishing trawler! You are quite the talk of the town. We've never seen a working boat like that one come in here before. Is it a lobster boat?" the officer asked.

"Scallop, actually," responded Rye.

"I heard that you were using the boat for a pleasure cruise. How unusual! You must tell me about this," continued Emmy.

Rye, caught off guard, responded, "I'm surprised you know so much."

"You must understand that everyone talks here."

"I am traveling on it in my quest to live in accordance with nature and also doing fieldwork for a book I am writing," Rye explained.

"Very interesting. And how is that working out for you?"

"I have made limited progress but am hoping that will improve shortly."

While Rye was talking to Officer Emmy, Nori managed to get Stems aside and tell him about her suspicion. Stems's only response was a whispered "oh shit."

"By the way, did any of you lose any money at the beach in the last few days?" the police officer asked.

"Maybe," Kaia said jokingly. "Did you find some?"

"Yes, actually. One of the local guys came in with five hundred American dollars and claimed he found it on the beach."

"I'm just kiddin', that wasn't ours," Kaia clarified.

"What happens if it's not claimed?" asked Kaia. "Does he get to keep it?"

"Perhaps. We'll see. We held him in case he stole the money. If no one comes to the station in the next few days and reports a theft, we'll likely release him and give him the cash."

"Hold him? You mean you locked him up?" asked Nori.

"Of course. You know, five hundred dollars is a lot of money for a local Bahamian. I find it's better to secure everything and everyone in a case like that until we can get things sorted out," the officer said to Nori. "Are you sure we haven't met?" he asked again, looking puzzled.

"Yes, I'm sure," she replied.

"The civility of a society can be judged by who it imprisons and how it treats its prisoners," Rye commented to Kaia.

"What's that?" the officer asked.

"Oh, nothing," Nori responded quickly. "Now's not the time," she added, looking at Rye.

"Well, excuse me, I see another couple I know at one of the tables. Please enjoy your time on our island, and I hope to see you again!"

As Officer Emerson walked off, Nori quietly said to Stems, "Looks like we made the right decision."

"No shit," Stems answered, finishing off his beer.

"Christopher, I've got a question for you," Kaia said, turning back to the bartender.

"Shoot."

"So, when we drove up the coast earlier this morning, we went through a little town. I think it was a town called Hopeville."

"Yeah, yeah, that's close to here," said Christopher as he mixed a drink for another customer.

"When we came through, it looked like everyone was setting up for a party or something."

"It's a party of sorts. The town is mostly made up of families of conch fishermen. They have a big get-together around this time every year. They celebrate the close of the last season and also the beginning of the next. They have a little ceremony. Kinda a blessing of the fleet, and then there's a big party afterward."

"That sounds pretty cool. Do you think we could go there?"

Christopher thought for a moment and then responded, "I think it would be okay. They'll know you are tourists, but they'll understand that you've come to celebrate with them. I can sell you a twelve-pack of beer that you can take with you, and then you won't show up empty-handed."

"Alright, cool, cool," said Kaia. "We got some beer in the car we could take."

"Probably should get some more," Stems interjected.

"You guys all down?" Kaia asked the rest of the group.

"Sure," said Nori.

"What the hell—why not?" said Stems. "But I think we should do one more round first."

"Alright, but I got another idea," Kaia said. "Nori, check it out. The tiki torches are all blown out, and the palm trees are moving pretty good."

Nori scanned their surroundings and noted the wind had picked up and said, "Check out the whitecaps."

"It's side-shore here, and I'm thinking we walk down this beach a little away from the restaurant, do a quick evening kite session, and then head to the party," Kaia suggested.

"Hell yeah," Nori agreed.

Christopher grabbed the fish tacos that had arrived from the kitchen and placed them on the bar in front of Rye, Stems, Kaia, and Nori, along with another round of beers.

"By Sirius, these tacos are exceptional," said Rye. "What kind of fish do they use here?"

"Probably dolphin," said Nori.

Rye nearly spit out his mouthful of food. "Oh my God. I don't eat mammals!"

"No, no, no," said Nori, laughing, "It's mahi-mahi. They catch them right off the reef here."

Chapter Twenty-Five

After eating, the four headed out to the car to get the kite gear. The wind continued to pick up and was blowing a steady twenty-five miles per hour. Stems grabbed a few beers from the case they had bought earlier and headed down to the beach to watch.

"Rye, it's blowing pretty hard. Maybe you should sit this one out?" said Kaia.

"Nonsense," Rye said, feeling confident from his earlier kite session. "Fortune favors the bold!"

Kaia, Nori, and Rye hauled the kite gear from the car and walked down the beach to a quiet spot around a hundred yards down from the restaurant where Stems had already camped out in the sand. The sun was setting, and the wind was really howling. Nori quickly launched her kite and headed out across the breakers and out into the open ocean.

Kaia then launched Rye's kite and walked over to him. "Okay, let's go easy and stay close to the shore. It's shallow out here for around twenty or thirty yards but then gets over your head. Like I said before, it's harder to learn in deep water. If you fall, don't panic. Try and keep your kite in the sky, and then you can use it to kite back toward shore."

"I understand," Rye said.

The two waded out a short way into the water. This put them out past some of the smaller breakers, but every fourth or fifth wave was larger and broke on top of them, putting Rye in the difficult position of trying to fly the kite and simultaneously get on the board in the turbulent whitewash. Every time he would get himself halfway situated, trying to dive the kite and standing up on the board, one of the larger waves would crash into him. This usually resulted in him losing hold of the board, and then he would need to start the entire process over again. After around fifteen minutes of this exercise, Rye was getting exhausted and was about ready to call it quits for the day. However, as luck would have it, there was a break in the larger waves, giving him the opportunity to put all the pieces together quickly and successfully. Rye dove the kite hard and felt his body quickly being pulled out of the water as he stood up on the board. The wind was much stronger than what Rye had experienced earlier in the day. It was exhilarating and terrifying at the same time. He tried to steady the board with some success, but this resulted in him going even faster. Rye could just make out Kaia screaming instructions to him on how to get control of the kite and slow down.

"Lift the kite higher! Go to twelve o'clock!" Kaia yelled.

Rye suddenly remembered Kaia's earlier explanation about why the kite pulls you faster and harder when it is parked lower in the sky and closer to the horizon, He successfully used the control bar to raise the kite higher into the sky. This slowed him down a bit but he was still being drug out to sea. By this point, Rye could no longer hear Kaia's instructions through the strong wind and decided he had better stop when, out of the corner of his eye, he saw some kind of large black and white bird flying very fast. "Perhaps some kind of frigate bird," he thought.

Rye glanced at the bird and then back at his kite as he tried to figure out if there was any risk of collision. He quickly dismissed the thought, realizing that the bird could obviously see the large kite floating in the air in front of it. But the bird was apparently daydreaming, and before Rye knew what was happening, it blasted right through the kite, leaving a gaping hole in it. The bird crumpled for a moment but regained its composure before hitting the ocean and then continued along its journey. But the collision caused the damaged kite to change direction abruptly, generating a powerful surge that launched the kite high into the air with Rye hanging on.

He floated twenty feet in the air and hung there for a moment in astonishment. He thought time had stopped. But it didn't, and the kite accelerated back down toward the water with Rye in tow, and both slammed into the water with a loud smack.

As he hit the water, he felt a sharp impact on the side of his face, and the force propelled him several feet below the surface. As he popped his head back up, he felt disoriented and unbalanced. He looked back at the shoreline and saw that he had covered over a hundred yards in the short time he was up on the board. He had now lost the board, which floated ten yards behind him, and in his confused state, he could not relaunch the damaged kite.

Kaia, who had observed the entire ordeal from the beach, was frantically swimming trying to reach Rye. As she finally closed in on him after several minutes, she called out, "Jesus, Rye, are you okay?"

"I'm not sure—I'm feeling a little dazed," he yelled back.

"Anything broken?" Kaia asked.

"My pride."

"Anything else?"

Rye took a quick inventory of his body. "My ear may have suffered somewhat of a trauma."

"Did that bird punch through the kite?" Kaia asked as she finally caught Rye and grabbed onto him.

"I believe it did. You did not happen to mention this particular contingency and the appropriate response in such a case."

"That's because I've never even heard of such a thing! Let's get back to shore. Where's the board?" Kaia asked, looking around.

"I think it's back behind us," Rye said, pointing to where he had last seen it floating.

Kaia spotted the board and quickly swam and retrieved it. With the board in tow, she returned to Rye and managed to relaunch the beat-up kite, then used it to drag them both to the beach.

"Damn, you okay, Doc?" Stems asked as he ran up to them when they arrived at the shore.

"I believe so, although I seem to have a bit of ringing in my ear."

"Is one ear or both ringing?" Kaia asked.

"I'm not sure. I think just the right one."

"That damn bird attacked you!" Stems said.

"I'm not certain, Stems, but I don't believe it was intentional," Rye answered.

"Sure as shit looked intentional to me!" Stems responded. "He drew his wings in like one of them stealth fighters and shot right through that kite!"

"You caught some serious air there. That's usually reserved for advanced lessons," Kaia said with a little laugh.

"I think I need to wait a bit before I undertake jumping," said Rye. "Is it just me or is the earth slanted to the right?" he asked as he looked out across the water while tilting his head to one side and trying to figure out why everything was askew.

"You want to see a doctor?" Kaia asked.

"No, I believe I will recover. As a rule, I disfavor doctors."

"That's good because medical care is pretty shitty here," said Kaia. "You scared the hell out of me. I don't know if I've ever swum that fast before."

Kaia realized she hadn't been keeping track of Nori with all the commotion going on. She looked back out over the surf just in time to see her jogging in through the waves with a large smile on her face. She quickly landed the kite and trotted over to the group and said, "Great session! What's up with you guys?"

"We had a minor mishap," explained Kaia.

"What do you mean? What happened?" asked Nori.

"Oh, a rogue pelican punched through Rye's kite and launched him. Really boosted him. I mean like big air!" Stems said.

"What?" asked Nori. "No shit?"

"I don't believe it was a pelican," responded Rye.

"Damn, Rye, are you okay?" Nori asked.

"I believe so," Rye said.

"So, we going to call it a night?" asked Nori.

"Up to you, buddy," Kaia said, looking at Rye. "You still up for a stop at the party?"

After a moment, Rye said, "Yes, I think we should go. I could gain some insights at this function. I've been thinking since our encounter at the sandbar that perhaps some of the local people here may have more to contribute to my writings than those passing through."

"That's the spirit!" Nori said.

Chapter Twenty-Six

As they drove back to the small town, Rye was becoming more excited about the prospects of the party. Although he had not given up hope of finding other travelers who shared his vision, he realized that perhaps the locals in this community might have a better understanding of what he was searching for. After all, these islands were known for their laid-back lifestyles, far removed from the rabid consumerism of the States. Perhaps he was in the right location for his journey but had just sought the wrong people.

Kaia, Nori, Rye, and Stems pulled up in front of the small field where the townsfolk had conglomerated in Hopeville. Even before they got out of the car, several people were looking over at them curiously.

The group exited the vehicle and paused to better survey their surroundings. Kaia had a twelve-pack in hand.

"What now?" Nori asked Kaia.

"Good question," Kaia responded.

Sensing their reluctance, a man working behind the makeshift bar yelled over to them, "Come on over! Don't be shy!" He was wearing a pair of dress pants and a long -sleeved button-down shirt.

A woman standing near him, wearing a colorful floral dress, yelled, "Yes! Come on! You're welcome here!"

Kaia smiled and yelled, "Hello!" and led the way with the others in tow. As Rye stepped forward, he stumbled a little, realizing that he was still a bit stunned from the earlier fall. As soon as they reached the large group of people, the man who had initially invited them over yelled out, "Okay, quick, everyone, let's tie them up!"

There was a pause and then several people in the crowd laughed.

Kaia handed the beer over for the communal collection of alcohol, and several curious attendees quickly surrounded Kaia, Nori, Stems, and Rye.

"We just happened to drive through the town earlier today and saw everything being set up and decided to drop by. Is that okay?" asked Kaia.

"Of course, of course, we are glad you came by. These things are intended to be events of celebration. They are open to anyone who wants to take part," responded a full-figured Bahamian woman wearing a dark-colored skirt and white T-shirt.

"So where are you from—America, correct?" asked one of the older men who had walked up. He was well-dressed and clean-shaven.

"That's correct," Rye answered.

"Which part?" asked the man.

"Stems and I are from Virginia," Rye said.

"We're from all over," Nori added.

"Have any of you been to Florida before?" the man asked.

"Sure, Nori and I spent a lot of time there," Kaia responded.

"You know, I went to Florida many years ago for work. I worked the sugarcane fields," the man said.

"How was it?" Rye asked.

"It was very difficult," said the man. "I did it for a few years and decided to come home. It was very hot there. Here, you know, even in the hottest part of the year, we still get a pleasant breeze to cool things off. Not there. Even then, I was not young enough for that job."

"If you don't mind me asking, what did you think of life there versus here on this island?" Rye inquired.

"Oh, I made good money there, you know, but by the time I paid rent for a place to live, a car to get to work, and all the other things you need there, I couldn't save much. You make more, but it costs more. After a while, I realized I was happier back here. Life is simpler."

"You feel it is better here, correct?" Rye asked.

"I don't know if it's better or just different. For me, it's better, though. When I was working there, I took a break for lunch one day and heard the boss man who owned the company talking to some other businesspeople. He was giving them a tour of the operation, and he was complaining to these men that his plane was too small and that he couldn't make it across the country without stopping for fuel. I heard him say that there were other people who had really expensive planes who didn't need to stop and fuel the plane even on longer trips. He said these other people had such a good life and that they lived a whole 'nother level."

The old man continued, "When I heard this, I laughed to myself and realized that you could never have enough in that country. You'll always want more. The other thing the owner was saying was how much he liked to fish, and he had a big, expensive boat to do this. He said one day when he made even more money, he would retire somewhere where the fishing was good and just do this. It hit me then that he was looking for what I already had back here. So I came back home."

Rye was mesmerized. Although he had been carrying his notebook, he suddenly realized he had forgotten to write down any of the conversation. "Do you mind if I take some notes?" he asked the man.

"Sure, why should I care? What for?"

"I am writing a book."

"Of course you are," the old man commented.

"So, based on what you have said, I take it that you're not a fan of capitalism."

"Oh, I wouldn't say that. What else you gonna do. Look at Cuba. Things aren't so great there. Maybe everybody's just gotta be a little less greedy."

"Is it difficult to get by on this island?" Rye asked.

"You don't make too much here, but I get by okay. When I was very young, I used to dive for conch like many in this town, but that's hard work for someone my age," explained the man. "Then I worked for a while at the big all-inclusive resort across the island, but I didn't like it. They didn't pay very well, and they made me work many long hours."

"I see," Rye said.

The old man continued, "Most of the locals don't really like the resort much. They don't treat us very well, but we see the advertisements they put on the TV about what luxury they have there. The people who come there, they don't really see us—it's like they look right through you."

An ancient-looking Bahamian woman listening to the conversation added, "Those people, they'd never come here to our party. Most never leave the resort. They don't spend no money in the community."

"This is true," the man agreed. "Anyway, now I do a little fishing and sell to the local restaurants. I make enough for what I need, which isn't much."

"So, I hear this is a celebration of the conch fishing season or something," Nori commented.

"They call it a celebration, but they should call it a wake," the old woman said, shaking her head.

"Why do you say that?" Nori asked.

"It's tough goin' nowadays," the woman said. "You used to make a good living catching conchs. Many of the families in this town have been doing it for five or six generations. When I was young, you could go right off the shore and catch as many as you wanted in the shallow water. It was a way for a family to get ahead. Now, there's not too many out there anymore. Men now sometimes got to go thirty or forty miles away from the island to find conch. Everybody wants conch now. All the tourists want conch. People off the island, too. Most of the conch now is being frozen and shipped somewhere else."

"She's right," the man said. "And even worse, the warm waters and big storms are killing them off."

"Is that right?" Kaia asked.

"Oh sure," the man said. "The big storms wipe out the underwater grasses that the conchs live in. Maybe sometime soon, there won't be any more conch around here. Just like in Bermuda and Florida."

"Still, it seems to me to be better here than in the States. After all, you've seen the problems there firsthand," Rye said to the Bahamian man.

"Look here. You need to understand things aren't perfect here, either. I came back, but things maybe aren't really that different. Everybody here wants better jobs and to make more money, too. Maybe it's even harder to do that here. Most of the jobs here are service jobs to make life better for the tourists, and it's hard to make much money. Everything's expensive here, too. It costs a lot to ship everything here, like food, and with a lot of tourists looking for vacation homes, houses are getting more expensive all the time. For me, I'm old and don't need much, but if you're trying to raise a family, that's different," the old man explained.

"Do you really need a house to live in?" Rye asked.

"What's wrong with you, man? You can't just live off fish and coconuts and live in the street! You hit your head or something?" the man asked.

The man's comments clearly disappointed Rye, and he did not know how to respond.

Kaia, sensing the awkward moment, tried to lighten the mood. "Actually, he did, just before we came here," she said with a little laugh. "Rye had a run-in with an enormous bird, and it didn't go well. He took a pretty good knock to the head."

"It ain't the first time he's taken a hit to the head, either," Stems muttered under his breath.

"You should get that checked out," the old man said.

The older woman listening to the conversation suddenly eyed Rye suspiciously and asked, "What kind of bird?"

Rye said, "I'm not sure. It may have been a frigate bird, but, by Sirius, it was a colossal beast—slim and very aerodynamic!"

"A frigate or maybe an albatross?" the woman asked Rye.

"Possibly either, yes," he answered.

"Either way, you get tangled up with one of those, it can be bad news. Maybe soon, things get bad for you," the woman said. "Then again, maybe not," she added with a shrug. "Either way, I think you'll get a visit from the spirit world."

A young woman in the group who was in a blue dress chimed in, "Pay her no attention. That's Obeah nonsense she's talking about."

"Obeah is illegal here!" the old woman shot back with a glare. "Don't be slandering me. I'm a good Christian. I'm just talking about good old truth."

"Who is Obeah?" asked Rye.

The old man explained, "It's not a who. It's a what. Obeah is an old religion. Sort of like voodoo here."

"You take care of yourself, mister," the old woman said to Rye. "That bird is no joke. He came here to teach you something."

Rye made a note in his book to avoid large, out-of-control birds, and then he slipped off to a less populated area of the yard with his three friends.

"You doin' okay, Doc?" Stems asked.

"I suppose. I thought I was really making progress for a moment, but I'm starting to feel that it may be difficult to locate those living their lives in accordance with nature. It seems that the tentacles of consumerism have spread further than I anticipated."

A man in his early twenties with dreadlocks and a T-shirt with Rasta colors wandered up to Rye and the others and said, "How you people doin'?" He told the group his name was Clinton. Rye and the others introduced themselves to the young man. Clinton was carrying a drink made from a coconut shell, and Rye could have sworn that he saw smoke rising from it.

"What are you drinking there?" Stems asked Clinton.

"Ah, this is rum with strongback mixed in," Clinton explained.

"What's that?" Stems inquired.

"Strongback is the bark from a local tree here. It's good stuff. Adds a little something extra," said Clinton.

"Why do they call it strongback?" Stems asked.

"Because it'll give you a strong back and make you irresistible to the ladies. You want to try it?"

"Damn straight!" responded Stems.

Stems took the cup and took a large gulp of the drink. "Damn, that's got a kick to it."

"Oh, you have no idea, but you will see soon!" responded Clinton, smiling.

"Would you like to try?" Clinton asked, holding out the cup to Rye.

Rye thought that perhaps this was one of those rare situations where he should accept this offer as a matter of local custom. Maybe the concoction had a ceremonial quality to it.

"Yes, I believe I will," Rye said as he accepted the drink, which went down hard and left a soapy aftertaste.

"There you go, Doc!" Stems said.

Stems, thinking about the fact that they still needed to drive back across the island in the dark to get back to the docks, asked Clinton, "What are the DUI laws like around here?"

"Oh, trust me, you don't want to get in a wreck if you have been drinking. You'll be in big trouble. They'll lock you up for sure," said Clinton.

"No, I get it, but how much are you allowed to drink legally? What is the blood-alcohol limit here?" asked Stems as he tried to gauge his own level of sobriety by closing his eyes and attempting to touch the end of his nose with his index finger.

"You can drink as much as you want and drive. That's no problem. Just don't get in a wreck. If you get in a wreck, you will be in serious trouble," repeated Clinton.

Hearing this response, Stems said to his fellow travelers, "Hell, no problem. I can get us back across the island."

Nori interjected, "That's a bad idea, buddy. You've been drinking all day. You'd probably run into Officer Emmy with our luck."

"More likely, he'd run into us but still lock us up," Stems whispered back to Nori.

"Rye, you haven't really been drinking. Can you drive back?" Kaia asked.

"I believe so," Rye said.

Stems pulled a joint out of his pocket and lit it up. "Want some?" he said, holding it out to Clinton.

"Yeah, man," Clinton said, taking a large hit. "This is good stuff," Clinton commented.

"I know my weed. Grow it myself," Stems explained.

Rye took down a few additional notes but then realized his writing was askew. "Perhaps we should call it a night," he said.

"Probably," Kaia agreed.

The group said their goodbyes and headed to the vehicle and piled in, with Rye taking the driver's seat. Kaia took the passenger seat, and Nori and Stems sat in the back.

Rye started the vehicle and blinked hard twice, trying to clear his head unsuccessfully. "I'm not sure if it is the fall I had earlier or the smoking drink, but I'm feeling unsteady," Rye explained.

"Well . . . damn," Kaia said. "Should we just sleep in the car?"

"Maybe, I sure can't drive," said Nori.

"Looks like the car it is," Stems said as he yawned and laid his head back.

"Rye, did you enjoy the kiteboarding?" Kaia asked.

"Certainly, but the ending was less than optimal," he answered, closing his eyes. He was still feeling somewhat unsettled.

"That was a crazy fall," said Kaia to Rye.

"Yes, it was impressive, I suppose," Rye replied. "But I'm thinking I might be better off staying away from airborne activities. I wouldn't mind giving surfing another shot, though. We would just need a better setting—somewhere with a more inviting environment. Is there somewhere we can find some beaches without those damn underwater porcupines?" Rye asked.

Kaia turned to Rye in her seat and said, "You know, I think we could find some spots like that. There's plenty of good surfing in the Caribbean, but some of the places are a little bit of a hike from here. What do you think about heading to Puerto Rico? I've always wanted to surf there, and I've heard they've got some incredible beaches."

"How far is that?" Rye asked.

"Not sure. It's a ways away. Maybe seven or eight hundred miles south from here."

"I see. Stems, do we have enough fuel left to go that far?" Rye asked Stems, who was already dozing off in the back seat.

"Yeah, we can at least get down there," Stems said with a large yawn. "Getting back may be a problem without fueling up, though."

"Back? Who said anything about going back?" Rye replied.

Part III

Chapter Twenty-Seven

Rye stared at the expansive white sandy beach from the deck of the *Miss Elizabeth*. It was a beautiful morning with only a few clouds in the sky and a light breeze. The temperature was in the mid-seventies. They had anchored the *Miss Elizabeth* about half a mile offshore. When they arrived the evening before, it was already dusk, and the views of the beach were now much clearer in the morning sun. The beach, which was nearly a mile long, had a heavily vegetated hillside behind it that sloped down toward the water. Both ends of the beach also had craggy rock outcroppings that jutted out into the sea and acted like bookends, framing the idyllic setting. One could have imagined they had found some undiscovered paradise as the beach lay deserted. However, scanning farther up the hillside, they could see a small town with several buildings, including a few hotels and restaurants.

"Today's the day, Rye. Time for your therapy session!" Kaia said.

"Yes. I am quite excited," Rye replied.

Rye, Kaia, and Nori climbed down into *Bassassin*, and after they were in the boat, Stems lowered the three surfboards, one at a time, with a rope.

"You sure you don't want to come with us?" Nori asked Stems.

"No, I'm just gonna hang out here today and relax in the sun," Stems said.

Rye noticed that Stems had already opened a beer.

Kaia quickly started the boat up and headed to the beach.

"Looks pretty good to teach, Nori," Kaia said as they approached the shoreline. It was high tide, and the small whitewash waves were breaking a hundred yards offshore and traveling all the way up to the beach.

As they approached the breakers, Kaia slowed down and matched the speed of the boat to the waves, then picked her wave to surf into the shore. When they reached the beach, Nori quickly jumped out with the anchor line and pulled the bow of the boat forward onto the sand while Kaia raised the outboard motor. Kaia and Rye jumped out into the shallow water. The three worked the bow of *Bassassin* well up onto the edge of the beach. Nori then pulled the anchor line tight and buried the anchor in the sand.

"Let's keep an eye on that, Nori," commented Kaia. "I don't think the tide is coming in anymore, but better to keep a close watch."

"Absolutely," said Nori.

"Okay, Rye, you remember our instructions?" Kaia asked.

"I believe so," said Rye.

"This water is pretty shallow a long way out, so we can probably just walk the boards out most of the way and then paddle out the last bit," said Nori.

"Remember, you'll want to paddle hard once you've picked your wave. When you take off, just jump up on the board like we showed you," explained Kaia.

Rye, Kaia, and Nori walked their boards out through the surf. Once they were waist-deep, they paddled out through the small break with no major difficulties. All three then sat on their boards, and Kaia and Nori went through their instructions one more time.

"You go ahead, Rye, and we'll sit back here and make sure you have it," explained Kaia.

"Understood," said Rye.

Rye's first several attempts to catch waves were unsuccessful. He didn't paddle hard enough, and the waves went gently past him. But then a slightly larger wave came in, and Nori told Rye to go for it and paddle hard. Rye caught the wave, jumped up, and rode nearly twenty yards before he fell off.

As Rye popped his head back out of the water, he could hear Kaia and Nori yelling words of encouragement from where they were still sitting on their boards offshore.

"Nice job, Rye!" Kaia yelled over the crashing waves.

"What did you think?" Nori added.

"Quite interesting!" Rye yelled back as he paddled in the direction of the shore.

"Where are you going?" Nori yelled.

"I'd like to make some notes about the experience!" Rye yelled back.

"Don't you want to ride some more first?" Nori yelled.

"Oh, certainly," Rye responded as he turned his board back around.

The trio caught several more waves over the next few hours of riding. The small surf was more tailored for a beginner, but Kaia and Nori still enjoyed the relaxing morning in the sun, taking multiple joyrides. By late morning, a handful of people started to trickle down to the beach from a path that led up to the town. As they arrived, they set up a few umbrellas and laid out beach towels, and several children started to play in the shallow surf.

"How about we take a break and check out the town?" Kaia suggested.

"Sounds good," Nori said. "I wouldn't mind a little something to eat."

"That's agreeable to me. There are certainly notes I would like to make," Rye explained.

The tide started to go out. *Bassassin* was now fully up on the beach, and the waves were building.

Inspecting the tender, Kaia said, "I think the boat will be okay. What do you think, Nori?"

"Yeah, the tide is still going out. Should be fine. May be tough pushing her back in the water, though."

"We can deal with that later. Let's bring the boards. Don't want them to disappear," Kaia said.

"Should we go find a doctor today and figure out what's going on with your ear? Is it still ringing?" Nori asked Rye.

"Yes, it's still ringing, but you know my views on doctors."

"Okay, but I think we should get it checked out at some point," Kaia said to Rye with her brow furrowed.

Kaia, Nori, and Rye followed the narrow jungle path that went up the hillside while carrying their surfboards. The path led to a dirt road on the edge of the small town. The town was larger than they had expected as the canopy from the surrounding trees concealed many of the smaller buildings from view along the shoreline. There were several small hotels, a few restaurants, and a grocery store they could now see from their vantage point.

They walked down the road to one of the small restaurants with outdoor seating called the Green Turtle and ordered some water along with several breakfast pastries. The three relaxed and chatted for an hour as Rye made multiple notes in his notebook about the potential implications of surfing on the theories of transcendentalism.

After they finished, Rye led the way back down the jungle path to check on *Bassassin*. But before he could even see the beach, he knew something was different. He quickly realized that there was a consistent roar from the crashing waves. As he emerged on the beach, Rye stopped in his tracks. He could see that the waves were much larger and breaking closer to shore. The wave height was well overhead. The sheer power of the water amazed Rye. He watched a large log get violently tossed from the surf onto the beach and then sucked back out. Rye imagined this would be his likely demise if he stepped foot in this water. Rye looked at Kaia and asked, "What do you think?"

"No way in hell you're going out there," responded Kaia, shaking her head.

"Oh, that's probably advisable. It really is imperative that I complete my book."

Chapter Twenty-Eight

Kaia looked down the beach and saw that *Bassasin* was still safe, grounded well above the breaking surf. "Well, we're not leaving here for a while until that tide comes in and the surf drops. Any ideas?"

Nori answered, "When we walked past the surf shop down the road, I saw a sign about hiking tours to a waterfall. How about a little nature walk?"

Rye and Kaia agreed, and the group walked back into town and then to the surf shop and walked inside. A young local kid was engrossed in repairing a surfboard he had propped up on a table in the middle of the shop.

"Hey, how's it going?" Kaia asked.

"Good, just fixing up a ding in my board," the boy said without looking up.

"I saw the sign out front about the walking tours to the waterfall. You guys doing any today?" Nori asked.

"No, not today. The owner is out, and I'm the only one here. You don't really need a guide. I can tell you how to get there," the boy said, finally looking up.

"Nice," Nori said.

"Just keep heading down the road farther inland," the boy explained. "Take your first right on the next road and head up a few hundred yards, and you'll see a path on your left. There's a little blue sign there that has a picture of a waterfall on it."

"Great, is it pretty cool?" Nori asked.

"It's not bad," the kid responded.

"Cool. Can we leave our boards here while we're gone?" Nori inquired.

"No problem. Just put them around back, and nobody will mess with them."

"Thanks," Nori said as the group departed.

After stashing their boards, Nori led the way down the road to the path that would take them to the waterfall, which they found with no difficulty. The trail had heavy vegetation and mud and sloped down to a stream that they could barely see from the road. It had also grown more humid this far inland from the beach and its sea breeze. The group worked its way down to the edge of the stream. They could see that the trail continued along the edge of the stream in the upstream direction.

"I guess that's the way we go," Kaia said as she took the lead.

The trail was slick and so overgrown with branches and vines that they had to climb down into the stream to get around them on multiple occasions. It was even more difficult to walk in the stream because the rocks were covered with slippery moss.

"How far did the kid say this hike was?" Kaia asked.

"He didn't," Nori answered.

"Ugh," Kaia said.

By the time the three made it about a mile up the stream, they were all tired and overheated. Also, not having expected this level of difficulty, no one had brought water for the trek. As they rounded the next turn of the stream, they saw a family coming back down the trail toward them. The husband, wife, and three girls were all wearing matching khaki shorts and button-down shirts, giving them the appearance of a small paramilitary squad. The girls appeared to be between the ages of four and ten. Rye, Kaia, and Nori watched as the man and woman waded out into the stream to get around a large tree that had fallen across the trail. They looked extremely haggard. The young wife was trudging in waist-deep water and trying not to fall while holding an expensive-looking camera above her head with both hands. The husband was following the wife with the youngest child on his shoulders and likewise was trying to traverse the slippery rocks and not fall over. The two older children had instead stayed on the trail and were trying to maneuver through the branches of the fallen tree that lay across the path.

As Rye got closer, he noticed that the shirts weren't khaki-colored but were originally white. They were just heavily stained with mud. The children also had mud smeared on their faces.

"How was it up there? Do we have much farther to go to get to the waterfall?" Kaia asked as the group approached.

"Don't ask," replied the husband. "It's still a long way up. I don't think you're even halfway there yet."

"How's the waterfall?" asked Nori.

"Damned if I know," continued the husband. "I didn't really even pay attention. By the time I got there, I was already thinking about how we were going to get back in one piece. It just gets more overgrown as you get farther up the trail, and the rocks seem even slipperier up near the top. The heat is ridiculous. At one point, our youngest daughter nearly pushed the oldest off a twenty-foot cliff in frustration. My advice, if you want it, is to turn back."

Kaia, Nori, and Rye looked at the family, looked at each other, nodded, and turned around and walked ahead of the slower-moving family back to the road. They had just emerged from the trail and started heading back to the beach when a man pulled up beside them in a four-door Chevrolet pickup truck. The man appeared to be in his late forties and had wavy dark hair and a thick Fu Manchu mustache straight out of the '70s. The truck was covered with dust but otherwise looked like a new model. As he pulled up, the driver said to the group in an American accent, "Hey, if you guys haven't tried it yet, there's a fantastic bar down the road close to the beach."

"Cool, we went to the Green Turtle earlier today. Is that the place you're talking about?" Nori asked.

"No, it's not far from it, though. You'll like this place more. It's much better. Want a ride?"

The group looked at each other and nodded in approval, at which point Kaia said, "Sure, if you got room for us."

The driver put the vehicle in park and motioned for them to jump in. Kaia went around to the front passenger seat, and Nori and Rye opened the rear driver's side door. When they opened their doors, they immediately noticed that the interior of the truck was not what they expected. Someone had removed the factory seating and replaced it with a loveseat up front and two small wooden stools in the back.

"This is some interior," said Kaia as she climbed in.

The man put the truck back into gear and explained, "I tried to cross a river that was a little too deep and flooded her. I found a mechanic to get her running again, but the seats were waterlogged and moldy, so I just ripped them out. Getting replacement parts for a Chevy down here is damn near impossible. I found this couch and stools at a second-hand store and jammed them in here."

"The couch looks like a nice place to take a nap," Nori commented.

The driver eyed her suspiciously through the rearview mirror, not sure if he was being ridiculed.

"Anyway, the food is good at this place, and it has an excellent outdoor seating area. I think you'll like it," the man continued. "You guys seen the nesting turtles yet?"

"No, that sounds cool," said Nori.

"Yeah, I do some arranged trips down to the beaches where they nest. They're just down south of us. I could set it up for you if you like. You can get in touch with me at the bar I'm taking you to if you decide you want to do the trip. I submarined my truck going to one of those beaches, but the rivers are down now. At least, I think they are."

"That could be fun," said Kaia as she looked back at Nori and discreetly raised one eyebrow.

"Here we are," the man said as they pulled into a small hotel and restaurant. "The bar and patio are just around back," he added as he pointed them in the right direction.

They walked down a small path that led from the parking lot area around the building to the back of the property, where they found a small bar with a half-dozen barstools and a simple concrete patio with a few plastic tables and chairs. There was one group of four people at one of the tables, but the others were open. They sat at a table close to the bar, and a few minutes later, a pleasant young waitress came and gave them menus. Kaia ordered a round of water for everyone and said they needed some time to figure out what they wanted to eat.

"At least we got some surfing in this morning," Kaia said.

"Yes, it was quite exhilarating," Rye agreed.

"Rye, I realize you haven't really been able to connect with any of the people you have been looking for so far on this trip, but maybe there's still hope," Kaia added.

"Perhaps," Rye said, thinking of the additional stops they had made as they island-hopped their way to Puerto Rico.

Most of the people they had encountered since departing the Bahamas who were living on their boats were similar to the two groups that were on the sandbar that evening. They kept running into unsavory and exploitive people that were taking advantage of others, or, alternatively, they were mindless drunkards. Rye actually described the second group in one of his journals as "boozy hyenas."

The people at the other occupied table at the bar appeared to be in their twenties and were speaking in German. There were two men and two women wearing bathing suits and T-shirts. One of these men heard Kaia's comment about surfing and shouted across to them in English with a German accent, "Ah, so you are surfers also. Did you go surfing this afternoon?"

"No, we did the hike from hell instead, but we got in a little surfing this morning," Nori explained.

"We went this afternoon, and it was incredible," said the man. "Come, you must join us and have some drinks. Move your table over."

Kaia and Rye picked up and moved the table while Nori carried the drinks so as not to spill them.

The man introduced himself as Felix and introduced the other man as Max, and the two women as Lena and Hannah.

"Nice to meet you," Nori said. "This is Rye and this is Kaia."

"Hello, nice to meet you," Max said.

"Are you here on vacation?" Nori asked.

"Actually, we are in college together at Heidelberg University but are doing research here in Puerto Rico. We are all Ph.D. candidates in environmental science. We drove down a few days ago from the cloud forest in the mountains to take a break and spend some time on the beach."

"So, how about you? Are you here on holiday?" asked Max.

"Not unlike yourselves, I am also doing some fieldwork," explained Rye.

"Very nice! We are staying here at the hotel. Are you here as well?"

"No, we're traveling by boat," said Kaia.

"Oh, that sounds cool," said the woman named Lena.

"Have you eaten? Let's get some food!" said Max.

"You read my mind. I'm starving," Nori said.

"Great," Max replied. He raised his arm to get the attention of the bartender, who came over to the table quickly. Max and the woman engaged in a fast-paced conversation in Spanish.

"So . . . she says they have a special they are recommending. It's a *casado*. They have a local woman who makes it for them."

"What's a *casado*?" asked Nori.

"It's a blend of a bunch of things they put together on a plate," Felix explained. "It's made with black beans, rice, and vegetables, served with tortillas and either fish or chicken. She said they have fish today. It is a very authentic dish."

"Sounds great," said Nori.

"Does everyone want to try it?" Felix asked, to which everyone responded affirmatively.

While waiting for the food to arrive, Rye noticed that the guy who had dropped them off in the truck earlier was behind the bar mixing drinks.

"The man working the bar actually gave us a ride here and recommended this place, but he didn't mention that he worked here," Rye commented.

Felix laughed and responded, "Yes, not surprising. He owns the place. Sounds like he was drumming up some business."

"So, how is the hotel?" Kaia asked.

"It's okay," Lena said. "It is not very fancy, but it was cheap, and we have been having a good time. We have done a little surfing, some sunbathing, and some drinking."

"Doesn't sound bad at all," Kaia said.

"So, tell me about your research. Perhaps we can trade some notes," Rye suggested to the group of German students.

"We are doing research farther inland on the east side of the island in the Yunque National Forest," Lena said.

"You said it's a cloud forest?" asked Nori. "What's that like?"

"It's incredible!" Lena said. "There's a thick cloud cover there that just hangs in the air. It's like you are constantly walking through a mystical fog in this beautiful foliage with ancient trees."

"Walking through a haze. That sounds like us back on our last night in Exuma, right Kaia?"

"Yep," Kaia answered, laughing.

"We have had some of those nights here as well since our arrival," Lena said.

"So, exactly what are you studying?" Rye asked.

"We are looking for a mycorrhizal fungi network within the large canopy trees in the forest," Lena explained.

"A network of fungus? Is that bad for the trees?" Nori asked.

"No, the exact opposite," Lena continued. "You see, there is a complex network of these fungi living underground, and this network lives in a symbiotic relationship with trees through their root systems. These mycorrhizal networks can facilitate signals or communications between trees. We are investigating this system in some of the largest and oldest trees in the cloud forest. Some of these trees are more than a thousand years old."

"Wow, so you mean the trees can talk to each other?" asked Nori.

"In a sense, yes," said Lena. "They use chemicals and electrical signals to communicate with each other through the fungi. This underground communication network looks very similar to neural networks in humans and other animals."

"So, what do trees talk about? I'd love to hear what small talk is like between trees—probably mostly talk about the weather," Nori joked.

"Actually, I think that *is* a topic of conversation. We believe they communicate about weather conditions like droughts as well as soil conditions and bug infestations. Things of that nature," Lena explained.

"You know, ecosystems are complex," Max added. "There is a great deal of competition out there, but there is a lot of mutual support as well. Because trees and other plants that exist in a finite area are competing for a limited amount of water and sunlight, you would think that nature would have them just looking out for themselves, but that's not always the case. Not only do trees use these underground fungal networks just to signal each other, but they will also sometimes use them to help each other. They will send nutrients through the networks to other trees that are struggling and more in need. There is interdependence between the trees in the system."

"That's really cool," said Nori.

"Yes, it is. Sometimes, the larger and more established trees will help the saplings that are trying to get established. Studies have shown that some trees can determine if a nearby sapling came from one of their own seeds and that they share more with their own progeny," Max continued.

"A bit of plant nepotism," Rye interjected.

"Yes, this is true," Max said. "But it's interesting—a tree does not limit itself to helping others from the same species either. It's not just the old helping the young, either. We have also observed young, healthy trees providing nutrients to old, weaker trees."

"Has anyone given any consideration as to *why* they might do this?" Rye asked.

"There may be no way to know," said Max. "Maybe it somehow helps them survive by having other healthy trees around them, or maybe they just like having company."

From reading Rye's notes, it was clear he was very excited about the conversation. He had stumbled across a group of young, educated people who were studying the environment. In a way, Rye saw them as peers studying closely related subject matter. After all, to live in accordance with nature, you obviously had to preserve nature. Of course, he felt his work was more important.

"Would you like to hear about my field study?" he finally asked.

"Yes, of course," Max said.

"I am on a quest to live in accordance with nature," Rye explained to his new group of friends.

"What does this mean?" Max asked, a little confused.

"I think it is obvious. But to explain further, I am emulating the life of Diogenes."

Felix, who was sitting across the table and was apparently familiar with the ancient philosopher, burst out with a laugh, spitting out a mouthful of his drink. "You mean that crazy old loon who lived in a barrel?"

Rye was caught off guard. "He was neither crazy nor a loon. He was one of the ancient Cynics," Rye corrected.

"Oh, I know who he was!" Felix said. "He was this idiot who walked around the market in Athens in broad daylight with a lantern, looking for an honest man," Felix explained to the group.

Hearing this, Kaia was glad she had convinced Rye to leave his flashlight on the *Miss Elizabeth*.

"He was trying to get people's attention!" Rye said a little louder than he had intended.

"He was a clown!" Felix shot back. "Living on the streets like a dog! Nothing more than a troll! If you're going to live your life like the ancient Greeks, at least pick a school that makes some sense. Or pick the Epicureans. At least those guys knew how to enjoy life! But Diogenes? He was just a gadfly buzzing around and bothering people."

"That's not all bad, you know. Socrates called himself a gadfly as well."

"You can't seriously be comparing Diogenes to Socrates," Felix scoffed.

"Oh, they're more similar than you might think, young man. They are just flies with different wings. Socrates was a bit of an elitist, you know. He was happy hobnobbing with the highfliers up in the clouds. Diogenes was happier buzzing around at ground level where he could poke, prod and occasionally bite," Rye argued.

"Living like a dog on the street—give me a break," Felix said. "If you really want to understand how best to live your life, you need to jump forward a couple of thousand years. Look at people like Nietzsche!"

"Who?" Rye asked.

"Nietzsche!"

"Who?" Rye repeated.

"Friedrich Fucking Nietzsche!"

"Oh, him! Don't be ridiculous! God is dead, and we have killed him. Blah, blah, blah! What a downer!" Rye said.

"You understand Nietzsche thought that this was a statement of freedom so that man could focus on more important aspects and embrace our collective potential," Felix said.

"By Sirius, I was teaching Nietzsche before your brain was purged of all original thought by the indoctrination of your elementary school teachers. Nietzsche wanted us all to embrace music and art and the creations of man," Rye said. "Well, let me ask you this. Have you ever seen a dog get overexcited about an impressionist painting or a classical symphony? I can answer that question with some confidence: no. Indeed, they tend to be much more stimulated by eating, drinking, and chasing the occasional plaything! I can tell you what you can do with your Nietzsche!"

Wanting to settle things down, Kaia interjected, "So, what's the surf forecast like tomorrow?"

"Much like today," Max quickly responded, also wanting to change the subject.

The group continued to chat about the weather and some other good surf spots farther down the coast for some time while both Rye and Felix sat stewing.

Noticing this, Nori said to Kaia and Rye, "How about we get out of here and go check on the tender?"

Rye jumped at the opportunity and, together with Kaia and Nori, said their farewells and left the restaurant to check on *Bassassin*. The boat was fine, but Kaia and Nori thought it would not be wise to attempt traversing the breakers as it was getting dark.

"Rye, maybe we should just grab a room this evening at the hotel we just left. We can surf in the morning and then head back to the boat afterward," Kaia suggested.

"Perhaps we could sleep in the jungle," Rye said.

"Are you crazy? There's stuff that lives in the jungle," Nori said.

"That's the point," said Rye. "If we're lucky, it might rain as well. After all, the Cynic philosophers believed that disciplining oneself to endure hardships, such as exposure to elements, was a foundational principle of living in accordance with nature."

"Rye, to be clear, I am not sleeping in the jungle tonight," Nori replied.

"Oh, fine. I'm certain we could survive, but if you insist," Rye said. "That being said, it is probably best that you keep me away from that Felix character. I could end up bashing him with my flip-flop."

The three walked back to the hotel and into the front entrance to avoid running into the German students in the bar area. A young Puerto Rican woman working at the front desk told them there was a room open with two queen beds.

"That works, I think. Rye, you can take one, and Nori and I can use the other," said Kaia.

The woman at the desk explained in clear English that it was a small cabana separate from the main hotel building and that there was a footpath through a side door that would take them to the hut. She then called into the little room behind the desk from which a tall, stocky man emerged.

"He is our security, and he will walk you back to the cabana," the woman explained.

The large man smiled back at them and nodded. Rye estimated that the man was nearly six and a half feet tall and over two hundred and fifty pounds. The man was clean-shaven and neatly dressed in long dark pants and a button-down, short-sleeved white shirt. The woman spoke to him quickly in Spanish, and the man nodded and motioned for the trio to follow him.

The security guard led them down a narrow dirt path that was dimly lit by a few tiki torches. As they approached the end of the path, they saw a concrete, cylindrical structure that was painted white and had a thatched roof. The man escorted them inside and showed them the room. There were two queen beds, each accompanied by bedside stands and a small kitchenette area consisting of a countertop with a couple of rough, unfinished cabinets above and below. There was also a small bathroom. A few paintings were strategically placed on the walls—one of a beach and another of a jungle scene, with an exotic bird sitting on a branch. There was also a decorative spear mounted to the wall. Feathers hung from the shaft of the bamboo spear, and just below it hung a decorative headdress made of feathers.

Kaia gave the security guard a thumbs up, showing she approved of the room, and the man left with a smile. Everyone in the group was tired from the long day and turned in to get some sleep.

"Goodnight," Rye said to his companions across the room.

"Goodnight, Rye," answered Kaia. "Goodnight, *mijn lief,*" she added, turning to Nori.

"Goodnight, Rye," Nori said. "And goodnight, *mpenzi wangu,*" she continued as she turned to her companion.

Kaia looked stumped and said, "Okay, you got me."

"Swahili," Noir said, smiling.

"Of course. Nice," Kaia said with a laugh.

Rye lay in his bed and lamented his various interactions on the trip so far and his repeated disappointments. The aloof and drunken boat people had no interest in any serious dialogue. The nice Bahamian man at the party thought Rye was addled, and then there was that damn Felix. Maybe the entire trip was a mistake. Still, he enjoyed surfing. Perhaps there was still more to living *in* nature that deserved exploration, he decided in the end. He eventually fell asleep but tossed and turned much of the night.

By the time the morning light had crept into the room, Rye couldn't sleep any longer. He sat up slowly and looked around and saw Kaia sleeping in the bed next to him, but Nori was nowhere to be found. As he scanned further, he spotted her asleep, sitting up and leaning with her back against the wall opposite the front door. Her head was leaning forward awkwardly, and Rye noticed she was wearing the feathered headdress that had been on the wall, and the bamboo spear was lying across her lap.

Still feeling groggy, Rye laid back down and continued to ponder his trip. He was reluctant to abandon his journey, but he also had to acknowledge that he had made little progress with his book. He had filled up several notebooks with notes of the trip but failed to find anyone who understood his quest, let alone anyone living the way Rye thought they should. Also, despite his best efforts to live in accordance with nature and minimize his possessions, he found that travel was much more expensive than he expected. The *Miss Elizabeth* was about out of fuel, and he was running low on cash. He could always look at transferring some of his remaining savings, but he really didn't want to do that. Diogenes didn't have a savings account, Rye reminded himself.

Across the room, Nori stirred and opened her eyes. She looked at Rye, stretched, and said, "Good morning."

Kaia then sat up as well. She looked over at Nori and said with a full-throated laugh, "What in the hell are you wearing?"

"Oh yeah, shit," said Nori, smiling. "There was something outside last night that was crazy loud. It scared the hell out of me. I didn't want to wake either of you up, but I was totally freaking out, so I used my pocket knife to take the screws out of the brackets holding up the spear. Then, I was like, what the hell, may as well go all in and wear the headdress, too. Next thing I know, I'm asleep on the floor."

"Quite fashionable," Kaia noted.

"Thanks," Nori replied. "What do you think I heard?"

"I don't know. Maybe you were dreaming," Kaia said.

"Nope. I was awake."

"I don't think they have any large animals here. You better put that spear back up on the wall so we don't end up paying for it. Besides, you really think that piece of bamboo would do anything?"

"Damn right," said Nori, jumping to her feet and thrusting the spear into the air several times.

The group gathered their few belongings. Nori re-hung the spear and headdress, and the three headed to the lobby area to find a different young woman now working the front desk.

"How was your stay?" she asked.

"Great," said Nori, "but I heard something really loud and scary last night. It was eerie. Do you know what that was?"

"It was probably the coqui. There are many around here," the woman explained.

"Are they dangerous?" Nori asked.

"No, of course not. The coqui is a tree frog that is very well known here. They make a unique sound, like a whistle, that sounds like *CO-KEE*. They are very loud but also very cute."

Kaia suddenly laughed. "Glad we had you there to protect us last night!"

The three swung back by the surf shop and grabbed their boards and then proceeded down to the beach to find their boat still safely located where they had left it. With the tide coming in, the gentle waves had returned. The group surfed for an hour and a half before they headed back to the *Miss Elizabeth* for some food. They had no problem relaunching the tender.

Kaia drove *Bassassin* out over the breakers, strategically nudging the gas when necessary to give the boat an extra boost to top the small waves. When they returned to the *Miss Elizabeth*, they initially could not find Stems, but they ultimately found him dozing shirtless in the sun in a recliner he had apparently dragged to the front deck. There were multiple empty beer cans scattered around him, and Rye wasn't sure if they were from the night before or from the morning.

"Nice to see you guys. I was thinking about sending a search party soon," said Stems, opening his eyes as the group approached.

"We spent the night instead of trying to come back out through some big surf," explained Kaia.

Stems stretched and yawned. "I figured. So how was the surfing?"

"It was good," said Nori. "You should have come with us."

"Thanks, but it's not really my thing," Stems explained.

Once the ladies went below to change, Stems asked Rye, "How's the book coming?"

"It's slow, Samuel. As things have turned out, this trip has been a bit more difficult than I expected."

"I know what you mean, Doc. I've always been one of those guys who likes to work hard and play hard. When I was out working on the boats, I'd go nonstop. Hell, even when I was just cutting grass, I'd get up a little late and smoke some weed during the day, but I still worked hard in the afternoon and didn't really start partying until the evenings. Problem is that out here right now, I just don't have much to do besides drink and smoke. I've been startin' a little earlier each day. Maybe it ain't the best thing for me long-term."

"Yes, the situation appears to be less than optimal," Rye said. "Give me some time to think things over. I would like to surf a few more days, and then we can make some decisions together. Perhaps we could go fishing this afternoon in the tender."

"That sounds good, Doc. It'd probably do me some good. Kaia and Nori going?"

"I'll ask."

"Tell ya what. Go check with them, and if they're down, you guys make us some sandwiches and I'll throw some drinks in a cooler and get the rods and tackle together. We can work our way offshore and do a little trolling."

Rye went below and found Kaia and Nori and asked if they would like to go fishing, and they agreed to do so. They then headed to the galley and made four sandwiches and grabbed some chips. Rye also noticed that the provisions were getting low. They all headed topside to find Stems.

Stems took the sandwiches from Rye and put them in a large cooler on the deck next to the fishing gear. The group then loaded everything and headed out for a day of fishing.

The sky had become a little overcast, and a light breeze was blowing. Stems asked Kaia to run the boat and told her to just head offshore at a fast idle while he started rigging the rods.

"I'll rig up three lines for you guys, and then I'll run the boat," Stems said as he pulled some lures out of a tackle box. Once he finished the rigging, he took the helm from Kaia and continued the course, heading offshore. He then dragged the heavy cooler closer to him and rifled through the ice to find a cold beer.

"Maybe get a nice dolphin today," Stems said as he scanned the horizon.

The waves had come up just a little, resulting in gentle-rolling two-foot seas. However, even this made the bass boat ride bumpy as it wasn't designed for offshore use. Stems continued to point the boat offshore but dropped the idle speed slightly to compensate for the larger waves.

"Anyone else want something to drink?" Stems asked as he finished his beer and reached into the cooler for another.

"How about water?" Kaia asked.

"I don't think I packed any of those," Stems said.

Rye sat quietly, thinking about Stems. He hadn't previously considered the fact that this trip might not be the best thing for his childhood friend. It was becoming clear to Rye that something needed to change. His thoughts then drifted back to the last class he had taught before he departed on the trip.

Noticing his silence, Nori asked, "What are you thinking about, Rye?"

"I was thinking about an exercise I was doing in my last class and something I was trying to convey to my students."

"What was the exercise?" Nori asked.

"In short, I was attempting to explain the perils of modern society. To do this, I offered them a choice of two alternative career paths."

"Okay, I'm intrigued. Tell me about them," Nori said.

"Certainly," Rye answered. "If the students took the first path, they would have a job that they loved. They would wake up every morning excited to go to work, and their job would be engaging and fulfilling. They would always have enough money for food and necessities, and they would make enough money to buy a modest but functional car and home. However, they would never become rich, and they would work until they died. If they took the second path instead, they would hate their job. They would dread going to work every day. It would not be interesting or fulfilling. They also had to agree to do this job for twenty years. However, if they took this path, they would make a tremendous amount of money. They could buy an enormous house and many expensive cars. At the end of the twenty years, they could then quit and travel and do whatever they wished. Do you know what most everyone picked?"

"Probably the money," said Kaia.

"That's correct," Rye said. "I had done this exercise in a few previous classes, and each time, eighty to ninety percent chose the money. I would then inquire further about why they would make this choice to demonstrate that they wanted these things so that others would know that they were successful. In other words, many of them were drawn to the money so that they could buy things to impress others."

"That's not surprising. Nori and I have talked about the pressure to buy stuff. That's not really their fault. It's what they've all been taught," Kaia responded.

"That's a fair point, but there is something else that bothered me about the last few times I did this exercise. I was getting more students who rejected these scenarios and demanded a third one where they have an enjoyable and fulfilling job where they also receive large financial compensation for their work."

"And that's a bad thing?" asked Kaia.

"I feel there is a certain amount of entitlement that is reflected in that belief."

"I don't know, Rye. I agree with the students on this one. Why settle?" asked Nori.

"My premise is that it's not always so easy to find that," Rye responded.

"You may be right, Rye, but you need to look at things from their point of view," Kaia countered. "I mean, Nori and I both had scholarships in college, so we didn't have any debt, but a lot of our friends had huge student loans and when we came out of school, the job market was crap. Students are going into debt to go to college because they want a better life, and they've been told that this is the way to get there. But as they get to the end of their college experience, they're finding that many of the jobs out there just suck. The reality is many of our friends didn't get the choices you described. Instead, they got the crappy job that didn't pay well, and they had to take it to make loan payments."

"I get your point, Kaia," Rye said. "It seems to me that many people are picking money over quality of life just to impress others."

"Actually, I think many of our friends in college wanted even more than what you are describing," Nori said. "The real prize—the trifecta—is a job where you make good money, have interesting work, and make a difference in the world," Nori explained. "I mean, I can see how some of your students didn't like how you framed the question. In the end, Kaia and I made our choices, but many of our friends didn't have that option. I just think there may be a generational divide here, but the younger generations don't really get a fair shake. Shit, I mean, it wasn't our generation that raised their kids, telling them they can have it all. We were the ones sold a bill of goods who had to adapt to reality quickly. Ever notice how our society is quick to congratulate parents when their kids do good things, like graduate from college? They say this because they think the parents had something to do with it, right? It's like your kids did well because you raised them right and gave them good advice. On the other hand, society isn't so quick to place responsibility on parents for giving bad advice. Instead, it's like, 'You guys just got to suck it up. No one ever said it was going to be easy.' Despite the rosy picture told to them growing up, a lot of our friends found that there was just a crock of shit at the end of their rainbow."

"We've had this discussion with a bunch of our friends stuck in jobs they don't like and can't quit," added Kaia. "They know it will take them years to just get out of the hole, and then what? Some of them are really struggling. They're trying to figure out if they're going to be stuck in some job they don't like for the next fifty years."

"Hell, that's just life," Stems interjected. "I ain't got no college education and taken plenty of jobs I didn't like. I took 'em 'cause I needed the money. Stayed with 'em as long as I had to until I found something better, then I switched. I like what I do now and will probably keep doing it until I can't anymore. I'll probably work the rest of my life."

"I get what you're saying, Stems. It's just that some of our friends are stuck with a lot of debt and feel they need to stay with a job they don't like so they can just keep making payments," Kaia said.

"Yeah, well, that's pretty much been my life. Always had debt to pay off and making it paycheck to paycheck. Didn't stop me from leaving jobs and finding new ones. Ain't no free ride in this life," Stems said.

"Fair, fair," said Kaia. "But just think how you'd feel if you had gone to college for four years and spent a lot of money and still found yourself no better off? Maybe even worse because of $100K of debt."

"Reckon that would suck alright," said Stems.

"You have all certainly given me something to think about," Rye conceded.

Stems steered the tender offshore a couple of miles and then ran parallel to the coast. The wind was picking up more, and the seas were continuing to build. The waves were now around three feet, but they were still gentle rollers, so the group could no longer see the shoreline when the boat was in the troughs of some of the larger waves. There were also more gray clouds showing up on the horizon.

"Getting a little rougher out here," commented Kaia.

"Yep, probably should head back in soon," said Stems.

Suddenly, there was a strike on Kaia's line. She yanked the pole up to set the hook and started reeling it in. The fish put up a fight, and it took around five minutes for Kaia to work a sleek-looking fish around three feet in length to the edge of the boat.

"Nice. Wahoo!" yelled Stems. "Don't have a gaff. Bring her up alongside, and I'll grab the line and pull it into the boat." Stems took off his shirt and wrapped it around his hand, and then when the fish was close, he grabbed the line and quickly pulled the fish up into the boat.

"We'll stake this guy and grill him tonight," Stems said as he worked to get the hook loose.

"Nice!" said Kaia.

Stems was still working to remove the lure from the fish's mouth as Rye moved closer to inspect the operation. "Want to put your finger in there?" Stems asked, holding the fish out so that the mouth pointed in his direction.

"Is it safe?" Rye asked.

"Nope," said Stems with a laugh. "He'll take a finger off if you let him. I know a guy who was fishin' off Florida. One of these suckers was chasing a smaller fish that the guy was reeling in, and the wahoo jumped right into the boat and bit the guy in the neck. Latched right onto him."

"Damn, that's crazy," said Nori. "Did it let go?"

"No, he's still attached to him to this day," Stems said, smiling and using a pair of pliers to get the lure free.

"Okay, ha, I get it. I mean, did it let go on its own, or did they have to remove it?" asked Nori.

"I think it just let loose, but he ended up with like forty stitches." Stems looked around and noticed the seas were still building. "Thinkin' we should head back. It's starting to get a little big."

"Sounds good," said Kaia.

Stems turned the boat in the direction of the shoreline where the *Miss Elizabeth* sat waiting for them. The wind was blowing offshore now and heading in, which meant that Stems needed to steer directly into the waves, which resulted in a rougher ride. Still, the boat was making slow but steady progress. Rye was sitting in the front and suddenly spotted something in the waves floating ahead of them. "Slow down for a minute, Samuel!" he shouted back.

Stems backed off the throttle and asked, "What's up?"

"There's something up ahead in the water. Run up on it slowly so I can see what it is."

"Will do, Doc."

Rye had the best vantage point from the front of the boat as they approached the object, and he shouted, "By Sirius! Quick Kaia, give me that boat hook back there!"

"What the hell is that?" Kaia said as she retrieved the boat hook and handed it to Rye.

Rye twisted the telescoping handle to the boat hook and extended it out to its maximum length. He reached for the object as they approached.

"What you got there, Doc?" Stems asked, standing up.

"It's bananas!" Rye yelled excitedly. "It looks like it's an entire stalk. They must have fallen off a tree into the water or maybe off a boat. There must be over a hundred of them here!" Rye hooked onto the bunch and attempted to land them in the boat.

"Hell no, Doc!" Stems shouted back frantically. "I told you bananas on a boat are bad luck! Don't bring those damn things on here!"

"It's fine, Samuel. I've considered your objections and decided that they are just superstition. There are enough bananas here to last me a month!" Rye shouted back.

"I'm tellin' you, Doc, keep them off . . . ."

As Rye hoisted up the bananas over the side gunnel of *Bassassin*, the expandable boat hook suddenly separated at the center joint. The bananas fell back into the water, and Rye lost his footing.

He stumbled backward, tripped over the middle seat, and flew into Stems. This, in turn, knocked Stems off his feet. The outboard engine at the rear of the boat was the only thing that prevented Stems from going into the water.

Stems and Rye both sat up, and Stems looked angry. "I told you those damn things were bad luck!" he shouted at Rye.

"I'm sorry, Samuel. Are you okay?" Rye asked.

"I think so. My back is gonna be a little sore, but I'll make it. Let's get the hell back in before this storm gets bad. Those clouds are looking mean."

Rye moved back to the front of the boat, and Stems sat back down at the helm, put the engine back in gear, and attempted to steer the boat back to shore.

"Damn it!" Stems yelled as he slammed the shifter back into neutral.

"Problem?" asked Kaia.

Stems stepped back to look at the engine and responded, "The steering is jammed up."

On closer inspection, Stems observed that he bent the hydraulic steering shaft at the rear of the boat when he fell into the engine. He went back to the helm and tried to turn the wheel again, but it was firmly stuck.

"What's the deal?" asked Nori.

"The hydraulics are jammed up," Stems said, rubbing his chin.

"Damn. Can you fix it?" Nori inquired.

"Hard to do with no tools out here."

"Can we limp home?" asked Kaia.

"Don't know. Let's try," Stems said. He put the boat back in gear and gave it a little throttle. He cranked hard on the steering wheel, putting his weight into it, but it still wouldn't budge. The engine was slightly turned to one side so that the boat was traveling in a large clockwise circle. The seas were continuing to build, and the sky was growing darker. Stems put the boat in neutral again.

"Any ideas?" he asked.

"Can you disconnect the hydraulic steering so we can turn the engine by hand?" asked Kaia.

"Not without some tools. She's bolted into the transom there. Besides, that engine is heavy as hell. I don't think we can turn it by hand," Stems explained.

Looking around, Nori asked, "Should we call someone for help?"

"We ain't got no radio, and my cell phone ain't got no service this far out," Stems said, looking at his phone. "Besides, even if we could call someone and they come looking for us, we're getting blown offshore right now and they might have a hard time spotting us. Next stop could be Spain, maybe."

"Anyone else have any ideas?" Kaia asked.

Everyone was silent.

Finally, Stems said, "Hold on a minute."

He climbed past everyone and made his way up to the front of the boat and lowered down the small trolling motor mounted on the starboard side of the bow. This small motor was designed to gently and quietly maneuver the bass boat for short distances in calm lake waters. It certainly didn't have enough power to transport the group back to the *Miss Elizabeth*, but Stems had another idea. He worked his way back to the driver's seat and put the large outboard at the rear of the boat back into gear. The boat began to move forward but again started its gradual clockwise turn. But this time, Stems used the foot control pedals mounted below the console to start the trolling motor. He pointed the small electric motor away from the boat at a ninety-degree angle. By doing this, he was able to offset the boat's tendency to turn clockwise and was able to control their direction. He basically created an improvised bow thruster.

Even though the trolling motor was periodically popping out of the water from the wave action, its thrust was still strong enough to work. If he needed to go left, he pushed harder on his foot pedal and gave more throttle to the trolling motor. If he needed to go right, he would just let off the throttle and the boat would come back around by itself.

Once he decided he had control of the boat, Stems said, "My momma didn't raise no dummy."

"Way to go, Stems," Nori said. "Maybe we'll survive today after all."

"You damn right," Stems replied. "Doc, stay up on the bow and keep some weight up there to help keep that trolling motor in the water, and don't be looking for any more damn stray fruit!"

With Stems steering in this manner, the small boat slowly plowed back through the waves toward the *Miss Elizabeth*. A couple of the larger waves broke over the bow, and Stems asked Nori to empty the cooler and use it to bail some of the water out as they traveled. At one point, there was a solid six inches of water in the bottom of the bass boat, sloshing around with a dozen unopened cans of beer that Nori had emptied from the cooler.

"Make sure you don't bail out none of them full beers!" Stems shouted to Nori as he drove. He then scooped one up out of the water and popped it open.

Rye was still riding up front and was becoming seasick. Still, he started to smile. Even as the weather continued to grow more perilous, his mood only improved. By the time the large droplets of water from the squall began to fall and Rye's nausea had increased to the point of him vomiting over the side of the boat, he was ecstatic.

"You okay, Rye?" Kaia asked, seeing him wipe his mouth off with his forearm.

"Yes! This is it!" Rye yelled back with a manic grin.

"This is what?" Kaia asked.

"The sublime!"

Chapter Twenty-Nine

It was nearly 5 p.m. and I was packing up and getting ready to leave the office for the day when my legal assistant buzzed me and told me that North Peterson was on the line. North was a well-regarded local attorney who primarily practiced transactional work and commercial real estate. Although we hadn't spoken in the last few months, we had always enjoyed a good working relationship.

I picked up the phone and asked North how he'd been.

"Great, thanks," he answered.

"What have you been up to?"

"As little as possible," North replied.

"You and me both. So, what can I do for you?"

"I thought I should give you a heads-up. Consider it a professional courtesy. I closed a small shopping center loan today, and afterward, I ran up to record the deed at the Yorktown clerk's office myself. Really, I was just looking for an excuse to get out of the *orifice* and take a break. I walk in and guess who's there?"

"I have no idea."

"Ernie Harker. He's up at the window talking to a clerk, and I can't help but overhear the conversation because I'm waiting behind him to record my deed. Ernie had apparently just filed some kind of motion and was asking for a hearing on an emergency injunction. He was being pushy—you know how he is—and tells the clerk he wants it heard tomorrow morning."

I felt my chest tighten and told North that I thought I knew where this conversation was going.

"I figured as much. The clerk asked if there was an attorney on the other side who needed to be given notice of the hearing. Ernie mentioned your name but tried to brush it off and said notice wasn't necessary because it was an emergency. Judge Burwell is sitting as a substitute tomorrow. You know how he always gets in early in the morning so he can see what's scheduled for the day and review the pleadings? The clerk agreed to set the hearing for 8:00 a.m.—an hour before the court is normally open. I could tell the clerk was a little uneasy about it, so I figured I'd give you a call," North explained.

I told North I appreciated it and that I owed him one.

"Not a problem. I know you'd do the same for me. It's kind of funny. When Ernie walked out, he went right past me, and I don't think he even recognized who I was. Hell, I've probably dealt with him in a dozen deals over the years. In the last matter I handled, I was negotiating a purchase contract with a junior associate with his firm, and she was doing a good job working through all the issues on the deal. Ernie got involved at the last minute and almost blew the whole thing up. We were able to salvage it, but it took a lot of work to get the clients settled back down. He's exceptional at seagull management, you know."

"What's that?" I asked.

"That's when a person gets involved with something complex late in the game. They swoop in, shit all over everything, then fly back out, leaving everybody else there to clean up the mess. Watch out for him, Jackson. He'll pee on your leg and try to convince you it's raining."

"Thanks again, North."

The following morning at 7:45 a.m., I arrived at the Yorktown Circuit Court building. There was only one deputy sheriff working in the front lobby as the courthouse didn't officially open until 9 a.m. The officer recognized me and opened a roped-off second entry point with a sign that read "Security Only" and waved me through, allowing me to bypass the metal detector.

"Good morning, Mr. Forelle."

"Good morning, John. What's going on?" I asked.

"Just counting down my time to retirement."

"How long have you got now?"

"I'll finish in about two years. I'll have put in a full thirty."

"What are you going to do then?"

"Something different, but I'm not sure what. I can't sit around the house all day. My wife would divorce me. Too much time together can be a problem. I'll probably take some low-stress job at a store or something. If anybody pisses me off too much, I can just quit and find something else to do. You must be here for the early hearing?"

"You got it. Judge Burwell's the only one I know who'll schedule hearings this early in the morning. The other lawyer on the case set this one up at the last minute," I explained.

"Oh, that must be Mr. Harker," the deputy said. "He came in a bit earlier. I think he's in the courtroom already. That guy's never friendly when he comes in, so I always make him go through the metal detector and check his bag. It never fails to piss him off," he added with a grin.

I smiled back and told him that I better get moving. "We're scheduled to start soon, and I don't want to be late."

"Have a good day, Mr. Forelle."

"You too, John."

I scanned the familiar lobby as I headed to the courtroom where our hearing was scheduled. I had spent a lot of days in this room, hanging out with police officers and other lawyers as we waited for our cases to get called. There was a large bronze Lady Justice in the dark back corner of the lobby where she stood resolutely, holding her sword and scales. A few years earlier, the installation of the titillating, bare-breasted statue in the conservative community had stirred up some controversy. After a local paper ran an article criticizing the exuberant cost for the metal maiden, the resident judge directed his staff to slide her back into a less conspicuous area of the lobby where she still stands today.

The lobby also had a plaque on one wall dedicated to a former clerk of the court who had taken all the town's land records from the courthouse and hidden them in an icehouse during the Civil War siege and subsequent occupation of the town by the Union Army. These records memorialized who owned what. All those who owned land in Yorktown were quite relieved the records were later returned. Still, the old clerk had to go into hiding because of threats to his life by some of those who didn't own any land. As they saw it, the clerk's actions had dashed their hopes of making any quick claims to vacant properties. You can't make everybody happy.

While the Union Army was in control of Yorktown, some brilliant young officer decided it would be a great idea to use the courthouse to store the troop's stock of gunpowder. Of course, the building exploded shortly thereafter. The courthouse was leveled, and the explosion also damaged the adjacent jail. The elation of the escaped prisoners was crushed when they realized that the blast also destroyed the nearby tavern, which was the only place to get a drink for miles around. By one account, a handful of the dejected escapees were so distraught by their inability to imbibe that they just walked back in through the gaping hole in the side of the jail and sat down with one of them muttering, "What's the point?"

As a side note, the Civil War was more of a skirmish in Yorktown, with the earlier Revolutionary War being the little village's main claim to fame. Historic Yorktown happens to be the location where Lord Cornwallis was forced to surrender to General

Washington, and the new courthouse is prominently located near the historical Revolutionary War and Civil War battlefields. A golf course was built over the battlefields in the 1920s for a private country club. There were plans to build a large hotel at the sites of past carnage, but the Great Depression caused the enterprise to go bust and the National Park Service acquired the land and rebuilt the redoubts as a plan B.

Across the room in the lobby of the courthouse opposite the portrait of the clerk, there was a shadow box that contained an old hatchet with a rusty head. A small brass plate with an inscription that hung below the hatchet explained that the hatchet was used to cut the rope for the first legal hanging in Yorktown in 1880.

Before I walked into the courtroom, I made a quick stop in the clerk's office and got a copy of what Ernie had filed the day before and almost laughed at the audacity of it. As I pushed open the two large wooden doors to the courtroom, I immediately spotted Ernie Harker sitting up front at one of the two counsel tables. There was also a court reporter near the judge's desk who was in the process of setting up her stenographic equipment and another tired-looking deputy sheriff leaning up against the jury box, staring into space.

Ernie heard the doors creak open as I came in, and as he turned around, he did a double-take.

"Oh, good morning, Jackson," Ernie mustered.

Before I could answer, the rear door of the courtroom opened and the judge emerged. We both stood up, as did the court reporter. The sleepy deputy popped to life and recited in a clear, audible, and practiced tone, "Oyez! Oyez! Oyez! All persons having business before this honorable court and the circuit court judge for the town of Yorktown, Virginia, are admonished to draw near and give their attention, for the Court is now in session. God save this Commonwealth and this honorable court."

Virginia had a mandatory retirement age of seventy for judges, but that didn't apply to substitute judges like Judge Burwell, who recently turned ninety. I had been before Judge Burwell a handful of times and knew that he wanted the lawyers in his courtroom to get to the point quickly. I figured that at his age, he had decided he didn't have that much time left to waste.

"Good morning, Counsel," the judge said as he sat down at his bench. "Please take your seats, gentlemen."

Once everyone was seated, the judge opened the file that he had carried out from chambers and said, "I have reviewed the pleadings and have some questions. Mr. Harker, you're representing the plaintiff in this action, correct?"

"That's correct, Your Honor," Ernie Harker said.

"Mr. Forelle, then I assume you are here for the defendant, Rye Smyth. Is that correct?"

"Yes, that is correct, Your Honor."

"Mr. Harker, it's your motion, so you go first."

I interrupted Ernie Harker as soon as he started to speak. "Your Honor, I would like to address a procedural matter first."

"That's fine," responded the judge. "What's on your mind?"

"The notice of this hearing. Or more accurately, the *lack* of notice of this hearing."

"I'm listening," the judge responded, glancing for a second at Ernie Harker, who immediately looked down and shuffled a few papers on his table.

"Mr. Harker filed a motion yesterday for this preliminary injunction and failed to give me fair notice of it," I explained to the judge. "It was just by happenstance that I heard about it and made it here this morning."

The judge turned to Ernie Harker. "Mr. Harker, is that correct? I had assumed you cleared this date with Mr. Forelle before you requested the hearing."

Ernie stood back up and buttoned his suit jacket. "Well, Your Honor, it's an emergency hearing. I wanted to get it before the court as quickly as possible, and I didn't know if Mr. Forelle would be available."

"Apparently, he is available. After all, he is here."

"Yes, that's correct, Your Honor. I see that now," Ernie said.

"Did you know he was representing Mr. Smyth?" the judge asked Ernie.

"Well . . . yes, he had filed an answer to the underlying suit, but—"

"In that case, you certainly knew you were required to give him notice of this hearing. I'm inclined to continue this until a later date if Mr. Forelle wishes me to do so."

"Your Honor, just so that you are aware, technically . . . on a preliminary injunction like this . . . the court can enter an order without notice to the other side under extenuating circumstances. I didn't really do anything improper . . . ."

"Mr. Harker, that's not going to fly with me," the judge said. "Yes, there are cases where that may be appropriate, such as when there is an emergency and you cannot get in touch with the other party and there is some immediate risk that requires quick action. But here, you clearly knew that Mr. Forelle was representing the defendant, and you could have easily given him a phone call to make sure he was available."

"I understand, Your Honor, but he is here, so I suggest we proceed."

"You can suggest it, but I am denying it unless Mr. Forelle wants to go forward."

My initial plan was to ask the judge to continue the matter, slowing things down and giving me more time to review Ernie's motion and prepare a response. However, I suddenly realized that I was likely making a mistake. Seeing now firsthand that the judge was already agitated with Ernie, I decided it would be better to go forward today, even though I had just reviewed Ernie's motion for the first time. After all, if I continued the case, the same judge might not be here the next time. Ernie could end up with a better draw, and any momentum I gained from his lack of notice today would be lost. Based on this, I said, "Your Honor, actually, I have reviewed the motion, and giving the matter some additional thought, I am agreeable to moving forward today."

"That's fine. Let's proceed then," the judge said. "Mr. Harker, it's your motion. What do you have to say?"

Ernie Harker tried to regain his composure. "Thank you, Your Honor. Well, basically, this is an action that I have filed on behalf of a group of buyers who say that Mr. Smyth's father agreed to sell a certain scallop boat to them. Mr. Smyth's father has passed away, and Mr. Smyth has refused to complete the sale. The case is pending."

"So, what's the emergency motion all about that is so urgent?" the judge asked.

"You see, Your Honor, Mr. Smyth has taken this very expensive boat on some kind of crazy joy ride without a licensed captain. The man who accompanied him on this trip, who has a history of failing drug tests, was fired from the local scallop company. Mind you, this is a steel trawler approximately 100 feet long. I believe the two have headed down to the Caribbean somewhere. This is a working boat and worth a significant amount of money. If Mr. Smyth and his substance-abusing compatriot ran this vessel up on a shoal and sank it, my client could suffer a significant financial injury. We don't even know if Mr. Smyth has insurance on the boat. As a result, I am asking this court to enter a preliminary injunction and order Mr. Smyth to return to the vessel's home port here in Virginia while this case is pending." Ernie Harker then cited a handful of Virginia Supreme Court opinions that supported the general position for the use of a preliminary injunction to preserve assets during the pendency of a case, especially where there was evidence that there was a high potential for loss or destruction of those assets while the case progressed.

"I see. Thank you, Mr. Harker. Despite your failure to give proper notice for this hearing, you have raised some significant issues," the judge said.

This was not what I wanted to hear, and I was having second thoughts about going forward with the hearing without having more time to prepare. The cases that Ernie cited to the judge were also in his brief, but I only had time to skim the brief and was not able to actually review the cases themselves. So, instead of focusing on the law, I attempted to poke some holes in his presentation of the facts.

The judge turned to me and asked me what I had to say about the motion.

"Thank you, Your Honor. I actually have a great deal to say," I said. "First, yes, Mr. Smyth has taken *his* boat on a little trip. He is perfectly entitled to do so. Second, yes, he doesn't have a licensed captain on board, but under the law, he is not required to have one. The boat is not being used for scalloping but simply for transportation. It is no different than if they took a pleasure craft out for a cruise. Mr. Smyth is a highly educated and respected college professor who has taken some time off over the summer and is spending it with his childhood friend on his boat. Most importantly, Your Honor, the word that Mr. Harker never used in his argument is the word *contract*. Notice that Mr. Harker said that Mr. Smyth's father agreed to sell the boat, but he didn't say there was a contract. That's because there is no contract. The senior Mr. Smyth never signed a contract, and Mr. Harker knows he doesn't have a case here without a signed contract."

"Is that true, Mr. Harker? Is there no sales contract?" the judge asked.

"Your Honor, that's not relevant to the motion today. I'm not asking the court to rule on the underlying contract case, just to order Mr. Smyth to return the boat while it's pending. It could take years to resolve the case."

Hearing this, I knew Ernie Harker's plan was to draw this case out as long as possible. Ernie planned to make the case as long, expensive, and painful as possible. He was going to wage a war of attrition, hoping Rye would give up the fight and agree to sell the boat.

"It's very relevant, Mr. Harker," the judge said. "You want me to enter a court order that requires that man to return to this state on his boat, and whether you have a chance of prevailing on the merits of the case certainly plays into whether I will enter such an order. Is there a written contract?"

"Your Honor, once again, I really don't wish to get into—"

"Yes, I realized that, but I do!" the judge interrupted. "Yes or no, is there a written contract?"

"Not as far as I know," Ernie Harker reluctantly answered.

"As far as I'm concerned, you don't have much of a case then, and I'm not going to order anything on an emergency basis. There's a good reason for the Statute of Frauds, and this case is a prime example. Your folks could come in and say whatever they want and the elder Mr. Smyth is dead, so he can't contradict any of it. Shoot, your clients could make up anything. That's why, in a purported deal of this size, a written contract is required to validate the claim," the judge said.

"But Your Honor, I'm looking out for this man's best interest. You know, he took a hard fall and hit his head before he left on this trip, and I have legitimate concerns about his ability to make good decisions. In fact, I think he is making *bad* decisions."

"A person is allowed to make bad decisions, Mr. Harker. Are you claiming he's not competent?"

"Possibly, Your Honor. I am still trying to gauge that."

The ninety-year-old judge was not happy with this line of questioning. I found out later from a colleague that around a year before our hearing, the judge had taken a fall and broken his hip. To make matters worse, one of the judge's children—who had never accomplished much in his own life— had suggested that it was time for the judge to step down from the bench. The same son also offered to take control of the judge's considerable finances and assets. The son told the judge that he was just trying to look out for the judge's best interests and prevent him from making bad decisions.

"Mr. Harker. There is a hell of a burden to declare someone incompetent, and you shouldn't be tossing that around lightly," the judge said in an agitated voice.

"I understand, Your Honor. I'm just trying to look out for this man."

"That's the second time you've said that now. You're not his attorney! Mr. Forelle is his attorney! You've sued Mr. Smyth! You have my ruling. I'm not granting your motion."

I had been standing silently and thoroughly enjoying the show when the judge turned to me and asked, "Is that all we have for today?"

The day had gone well, but I was thinking that all I had really accomplished was to give Rye some time. The judge wasn't going to order Rye to come back, but Ernie could still move forward with his case and tie things up for my client for a long time. Even worse, he could make him spend a great deal of money defending the case. There's an old adage in the practice of law that you shouldn't ask for anything from the court you can't say with a straight face. I did my best to appear serious as I said, "Thank you, Your Honor. Based upon Mr. Harker's acknowledgment that there is no contract, I would like to make a motion to dismiss this entire action at this time."

"I appreciate your position, counselor, but I don't believe that's within my power to do today. You haven't filed a motion to dismiss asking for that relief, and I don't believe I can do that without a formal motion."

"Your Honor, there's no other way to prevent my client from expending significant funds defending a case without merit. Mr. Harker has suggested that this case could take years. I don't see any reason to put my client through that when there isn't even a basic contract. I just think it would be appropriate to dismiss the case now so that my client doesn't incur a lot of unnecessary attorney's fees."

"I understand your argument, and I'm sympathetic," the judge said. "Lawyers getting paid by the hour are one of the few professions that I know of where a person actually makes more money for being inefficient. That being said, I don't believe I can procedurally dismiss the case at this point."

I was disappointed knowing that the case was going to continue, but at least I gave it a shot. The judge next turned to Ernie Harker and said, "I'm inclined to deny Mr. Forelle's request to dismiss the case at this point. Anything you wish to add, Mr. Harker?"

"Yes, Your Honor. Yes, I think you are absolutely correct that you cannot dismiss the case today. Even if Mr. Forelle could make an oral motion to dismiss the case today, he also would have failed to give me proper notice of the motion. It would be completely inappropriate."

The judge paused for a moment. "Perhaps the issue really is a failure to give notice more than not having filed a written motion," the judge mused aloud.

"Absolutely," Ernie Harker said.

"In that case, I think you have a bit of a problem, Mr. Harker. After all, you failed to give Mr. Forelle notice of your preliminary injunction, so I don't think you are really in a position to claim you haven't been given notice of his notice to dismiss. You have unclean hands," the judge explained. "I'm going to grant Mr. Forelle's oral motion and dismiss the case. There's no reason to put Mr. Smyth through the unnecessary ordeal of extended litigation."

Ernie Harker had made a classic mistake of talking too much and, in doing so, had managed to snatch defeat from the jaws of victory. He was flabbergasted.

"I object, Judge. This is totally out of line."

"Your objection is noted," the judge replied.

"I will almost certainly appeal this ruling," Ernie added.

"That's within your right to do so," the judge said flatly.

Ernie's threat of appeal made me nervous at first, as I felt the ruling could be reversed by a higher court, but Ernie never filed an appeal. Ernie's decision not to go any further may have been because of the judge's remark about Ernie having "unclean hands."

The doctrine of unclean hands says that if you come into court asking for equitable relief, you need to have clean hands to do so. If I recall correctly, I think this idea first came out of some papal edict in the eleventh or twelfth century. The concept was later adopted by England and then ultimately, Virginia. You don't hear it being raised very often in courts today, but that doesn't mean it's not still valid. Ernie opened himself up to this defense when he failed to give me notice of his motion. Frankly, the unclean hands doctrine hadn't crossed my mind until the judge raised it. That's one thing about old judges—some of them have a lot of history packed away up there.

After ruling in my favor and deciding the entire case was frivolous, the judge went as far as to order Ernie to reimburse Rye for my attorney's fees. When Ernie objected to this, the judge spun around in his large black chair and just sat there. This left Ernie Harker arguing to the back of the chair with the judge tucked out of sight. The judge had clearly had enough. In the end, it wasn't any brilliant work on my part that won the case. Instead, it was a bit of luck in drawing a favorable judge and then mostly sitting back and watching Ernie dig a hole for himself. Things could have gone much worse on a different day with a different judge. I was relieved that I would be calling my client with good news instead of explaining that I had lost based upon a last-minute decision to go forward with a hearing for which I was not prepared.

Chapter Thirty

When Rye woke up early the next morning and walked outside, he found Stems asleep once again on the couch. The scattered, crumpled beer cans surrounding him had become a common fixture on the boat at this point. Rye saw Stems's eyes crack open as he got closer.

"Good morning," Rye said.

"Morning," Stems said in a groggy voice as he slowly sat up. He had grown a scruffy, mostly white beard over the last few weeks.

"I think I'd like to go back to shore and get in an early surf session this morning, Stems. Would you mind if I used *Bassassin*?"

"No problem, Doc. Help yourself."

"Do you think you can fix the steering?" asked Rye.

"Already done it. Once I got some tools, I got things mostly straightened out. The steering's a little rough, but she works okay for now."

"That's excellent. If it requires additional repairs, I'll be happy to pay for those."

"Don't worry about it. Don't you want to wait for the girls today?"

"No, I'm eager to go. I think I can handle it. Tell them I'll be back in just a short while," replied Rye.

"You sure you want to try to beach that boat by yourself this morning? You want me to come with you?" Stems asked, looking a little concerned.

"If the surf is like yesterday morning, I don't think it will be a problem and I won't stay very long. We figured out the other day that you need to get in and out of there at high tide. If I get close to the shore and if things don't look great, I won't land the boat—I'll come back and get some help instead."

"Okay," said Stems. "Happy to help if you want it."

"Samuel, I haven't forgotten about our conversation yesterday concerning our long-term plans. I would like to surf a bit this morning, but when I return, let's sit down and talk about things."

"Sounds good, Doc."

Stems helped Rye load the surfboard, and Rye was underway within twenty minutes. It was another beautiful sunny day, and as Rye approached the beach, he saw the waves were small. As he came up on the first breakers, Rye picked a gentle wave to surf in, just as he had observed Kaia do. As the boat approached the beach, he backed off the throttle and gently ran the bow up onto the sand, jumped out, and secured the boat with the anchor line. Because he was by himself, he could not pull the boat up very far but felt it was secure enough for a short surf session.

Rye felt a certain satisfaction at successfully landing the boat by himself. He looked around and confirmed he had the beach to himself. This is what he needed—a little alone time to relax and evaluate his next move.

Rye grabbed the board and paddled out. He managed to catch a nice wave on this first attempt and rode it almost back to the beach before he fell off. Over the next hour, he successfully caught several additional waves and was feeling more relaxed and comfortable on the board.

Perhaps this is a good way to spend your days, Rye thought.

Checking the tide, Rye decided he had time for one more ride if he was fast. He took a couple of large strides back out through the small breaking surf and then stepped on something sharp. Although the pain was not terrible, he decided that it was best to call it a day after all, so he retreated to the beach to inspect the wound and prepare to return to the *Miss Elizabeth*.

Rye laid his board on the beach and sat down to inspect the bottom of his foot. He could see a small V-shaped puncture midway between the heel and the ball of his right foot. The cut was only a half-inch long, but it looked deep. Even more disconcerting, the pain from the gash wasn't subsiding but was getting worse and migrating up his calve. Rye's heartrate rapidly accelerated and he began to sweat as he realized he had likely been poisoned.

Looking for help, Rye left his board on the beach and quickly hobbled down the jungle path toward the small town while trying to avoid getting dirt in the cut. As he emerged onto the dirt road, he paused and realized he didn't know where to go. He didn't even know if there was a doctor or clinic in the town. He leaned up against a tree, clutched his foot, and tried to collect his thoughts. The burning pain sensation now reached all the way to his groin. Rye looked around and saw two men working on the utilities about twenty yards down on the side of the road next to a beat-up orange pickup truck. The men also noticed him and could tell that he was in some sort of distress, so they walked over to him to investigate.

Both men were wearing overalls, and as they approached, the taller of the two men said something in Spanish that Rye didn't understand.

Rye responded, "Do you speak English?"

Both men shook their heads, showing that they did not, at which point Rye pointed at his foot and grabbed it with both hands and grimaced to convey the fact that he was in pain. The men inspected the wound and then spoke to each other in Spanish. The larger man asked, "*Caliente?*"

Recognizing the word for "hot," Rye responded, "*Si—mucho caliente*," as he grabbed his shin and then his thigh.

The two men spoke to each other in Spanish again, and then the taller man quickly walked back to their truck on the side of the road.

The shorter man stayed with Rye and shook his head and said, "*Muy mal!*" several times with a serious expression. The other man returned from their truck and handed Rye four small pink pills and a bottle of water. Rye didn't know what the pills were but decided—rather hastily—that his best course of action was to take them all.

Both Puerto Rican men just shook their heads, and then the shorter man turned to Rye and very slowly enunciated the word "*gasolina*," repeating the word several times. Rye assumed that the word meant gasoline but did not understand what they wanted him to do. He speculated it was most likely one of two things—either they thought he should dose his foot in gasoline to help the pain, or he was, in fact, going to die, and they were planning to dispose of this body by way of a makeshift jungle cremation. He suddenly realized he had no idea what type of pills the men had given him. He decided that the best plan at this point was to return to the boat and seek help from his friends there.

Rye thanked the men as best he could and retreated down the jungle path while waving goodbye. The two men looked at each other and shrugged their shoulders and headed back to their truck.

Rye hurried back to *Bassassin* in a half-panic. He quickly threw the surfboard in the boat and then likewise tossed in the anchor and anchor line. The tide had not changed significantly, and Rye managed to unground the boat. He spun the boat around and got the boat engine started and headed back out toward the *Miss Elizabeth*. He was still in pain but was also beginning to feel a little woozy and lightheaded. In his haste to get back to the scallop boat, he did a poor job of timing his exit through the breaking waves and took a large wave over the bow, resulting in the boat partially flooding. Luckily, the boat remained afloat, and Rye kept the throttle down as he made his way back to his friends.

When he pulled alongside the *Miss Elizabeth*, he realized that someone had pulled up the rope ladder, so he called out for help.

Almost immediately, Stems poked his head over the side of the hull and yelled down to Rye, "You okay, Doc?"

Seeing Stems, Rye yelled up again, "Frankly, I don't know!"

Stems threw down the ladder, which Rye climbed up despite the pain and numbness in his leg. Kaia and Nori heard the ruckus and immediately came over to see what was going on.

"What's up, Rye?" asked Kaia.

"I think I've been poisoned," Rye explained.

"By who?" said Nori, confused.

"Not by who, by what," Rye clarified. "I stepped on something in the water."

"Did you see what it was?" Kaia asked.

"No," Rye responded. "Are you aware if there is any type of Puerto Rican poison death fish or similar creature in this vicinity?" Rye asked.

"Let me see it," Nori said.

Rye sat on the deck and lifted his foot to show Kaia and Nori.

"That's a stingray, I think," Nori explained.

"Is it fatal?" Rye asked.

"No, but they hurt like hell," Kaia said.

"A couple of local gentlemen gave me several pink pills. What do you think they were? The pills, I mean," Rye said.

"How the hell should we know?" Nori asked.

Rye realized that his head was really spinning now. "When the two men started to converse about gasoline, I decided it was time for me to depart," explained Rye.

"Are you in any pain?" asked Stems.

"Yes, it started in my foot, and now it's crept up to my groin. Is that bad?" he asked the group.

"Don't sound none too good," Stems said with a furrowed brow. "If you're in pain, you may want to try tequila. It's helped me get through a few injuries in my life."

"Samuel, I appreciate it, but as I explained before, alcohol has no effect on me," said Rye.

"I've been thinking about that, Doc. I'm guessing maybe you just ain't tried enough at one time. Give me just a minute," Stems said as he disappeared below deck and reappeared shortly after with a bottle of tequila.

Stems took a big swig and then handed it to Rye. "Tilt this up, and don't hold back."

With a shrug, Rye turned the bottle up and drank nearly a quarter of it. "Do you think that is sufficient?" he asked Stems.

"We'll see," Stems replied.

"You know, for stingrays, I've heard that if you get in hot water, it will really take the pain away. Not sure why it works, but they say it does," Nori said.

"We don't have a bathtub on the boat, but we got a couple of empty fifty-five-gallon barrels," said Stems. "We can run a hose out here from the shower in the head and pump some hot water in one."

"It's worth a shot," Nori answered.

Stems and Nori rolled one of the empty barrels out to the center of the rear deck and ran a hose to it from below while Kaia sat with Rye.

"How are you feeling, Rye?" Kaia asked as Rye lay down on his back and stared up at the blue sky.

"Contemplative," was all he could muster in response.

"Hang in there, Rye. I really think this will help," explained Nori.

Once the barrel was around two-thirds full, the group got Rye to his feet and helped him hobble over to it.

"How we going to get him in there?" asked Stems.

"We'll lift him up," Kaia said. "Between the three of us, we can get him in there."

With some effort, they were able to do so, and Rye slid down and sat on his knees in the chest-deep water.

"How's that feel?" asked Stems.

"Surprisingly good," said Rye.

Once Rye was submerged in the barrel, he noticed that the pain dissipated almost instantaneously, but he felt a bit like a lobster on a stovetop. His head really swam as he tried to comprehend what had transpired over the last few hours.

"I wonder if we should get him to a hospital?" Nori asked Stems.

"Hell, I got no idea where one is," Stems replied.

Overhearing the conversation, Rye said, "I'm actually starting to feel better. Just let me be for a bit."

The group looked at each other and reluctantly agreed with Rye's wishes.

"Let's keep a close eye on him for a while," said Kaia.

"I just need a little rest," Rye muttered again as he closed his eyes. He felt the hot sun on his face as he dozed off.

Chapter Thirty-One

Rye crawled out of the barrel, which was now on its side. He was no longer on the *Miss Elizabeth* but in a plush green clearing that directly abutted a stunning waterfall. Rye guessed that this was the waterfall that awaited him at the top of the hike that he had failed to complete with Kaia and Nori. He deduced that his friends had carried him there as he dozed in the barrel. He scanned the area for them, but they were nowhere to be found.

The temperature was now cooler in the jungle's shade. He climbed to his feet and walked across the soft grass to a deep blue basin of water at the base of the waterfall and kneeled. Using his hands as a cup, he took several deep gulps of the cold water. As he turned back around and inspected the clearing more closely, he saw that there were several fruit trees. He recognized the starfruit on one tree and picked a few. One of the other trees had some type of yellow fruit that looked like a cross between a mango and a lemon, and he grabbed a few of those as well. He carried them over to the basin of water and waded in to clean the fruit.

He was stooped over washing the fruit when a man called out to him in a cheerful voice, "Hello, sir, how are you doing today?"

Rye looked up and saw a man who was wading up the stream toward him. The man, who was smiling broadly, appeared to be in his forties with a clean-shaven face and immaculate dark hair parted neatly on the side. He wore an impeccably tailored navy blue suit with a white button-down shirt and red tie. He was also barefoot and had rolled up the pant legs of his suit knee-high.

"Hello, good sir. What are you doing here?" Rye asked as the man approached.

"I'm looking for you, of course," the man answered.

"May I ask who you are?" Rye inquired.

"That's a perfectly reasonable question," the man responded. "I am the governor of Puerto Rico. Are you enjoying your stay in our fine country?"

"Yes, I am actually, except perhaps some of the poison-excreting wildlife."

"Ah . . . the stingrays. Yes, they can be a bother at times. I'm sorry about that. Otherwise, your trip is going well, I presume."

"Yes, it is, thank you," Rye said.

"I've come up here to discuss your situation."

"What do you mean . . . my . . . situation?"

"I would like to discuss your recent life journey and whether I might persuade you to 'get back with the program,' as they say."

"And what program would that be?" asked Rye.

"I mean, get back to being a productive citizen. It's one thing for a highly educated person to throw all that away in the United States, but down here, it's simply unacceptable. I mean, look at you. If you would get on board with things, you wouldn't have to be washing fruit in a stream. Instead, you could just purchase your fruit in the grocery store where they wash them for you."

"Let me ask you this," Rye said. "Why are you wearing a suit? It doesn't look very comfortable for this type of outing."

"It is what is expected for a man of my stature."

"Perhaps if you were willing to wash your own fruit in a stream, you wouldn't need to worry as much about your stature, and you wouldn't find yourself wading up a stream in a suit," Rye retorted.

The governor just smiled back at Rye.

"Why do you care, anyway?" Rye asked.

"We are not a large country. If others took up your pursuit, I fear there could be an economic collapse. I mean, don't get me wrong, we are all about a good time here, but you need to respect the process. It's time that you quit living like a bum and pull your own weight."

"Respect what process?"

"The government . . . society . . . all of it."

"I'm sorry, but I'm not interested in that. I am content."

The governor shook his head sadly and said, "I was afraid that this might be the case. Then I guess it is time to begin the trial."

"The trial? What trial?"

"*Yours*, my friend," the governor responded with a sad but determined look. "Ah, here they come now."

"Who?" Rye asked.

"The jury, of course."

Rye looked downstream from where the governor had come and saw several men and women working their way up toward them. Like the governor, the men were wearing suits with their pants rolled up, and several women were wearing skirts or dresses and carrying high-heeled shoes.

As they approached, the governor yelled, "Attention, everyone! It is time to get started. Please, please, it's time to gather around and begin."

"Before we commence, you should properly dress yourself," the governor said, eyeing Rye's shorts and T-shirt.

"What's wrong with the way I'm dressed?" responded Rye. "We're in the jungle, after all."

"Yes, but these are formal proceedings. I mean, shoes are optional, but you should otherwise show some respect to the authority here. Do you have your academic regalia with you?"

"Why on earth would I have that with me?"

"It's not a problem. I was prepared for this contingency, you see. My valet has brought a set of dress robes for you," the governor said. He then spun around and shouted back to one of the approaching men who happened to be carrying a suit bag over his shoulder, "Please bring forward the proper attire for this gentleman, and quickly!"

The man carrying the suit bag hurried over and handed the bag to the governor, who unzipped it and handed Rye a set of black academic robes with dark blue velvet trim.

"The dark blue represents the school of philosophy, correct?"

"Yes, but this really does not seem like the proper venue for dress robes."

"Nonetheless, please hurry up and change. I have a particularly busy schedule today and I would like to get this done and get on to a few other things."

"Oh, fine," Rye said, sounding exasperated. He quickly shed his clothes and put on the robes.

"Don't forget the cap," the governor said, handing Rye a cap and tassel, which he put on without saying a word.

"Much better. Now it is time for a formal reading of the charges," the governor said as he reached into the inside pocket of his suit and pulled out a folded-up piece of paper. "Rye Smyth, you're charged with heresy, breaches of etiquette, and corruption of the youth. Oh, and contempt of court for dressing inappropriately for your trial. How do you plead?"

"Not guilty, of course."

"So, then, do you deny that you have attempted to get others to abandon their responsibilities?"

"Well, that depends. What do you mean by responsibilities?" asked Rye.

"All of the things that a productive society requires."

"I think I have attempted to make my students aware of what they perceive—or have failed to perceive—as their societal responsibilities and helped them make their own judgments as to whether those responsibilities are appropriate. I have tried to make them aware that the only real responsibility is to live in accordance with nature. Anything else is dishonest," Rye responded.

"I'm not talking about your students. That's outside my jurisdiction, you know. I mean here in Puerto Rico. Some of those whom you have met along your journey here."

"I don't know. Have I? I mean, perhaps to some extent, but not explicitly. Maybe by way of example."

"Yes! Exactly! That's more dangerous! They see you doing it, and they may decide to follow your course. Do you deny the risks?"

"Oh, I don't know. Would it really be that bad? I mean, take a look at the world we are in right now. We have excesses in much of the world, and many of those who have the most still feel discontent. Other people are starving, and the environment is on the brink of collapse. While all this is going on, the vast majority of people are just working in the same unfulfilling jobs and will do so until they are too sick or too old to continue. It really doesn't sound that great, if you think about it."

"As I said, that's not what we are about here in Puerto Rico."

"I understand your point, but aren't you being just a little disingenuous? You advertise things are more relaxed here, but isn't much of your economy based on tourism? And aren't those one-week vacations just another means of control? People come here from other countries for a temporary reprieve and then go back and spend the rest of their time toiling away. They then save and scrimp together enough money to escape for another week or two the following year. And by the way, I've seen plenty of poverty since I've been here as well. I'm not convinced that things are as different here as you would like to pretend."

The governor grinned and said, "We have many Americans that come down here in their big boats and crews and spend lots of money. You aren't as different as you would like to pretend, either. Do you have anything else to say in your defense?"

"No, I think that pretty well sums things up."

"So, let us 'cut to the chase,' as they say."

"By all means then, let's proceed," Rye responded defiantly.

"I am finding you guilty."

"I see," said Rye. "I thought the people with us were the jury."

"They are, but just for the sentencing. I determine guilt or innocence. We have a tradition in our country. You can propose a sentence to the jury. They don't have to accept it, but if you show some contrition, I think it would bode well for you. Perhaps you should propose banishment. Get on your boat and sail away to somewhere new. How about that? That would not be so bad, would it now?"

"That's an interesting idea," Rye said. "Instead, for my punishment, how about you agree to pay for my food and expenses for the rest of my stay? I am actually finding it more difficult than I expected to provide myself with the basic necessities of life. As a result, it would be very helpful if you would provide these for me so that I can focus on the more important tasks at hand."

"So, you mock us then?" the governor said, sounding disappointed.

"No, I just think I've provided a valuable service. Seems to me that free food would be appropriate remuneration. Mind you, I think I can live primarily off the fruit from these trees, but a few supplemental food items would be helpful. There was a rice and beans dish I had the other day that was quite enjoyable."

The governor looked around to the men and women still standing shin-deep in the water. "You have heard his proposal. In the alternative, I feel I have no choice but to propose death by stingray venom. Do you all agree?"

In response, the entire group of observers responded in unison, "Agree!"

"Wait," Rye said. "I'm a bit confused. *Whom* do you agree with—me or the governor?"

Chapter Thirty-Two

When Rye woke up, he was feeling much better and was relieved to find himself alive. He sat up in his bunk and rocked his injured foot back and forth as he thought about the crazy dream he had. The foot was a little tender but was no longer aching or burning.

Rye peered out through the porthole of his cabin and saw that it was twilight. He didn't remember coming back to his room and concluded he must have slept most of the day. He got to his feet and, although he still felt a little unsteady, made it up to the deck to find Stems lying on the couch asleep.

Stems heard Rye walk over. He slowly sat up and asked, "Hey Doc, how you feelin'?"

"It appears that I slept all day," Rye responded.

"Day and night," said Stems. "I reckon you were out eighteen hours or so."

Rye looked confused and asked, "What time is it?"

"It's around seven in the morning," Stems explained, as he stretched and looked at his watch. "What do you remember from yesterday?"

"Some pills, tequila, hot water and then . . . the rest is a little hazy," said Rye, searching his memory. "I think I was on trial."

"I take it you didn't fare that well. Before we put you to bed, you knocked the barrel over and crawled out on the deck. You pulled off your clothes and were rummaging through everything. You said you were looking for some kind of robe."

"Oh my," said Rye, not remembering any of it. "Did our guests see *all* of this?" he asked.

"Oh yeah, it took all three of us to corral you and get some clothes on you," Stems said, grinning.

"Oh, God."

"Don't sweat it, Doc. At least you got yourself a nice tale to share."

"Thank you, Samuel. That is at least some consolation to hear. You know, at one point in my life, I went to the gym regularly. I did many repetitions of squats, and they really do help build up the glutes."

"What's that now?"

"You said I have a nice tail?"

"Yep. If you decide to go back to teaching, I reckon it's a tale you could share with your students."

"I can assure you that would be highly inappropriate."

"If you say so. Speaking of the ladies," Stems said, spotting them emerge from below deck.

"Morning, Rye," Nori said first. "Decided to wear some clothes today?"

Kaia just smiled and said, "Don't worry about it, Rye. It can happen to the best of us."

A little later in the morning, after Rye had grabbed a bite to eat, Kaia suggested they head to shore to locate a doctor for Rye and make sure his foot didn't get infected.

"Do they have a doctor in town?" asked Rye.

"I expect there's one around somewhere. We can go ask at the surf shop," said Kaia.

Rye reluctantly agreed, and by midmorning, Kaia, Nori, and Rye set out on *Bassassin* and headed to the shore. Kaia was driving and purposely maneuvered around the rear of the *Miss Elizabeth*. She pointed to the boat's stern and said, "Rye, we did a little work after you finally fell out yesterday afternoon."

Rye looked back at the boat and saw that the stern now contained the following names:

Miss Elizabeth

aka

Fat Lily

aka

My Barrel

aka

The Streaker

Rye sat stone-faced at first, making Kaia and Nori a little nervous that they had overstepped, but then he raised his eyebrows and released a slight grin that quickly grew to a broad smile.

"By Sirius!" he said. "I think you coined the perfect term describing my present mission! Would you mind if I used that for my book?"

There was almost no surf when they arrived at the beach, making it easy to run into the shore. After landing the boat and seeking directions at the surf shop, the trio discovered that there was indeed a doctor in town. She was an American physician who had retired in the area. The guy working in the surf shop gave them directions and described what the doctor's home looked like. Her house was around a half-mile down the road. Although Rye's foot was tender, he was able to make it there with some effort.

They discovered the house that matched the description. It was a small, simple, single-floor structure built out of concrete block, but it was well-kept and had a nicely landscaped yard. There was also a large gated fence surrounding the property.

"The guy at the surf shop didn't mention anything about a fence," commented Kaia. "There's a call box. Should we ring it?"

"Yeah, I mean, that's what we came here for," said Nori.

Kaia didn't have a chance to respond as two large dogs, spotting the strangers at the gate, ran to the fence and started barking ferociously. The dogs were black with white spots and had long, narrow snouts.

The barking quickly progressed to snarling when the dogs started jumping up against the gate. Apparently hearing the ruckus, a woman opened the front door and yelled, "Yes? Can I help you?"

"Hi!" Kaia yelled back over the spastic, frothing dogs. "My buddy here stepped on something yesterday, and we think it was a stingray. The guy down at the surf shop said you might look at it for him."

"Certainly," the woman called out. She then yelled "Heel!" to her two dogs, who retreated, but only after a few final menacing barks at the strangers. The doctor then hit a button that opened the gate, allowing Rye, Kaia, and Nori to enter. The woman had a generous smile and invited them inside her well-decorated home, introducing herself as Gabriela. She looked thin, healthy, and tanned. The doctor was wearing shorts, a short-sleeved, button-down shirt, and flip-flops, and had shoulder-length white hair. Rye estimated she was in her early seventies, which was good as Rye was convinced that someone in their seventies was more likely to have dealt with some level of illness during their life.

The doctor walked them through the home, and as they came into the back room, they observed a commanding view of the ocean through multiple large windows. It wasn't apparent from the front, but they could now clearly see that the home was built on the side of a cliff that sloped away from the back of the house.

"May I offer you something to drink?" the doctor asked.

"No, we're fine," Kaia said, answering for the group.

"Wow, some view!" Nori said to the doctor.

"Yeah, beautiful," Kaia added.

"Thank you. I enjoy it. It never gets old," the doctor responded. "It is my mullet house."

"Your what?" Nori asked.

"Mullet house. Simple and clean-cut in the front and more of a party in the back."

Nori laughed.

"So, what's brought you to the islands?" the doctor asked.

"I am attempting to live in accordance with nature."

The doctor paused. "So, you are a fellow Stoic," she said finally.

"No, a Cynic, actually," Rye responded.

"Really?" she asked. "I've never actually met one. How unusual. How is *that* going?"

"Actually, not particularly well," Rye responded. "It appears to be more difficult to sustain this lifestyle than I had imagined."

"I would think so," the doctor said. "Let's take a look at that foot."

Rye slid off the flip-flop and raised the bottom of his foot for the doctor to see.

The doctor removed a pair of reading glasses from her shirt pocket and put them on, then proceeded to carefully inspect the V-shaped wound.

"Interesting. It certainly looks like a stingray. Did it burn?" asked the doctor.

"Yes," said Rye. "The pain worked its way up my body."

"Did you ever see it?" the doctor asked.

"No," said Rye.

"You say this happened yesterday?"

"That's right," said Rye. "Not a very pleasant experience."

"How is the pain level now on a scale of one to ten?"

"Quite low now. Maybe a two or three," Rye responded.

"Are you having any other symptoms, like a fever, headache, or anything of that sort?"

"No, I really feel pretty good," Rye said.

"I suspect it was a stingray, and you aren't showing any signs of infection. I would monitor it. If you get any swelling or redness, I would get an antibiotic."

"Thank you, Doctor," Rye said.

"Doctor, would you also mind taking a look at Rye's ear?" Kaia asked.

"Certainly. What's the problem with your ear?"

"Before I came here, I took a fairly hard fall in the water back in the Bahamas."

"Okay," said the doctor. "What were your symptoms?"

"I was a little dizzy for a few days. I also have some ringing in my right ear."

"Yes, that sounds like a concussion," replied the doctor. "How are those symptoms now?"

"They all got better after a few days, but the right ear is still ringing significantly. Frankly, it does not seem to function that well."

"Let me check it out."

She disappeared into a separate room and returned a few moments later with a few medical instruments, and then she sat back down next to Rye. She used an instrument with a light to look into both of Rye's ears.

"They both look fine," she commented.

She then picked up what appeared to be a tuning fork.

"Are you going to play us a tune?" asked Kaia.

"In a manner of speaking, yes," replied the doctor as she gently tapped the instrument on her knee and then held the base of the tuning fork to the bridge of Rye's nose.

"Is the ringing louder in one ear than the other?" the doctor asked.

"Yes, it's much louder in the right ear," said Rye.

"Unfortunately, I'm sorry to tell you that's not good news," said the doctor with a concerned look. "That likely means you have conductive hearing loss in that ear. Probably some kind of cochlear concussion, I would guess."

"Can it be treated?" asked Kaia.

"I don't think there is much they can do. But it's not really my area of expertise."

"Will the hearing come back?" asked Nori.

"I'm not certain, but I suspect it's unlikely. Still, you should get this checked out back in the States when you return."

"It's really of no concern," Rye said. "I had actually expected this. Luckily, nature has built-in redundancy. How much do I owe you?"

"It's on me."

"Really, I don't mind paying," Rye said.

"No, it's okay. I do this kind of thing as a local service. There's no other doctor close by."

"So did you retire down here?" asked Nori.

"Maybe it is more accurate to say that I quit up there. You see, I still do a little work at the clinic down the road on a volunteer basis, and I do a bit of massage therapy to make a little money."

"Why did you pick Puerto Rico?"

"I worked in a hospital in the States most of my career. I made a lot of money and retired around five years ago.

Unfortunately, I allowed a trusted friend to invest almost all of my retirement accounts, and it turns out he was a crook."

"That's terrible," Nori said.

"Perhaps. But, as luck would have it, I had a little money tucked away in an account I had not given him access to. It was enough for me to buy this home. I am actually much happier now than before I lost the money. You see, I failed miserably in retirement. I feel more productive now."

Rye suddenly wished he had brought his notebook.

Chapter Thirty-Three

Rye, Kaia, and Nori had just arrived back at the *Miss Elizabeth* when I called to give them the news about the case. Stems recognized the number and immediately handed the phone to Rye, who apparently then walked up to the front of the boat for some privacy.

I told Rye I had some great news for him. "Ernie Harker tried to pull a fast one, and it backfired. The judge dismissed the whole thing," I explained. "Not only that, but the judge ordered Ernie to pay your attorney's fees, so you're not going to owe me anything."

I could tell Rye was relieved.

"That's great news, Jackson. Nice work. Thank you for your help."

"It's my pleasure. What did he offer you for the boat anyway?" I asked. "You never told me the number."

"I believe it was around $100,000."

"Well, here's the kicker, then," I told Rye. "I checked around some, and it turns out that Ernie was in on the buy with a few other folks. That's why he was pushing so hard. I talked to someone else down at the docks, and they confirmed that the *Miss Elizabeth* needs some work and may not be worth much in terms of the boat herself, but she's got a license for harvesting scallops, and that license is worth a whole lot of money. If you would have sold the boat, the license would have gone with it."

"Out of curiosity, what is the license worth?" Rye asked.

"Apparently, the market rate is always fluctuating, but it has gone up significantly in the last few years. I think it's somewhere between eight and ten million dollars at the moment. That's great news, isn't it!"

"Oh God, do you know how much responsibility there is to determine what to do with that much money!" Rye said.

It was not the response that I expected. We talked for a few more minutes, but I could tell he was distracted. I told him congratulations and to enjoy his trip and suggested we get together when he returned.

When Rye rejoined the others, Stems immediately asked Rye about the status of the events.

"It was very . . . interesting," Rye responded. "Jackson won the suit. It's a lot to digest, and I'm still trying to figure out how this might affect my plans."

"Hell yeah!" Stems said.

"Also, he told me that the license for the *Miss Elizabeth* is quite valuable."

"Shit, Doc, I could have told you that. Remember, I worked down there at the docks. Everyone down there knows that."

"Why didn't you mention this to me, Samuel?"

"Figured you knew. I was guessing that's why you were fighting to keep the boat so hard."

"I see," was all Rye said.

"Hey, I got an idea. How about we all head into shore and celebrate tonight and we can talk about plans tomorrow?" Stems suggested.

"I see no reason not to," Rye said, still a little stunned.

Later in the day, the group headed out on *Bassassin*. Once they had the boat beached and secured, Stems asked, "Where y'all want to go?"

"There are the usual bars down the road," Kaia suggested.

Stems scanned down the shoreline and eyed an expansive white building that was propped up on a protruding cliff at one end of the beach. "What the hell is that place up there?" he asked.

"One of the locals told me about it. It's a high-end place," Nori responded. "It's got great views, but the drinks are overpriced and watered down."

"That just means we'll need to drink more of them. I bet we can get a great sunset from up there," said Stems. "What do ya think, Doc?"

"Why not," Rye said.

Instead of walking through the jungle trail, the group walked down the beach and found a rocky path that led up to the rear of the building. They emerged at the top of the cliff to find themselves on an exquisitely manicured lawn where a young family was engaged in an intense game of croquet. Behind the lawn, there was a veranda extending off the rear of the hotel with a bar where a group of people were singing karaoke.

Stems led the way past a handful of round tables covered with white linens and then across a small dance floor to the bar and ordered a round of drinks for the group. Kaia suggested they all join in on the karaoke. Everyone agreed except for Rye, who took a seat to contemplate his current situation. As the rest of the group made their way back across the dance floor to the small stage, Rye drank an overpriced bottle of water and thought about what he wanted to do with this life.

After a few minutes, a thin, smartly dressed woman sitting a few barstools down from where Rye was perched approached him with an unmistakable Southern US accent and said, "I haven't seen you here before. Did you just get in?"

"No, we have been in town for some time," Rye said, not particularly wanting to get into a conversation at the moment.

"Heading back to the States soon?" she asked.

"I am actually trying to decide that at the moment."

"We're down here for a week, and then we've got to get back. Where are you from?"

"Virginia."

"That's nice. We've been there a few times. We're from Texas. I'm Billie, by the way."

"Hello. I'm Rye."

"What an interesting name. What do you do, Rye?"

"I do many things."

"I mean, what do you do for a job? You know, to make money," the woman said with a laugh.

"I'm not certain that I believe in that concept, but suffice to say, prior to starting this trip, I was a professor. I am trying to decide if I still desire to continue as one."

"So, what did you teach?"

"Philosophy."

"My husband, Clay, is over there telling fish stories about our charter today. He's the one in the blue T-shirt," she explained, pointing to a large man with his back to them who was talking to a group of men. "He retired recently. He was in federal law enforcement, but we're not supposed to tell anyone about it."

"Has he retired from this profession or society more broadly?" Rye asked.

"I really don't know what you mean. He was with the ATF— The Department of Alcohol, Tobacco, and Firearms. But don't tell him I told you."

"Such a strange combination," Rye commented. "It occurs to me that they oversee several of the leading causes of death in the United States."

"What's that?" the woman asked.

"Alcohol and tobacco are some of the leading causes of death by heart disease, stroke, and cancer. As for guns, well, that's obvious. Although you would think they would also want to regulate cholesterol if they were really trying to cover their bases. In such a case, I assume they would need to change the acronym."

"That's interesting; I never really considered that," the woman said. "It certainly has been wonderful weather this week. I was getting so hot back home. We really needed to get away."

"It's going to keep getting hotter," Rye said.

"Yes, late July and August tend to be the worst here. That's what one of the locals told me."

"I'm sure, but what I mean to say is that it's going to keep getting hotter *everywhere* with climate change."

"Oh, we personally don't believe in that," the woman said. "That's the case with most of our friends in Texas, too. We're from Beaumont, you see."

Rye perked up. "Interesting. I have heard there were still a few out there, but I haven't met one in many years."

"Someone from Beaumont?" the woman asked.

"No. A person who doesn't believe in climate change."

"Oh, I realize there's some debate around it. Is it real? If it is, is it manmade or just a natural cycle? All these unanswered questions. But personally, we just don't buy it."

"I can tell you that there is no debate about it in academic circles," Rye said.

"Well, I mean, there's just strong moral arguments on both sides. Do you know what I'm saying?" the woman said, still smiling.

Before Rye could respond, the woman's husband came up and said to Rye in a booming voice, "How's it going there, Buddy?" He then immediately turned to Billie and asked, "You ready to get out of here?"

The man leaned in between his wife and Rye and set an empty whiskey glass down on the bar with a loud thud. Rye estimated that the man was well over six feet tall and 220 pounds. His face was ruddy.

"Let me finish my drink first," the woman responded. "So, Clay, this interesting man is a professor, and I have just been telling him how this global warming thing has arguments on both sides."

"Absolutely!" Clay said.

"Actually, I was just telling your wife that I didn't really understand that statement. I mean, the science is clear that climate change is occurring," Rye explained.

"Well . . . you know, it could be just a natural weather cycle or something," Clay responded.

"No. Not really. The scientists are clear about that as well. It is manmade. If you review the reports by the Intergovernmental Panel on Climate Change, it is very clear," Rye said.

"I don't trust those things—that's like the UN or something, I think. Hell, I don't even trust our own government on this stuff too much, and I spent my life working for them. Can't really tell you what I did, but I can tell you that the government doesn't always tell you like it is a hundred percent of the time," Clay answered. "I know these things, but I can't really tell you *how* I know."

"I can assure you that what these scientists are saying is based on good science. If you were to look at the ice core samples that they have taken from Antarctica, it substantiates what I am telling you. Some of these samples go back nearly a million years. You see, when the water freezes, it encapsulates small pockets of air that we can test for levels of greenhouse gases throughout the years. It's quite fascinating. The data shows that the concentration of carbon dioxide was basically stable over the last thousand years. However, at the beginning of the industrial revolution, the levels rose precipitously."

"I don't believe any of that. That sounds like a bunch of false data made up by people wanting to get government grants," Clay said.

Rye could tell that the big man was getting agitated, which Rye found perplexing.

"I don't understand why people who don't believe in climate change get angry about it. I mean, for the sake of argument, let's say you are correct. If so, we've made some effort and spent some money to make the planet cleaner. Is that really an immense problem? But if you're wrong and we fail to act, it could be a mass extinction event. It could result in the possible end of humanity and much of the other life on Earth," said Rye.

"I mean, there's been other mass extinction events in history, haven't there?" asked the large man.

"Yes, but that doesn't mean we want to create another, does it? And there's never been a manmade one before," Rye said.

"Look, if God destroyed life before, we couldn't do anything about it, and if he intends to destroy all life on Earth again, we can't really do anything about that either," replied Clay in an animated fashion as he rocked back and forth on his feet.

While this conversation was going on, Rye's friends were singing karaoke and paying little attention to what was happening.

Stems had looked over once, and from what he saw, it just appeared Rye was engaged in a spirited discussion with a friendly couple.

"I don't think bringing religion into this argument is going to help your case," Rye said. "Do you really think that if God has given us this beautiful planet to use, he or she would be thrilled with us destroying it?"

"I don't question the will of God," Clay said. "Besides, like I said, all that data may be just made up. You haven't actually *seen* these ice samples yourself, have you?"

"Actually, I *have* seen them," Rye said.

"Come again," Clay said.

"Yes, it was a fascinating experience. I, along with two colleagues, one of whom was a sociologist and the other a psychologist, spent the winter at McMurdo Station, which is the United States Antarctic research station. The population of the base plummets that time of year as there are not many people who winter over. We were doing multidisciplinary research on effective means of communication and conflict management in stress-inducing environments. The temperatures can get seventy below down there, and it is continuously dark in the winter. If that's not stress-inducing, I don't know what is. It was extraordinary! While I was there, I had the opportunity to observe the ice samples firsthand," Rye explained.

The large man was skeptical. "So, you're telling me that you spent the winter at the South Pole?"

"Not quite the South Pole. I believe we were a little over eight hundred miles from the pole itself, but relatively speaking, we were close," Rye said. "We made some exceptional progress on conflict de-escalation research. For example, if I were to say you were an ignorant person, this would be more of a direct attack on you. Instead, I should be more precise and explain that you are simply ignorant as to the subject matter at hand—climate change, I mean. Although, I have always been better at studying conflict management in the abstract than in practical implementation."

"You calling me an idiot or something?" Clay said, stepping in a little closer to Rye with his face reddening further.

"Now, honey, no reason to get angry," Billie said, looking concerned.

"It seems I have misapplied the technique again," Rye muttered. "Of course not. I would never presume to call you an idiot. Did you know that the word 'idiot' comes from the ancient Greek word *idios*, which basically translates to someone that follows their own personal way and rejects societal engagement? I suspect that this is more akin to *my* actions than yours if you consider your prior tenure at Alcohol, Tobacco, and Cholesterol," Rye said, trying to defuse the situation.

Clay turned to his wife and nearly yelled, "Damn it, Billie! You need to quit running your mouth! You know we're not supposed to talk about that!" Then, turning his attention back to Rye, he added, "As for you, I'm not sure what the hell you're saying, but I don't like it! Best I can tell, you're making fun of my career and also saying that I'm dumber than an idiot."

Rye said nothing as he tried to consider the appropriate response to de-escalate the conflict.

Clay apparently mistook Rye's delayed response as confirmation of an insult. The man suddenly drew back and took a swing at Rye with his right fist. Seeing the telegraphed punch coming his way, Rye quickly but gracefully stepped to the side and blocked the attack with his left hand. He then jumped high into the air and, spinning 360 degrees, perfectly landed a kick to the side of the man's face. Clay was knocked out cold and fell to the floor with a thud as

Billie screamed. Rye hovered over the fallen man and quickly kicked off one of his flip-flops and slipped it onto his right hand and scanned the crowd, ready to defend himself in the event any of the man's companions decided to engage with him.

Chapter Thirty-Four

Rye's friends caught the end of the conflict and came running over. Clay began to sit up but was groggy. Billy was hysterical. Stems suggested that the best course of action was to leave, which the group did immediately.

As they quickly descended the hilltop on the way to their boat, Stems said, "Damn, Doc, I ain't never seen nothing like that before. You must've been near two feet off the floor when you kicked that guy in the face. You really know that karate stuff, don't ya!"

"Of course, Samuel. I thought I fully explained this to you before," Rye said. "That man is just lucky I didn't happen to have a towel within reach!"

"Yes—yes, he is," Stems replied, smiling as they scrambled down the rocks.

"What did you get in a fight with him over?" Nori asked as they reached the beach.

"I'm not sure, actually," Rye responded. "I think it was either climate change or my explanation of conflict avoidance."

"Doc, you do have the ability to piss some people off on occasion without even trying," Stems said.

"Why do you think that is, Samuel?" Rye asked.

A few hours later, Nori joined Rye on the back deck of the *Miss Elizabeth* as he leaned up against the rail and stared back at the thick forest that rose up the hillside from the beach.

"What are you doing?" Nori asked.

"I was thinking about my father, actually."

"Stems mentioned to me that you lost him not long ago. What was he like?"

"Very different from me. He came from a family with no money and worked very hard to get ahead. He was good at what he did. People who worked with him told me he could be tough, but he was fair and very loyal. Even though we didn't share many interests, we cared about each other very much. He had a *different* relationship with the men he worked with than he had with me."

"What do you mean?"

"You know, he never spoke to me about his business the way he did with others. He probably figured I wouldn't understand it, and he may have been right. Still, he left me this boat and I guess he decided, in the end, I'd figure out what to do with it. I'm sure he knew it was worth a lot of money, and I expect he wanted to leave it to me as a legacy of sorts," Rye said.

"I'm sure he cared about you very much, Rye. So, you still got plenty of time to get back for fall classes if you wanted to, I guess. What's your plan? Are you going back?" Nori asked.

"That's a good question. I guess I need to decide what I really want to do. Having too many choices can be a problem."

"No doubt. So . . . what are you thinking?"

"I've been thinking about a lot of things. For one thing, I wonder if this lifestyle really fits me. I mean, I haven't been at it that long, but I've sustained a few bumps and bruises. If things keep up at this pace, I'll be a physical wreck in no time."

"Yeah . . . well . . . you would probably get better at these things with time. I mean, I remember the first time Kaia and I tried kiteboarding. I launched myself into an apartment building behind the beach!"

"I expect I *could* get better with this mode of living. Still, the bigger question is what *should* I do? I set out on this journey to live in accordance with nature and hopefully find others who were doing the same. And of course, there's the book that I wanted to write."

"How's the book coming?"

"Not worth a damn, really. It all fell apart when I fully realized that I haven't lived the lifestyle I intended when I left on this trip. Let's face it; I've really been a half-assed Cynic at best. I have a boat with all kinds of conveniences on board, and I have already gone through a good deal of money. I don't think I am committed enough to live a truly minimalistic life—to live off the land. It's a shame, too, as I really liked the *idea* of living that way."

"I get it. It's not always an easy way to live. Kaia and I have moved around and gotten pretty good at it, but it can be tough sometimes. You're not the first one to romanticize it. We've run into that all over. We're traveling for months and living in some tents and shacks, and we run into some rich guys that flew in for a week of surfing who are staying at some bougie hotel and they're like—wow, we wish we could do what you guys are doing! I'd heard the same line so many times that I got annoyed at one dude and kind of snapped at him. I told the guy all he needed to do was to sell all of his shit and buy a tent, and then he could come sleep on the same patch of dirt we were camped out on."

"How'd he react?"

"He quickly changed the subject and then wandered off. Don't get me wrong, Rye, I wouldn't change our lives, but sometimes I miss all the stuff that makes you soft."

"What will you and Kaia do next?" Rye asked.

"Hard to tell. We'll probably spend some more time here until it's time to leave."

"When do you know it's time to leave?"

"That's a tough one. We'll stay as long as the surf is good and the vibe is right. It's easy to start thinking about the next spot where you're going to find true happiness, but it doesn't work that way. You're only going to find that by looking inward. You also want to be sure not to overstay your welcome anywhere. You need to leave while there's still good energy around—before things sour. Sometimes, you stay put half a year; other times, it's three days and you can already feel it's time to leave. I also think I keep a little bit of a wall up so leaving isn't so hard. You know, it's easier to leave when you're always leaving," she added with a shrug.

"Let me ask you something else, Nori."

"Shoot."

"Back when we were fishing, you brought up the idea of a trifecta. It was a job that paid well, was engaging, and helped to improve the world, if I recall correctly."

"That's basically it," Nori said.

"Do you think you will ever achieve it?"

"Actually, I think we're living it now," Nori said. "Kaia and I have talked about it before. We don't make a lot of money, but it's enough for us to travel and do what we want, and we love what we do. There's always something new to learn. And, you know, we bring some joy to others by traveling the world and exchanging energy with them. We're just trying to be kind human beings. Maybe it's not really saving the world stuff, and I'm sure some people would say we're just dicking around because we don't get paid for a lot of what we do, but I'll take it over a culture that rewards selling a bunch of crap to people, most of which will end up in a landfill in a few years. So, yes, all in all, I guess you could say we're living the trifecta. You just got to remember that it's all relative. I guess maybe you can achieve some level of the trifecta in any job. Maybe it's more about how you do that job."

"Ah, what you're talking about is moderation."

"I guess . . . yeah," Nori said.

"I've never been very good with it. Besides, who'd want to read a book about moderation? Where's the fun in that?"

The two stood quietly for a moment as Rye continued to stare back at the shore. Finally, Nori asked again, "So, are you going back?"

Rye continued to gaze quietly at the land they had just left and then said, "I'm sorry, I can't hear very well. What were you asking?"

THE END

AFTERWORD

After I completed my initial draft of this book, I decided to take a look at the USPTO website and find the crazy patent for the "dornet" that the guy down in the Bahamas told Rye about. It turns out the patent wasn't just limited to post-apocalyptic ducks. In fact, the inventor had envisioned the molestation of multiple types of stuffed animals, including bunnies, squirrels, and teddy bears. I found the bear design particularly intriguing. I guess you could call this one the "bornet." When you submit patent applications, you often submit drawings to illustrate them. The inventor included an illustration for the stuff bear as an example, and I have attached it below.

If you weren't aware, bear belong to the family of mammals referred to as "Ursidae," but in my mind, the drawing had more of a "Rodentia" quality to it. There was also something vaguely familiar with this particular illustration and it took a few days for me to remember what it reminded me of. Not long ago, I made a trip to Manhattan to visit one of my daughters and had the occasion to ride the subway. This was during the height of a rat overpopulation problem that had been covered extensively by the news media. I am confident now that I saw something nearly identical to the above sketch that was lying off in a dark corner of a rather dank loading platform.

As to a different subject, I would like to make an obvious disclaimer. I would like to acknowledge that I have absolutely no formal training in philosophy. Despite this, I have done my best to chronicle Rye's adventure and describe what he was attempting to do. While writing the book, I did a great deal of research about the ancient Greek Cynics. Reading Rye's notes about his encounter with the doctor in Puerto Rico also sent me down the rabbit hole of Stoicism. I found the Stoics fascinating. For those of you unfamiliar with them, they were a group of philosophers that came along after the Cynics. As I understand it, they borrowed a few things from the Cynics, including the idea of living *in accordance with nature*. However, the Stoics were more measured in their approach. They believed in adhering to societal rules and also advanced the importance of living a life directed toward the common good.

Comparing Stoicism and Cynicism got me thinking back about those German students Rye encountered in Puerto Rico. They were studying not only how trees communicated with one another, but also how they would sometimes share vital nutrients to help each other survive and thrive. This led to a bit of a revelation for me. Maybe Diogenes had more in common with the Stoics than he realized. I did a little digging and discovered that scientists believe that we share over fifty percent of our DNA with trees. We also share over eighty percent of our DNA with dogs. So, if helping one another is ingrained at a fundamental level in trees, isn't it likely that it is also ingrained in dogs, and even us? Maybe living *in accordance with nature* means more than just lounging in the sun? Maybe it means we are *intended* to help each other along our own journey? It's just a thought, but what the hell do I know. After all, I'm a lawyer, not a philosopher. I'll have to Rye about this next time we meet down at Bar 17.

ACKNOWLDGEMENTS

First, I would like to thank Rye Smyth for generously sharing his written notes and oral recitations of the events I've described. They were essential to telling this story. I'm also grateful to Stems, Nori, and Kaia for your insights and support. Without your cooperation, this book could not have been completed.

I would also like to acknowledge and thank Dr. David Dooley. David was a psychology professor (not at Tidemarsh) and a mentor to Rye. As far as I know, he was the first to deliver the "Two Paths" lecture to his students—a talk he used to encourage them to reflect on what they truly wanted out of life. Rye felt the message was so important that he adopted it shortly after he began teaching at Tidemarsh University.

Speaking of Tidemarsh University, I would also like to thank their publishing arm, Tidemarsh University Press, for agreeing to publish this book. Although the current chancellor and I have had our differences, I still have a soft spot for my alma mater.

Of course, I would like to thank my family and friends for their support throughout this undertaking. Over the years, I've shared many of the thoughts and ideas explored in this book with them, and they have never ceased to amaze me with their own insights—many of which compelled me to reconsider matters I once held with near certainty.

I suppose this is also a good time to mention that Rye wasn't the first person I've known to take a scallop boat on a leisure cruise. Back in the 1970s, my law partner's father and a group of his friends loaded up one of these spartan boats with pallets of food, beer, and whiskey and set off on a weekend odyssey. Apparently, on the first night, everyone—including the captain—got drunk and passed out, leaving them adrift in the Gulf Stream. When they woke up the next morning, they had drifted sixty miles north. Fortunately, they made it back in one piece.

A special thanks to my fellow kiteboarding and surfing travel companions, who have circumnavigated the globe and consistently served as ambassadors of goodwill and fun. Their reflections on the realities of life on the road have been deeply insightful. There's no doubt in my mind that the world is a better place because of them, as they've each worked to create their own version of the trifecta.

And finally, a heartfelt thanks to all my friends, professors, martial artists, and fishermen—and fisherwomen—who've inspired me to write this book. You are all *the best*!